# LIBERTY STATION

## BOOK ONE OF THE HUMANITY UNLIMITED SAGA

YOWLING
CAT PRESS

BOOK ONE OF THE HUMANITY UNLIMITED SAGA

# LIBERTY STATION

*Humanity will be free...*

*...no matter the cost!*

# TERRY MIXON

BESTSELLING AUTHOR OF *THE EMPIRE OF BONES SAGA*

*Liberty Station*
Copyright © 2015 by Terry Mixon

Published by Yowling Cat Press ®
Print ISBN: 978-0692531907
Edition date: 12/30/2017

Cover art - image copyrights as follows:
BigStockPhotos.com/goinyK
DepositPhotos.com/Antartis (Anton Balazh)
DepositPhotos.com/Iurii (Юрий Коваленко)
DepositPhotos.com/steho (Stefan Holm)
DepositPhotos.com/algolonline (C Atkinson)
Donna Mixon

Cover design and composition by Donna Mixon

Print edition interior design composition by Terry Mixon and Donna Mixon

Audio edition performed and produced by Veronica Giguere
Reach her at: v@voicesbyveronica.com

# TERRY'S BOOKS

You can always find the most up to date listing of Terry's titles on his Amazon Author Page.

## The Empire of Bones Saga
*Empire of Bones*
*Veil of Shadows*
*Command Decisions*
*Ghosts of Empire*
*Paying the Price*
*Reconnaissance in Force*
*Behind Enemy Lines*
*The Terran Gambit*

*The Empire of Bones Saga Volume 1*

## The Humanity Unlimited Saga
*Liberty Station*
*Freedom Express*
*Tree of Liberty*

## The Fractured Republic Saga
*Storm Divers*

## The Scorched Earth Saga
*Scorched Earth*

## The Vigilante Duology with Glynn Stewart
*Heart of Vengeance*
*Oath of Vengeance*

Want Terry to email you when he publishes a new book in any format or when one goes on sale?
Go to TerryMixon.com/Mailing-List and sign up.
Those are the only times he'll contact you. No spam.

# DEDICATION

*This book would not be possible without the love, support, and encouragement of my beautiful wife. Donna, I love you more than life itself.*

## ACKNOWLEDGEMENTS

Once again, the people who read my books before you see them have saved me. Thanks to Tracy Bodine, Michael Falkner, Cain Hopwood, Rick Lopez, Kristopher Neidecker, Bob Noble, Jon Paul Olivier, Tom Stoecklein, Dale Thompson, and Jason Young for making me look good.

I also want to thank my readers for putting up with me.
You guys are great.

# 1

---

Harry Rogers watched the target's house through his night vision scope. A guard patrolled the roof of the Italian villa slowly, with no idea that someone had him dead in his sights. Satisfied the guard wasn't going anywhere, Harry clicked his transmitter once to let his team know he was ready. A pair of clicks on the encrypted frequency acknowledged his signal.

The other members of his team were already in place. All they needed to move this mission from recon to assault was for him to give the word.

He scanned the rooftop once more and spotted a second guard near the rear of the house. That one was smoking. Didn't he know that was bad for his health?

Harry clicked his transmitter three times. Then he took a deep breath, lined up on the furthest man, and fired. The target stood just over two hundred feet away from the tree Harry had chosen for his nest. That range was a snap with a sniper rifle, but chancy with a tranquilizer dart. Good thing he'd practiced.

The man made a small cry, scrabbled at the dart embedded in his back, and collapsed. The closer man turned toward the commotion, giving Harry a clear shot at his unprotected rear. He went down just as easily as his friend had.

His people checked in once they'd neutralized the two guards at the back of the property, the two in front, and the man in the gatehouse. Time to move the operation to phase two.

Harry climbed down the Italian stone pine as noiselessly as he'd ascended. Tree climbing spikes made the ascent easy.

The tall trees at the edge of the yard made for dark shadows this early in the morning. He enjoyed their scent as he made his way toward the clearing. A hint of the sea mingled with the trees. He really needed to take some time off to unwind.

He crossed the clearing below the imposing mansion and up to the back of the villa just as his people were securing the unconscious prisoners. The next set of guards would find them just before dawn and the manhunt would be on. The clock was ticking.

Less than a minute later, the rest of his people ghosted in out of the dark. They were almost invisible in their grey on black camouflage. Their night vision goggles made them look like monsters to the uninitiated.

If this had been a hard entry, they'd have blown the doors and come in firing. He and his people had more experience at that than any seven people should have. War did that to people.

Thankfully, this was a snatch and run. They'd only kill if they had to. These guards were only doing their job. They didn't deserve to die for their master's poor decisions.

That wasn't always the case. Some opponents deserved lethal force.

The interior guards on this mission expected their exterior compatriots to warn them of any intrusion. Hopefully, his people would take them out before they realized their error.

Jeremy Gonzales, his security expert, had the doors open in just a few seconds. The target hadn't activated the electronic alarm. Of course not. He had armed guards. Harry and his team raised their night vision gear as they came into the lighted interior.

The staff lived on site, but in a different building. At three in the morning, they wouldn't be up for a few more hours. All Harry needed to worry about were the two guards in the building. IR had one of them in the kitchen—probably snacking, another bad habit—while the other was up on the second floor.

The team split without a word. Two of them moved toward the kitchen, two of them went toward the front of the house, and he led the remaining pair up the stairs.

The interior of the villa was every bit as lavish as he'd expected. Fine antique furniture filled the side rooms and expensive looking art filled the niches. The thick carpeting deadened even their careful steps as they went up to the next level.

A tiny fiber optic wire around the corner showed the upstairs guard examining one of the paintings near the far end of the hall. The man had a magnifying glass. He must be an art lover.

Harry leaned out into the hall and shot him in the ass with a dart. That was going to be tough for him when his friends teased him later.

That's where the plan went off script. This guard managed to bring his weapon around and squeeze the trigger before he collapsed.

Harry ducked back as the automatic weapon ripped through the silence and disintegrated the corner beside him. The man only got off one burst, but that was enough to ruin the element of surprise. Hopefully it wouldn't be loud enough to wake the staff.

"Blow the power and communications," he said over the team channel as he surged around the corner. He flipped his night vision gear down just as the lights went out. They'd cut the landline and a cell jammer would keep anyone from calling for help.

He raced to the end of the hall and kicked the door open. There were two people in the room, a very fat man digging in the nightstand and a shrieking woman in the bed with the sheet pulled up to her chin.

Harry darted the man and watched him crumple with a sense of satisfaction. A second shot took out the unknown woman. She'd wake up in the morning with a headache and damaged pride.

There hadn't been any shots from below, so his people had neutralized the man in the kitchen. Clean sweep.

He made a pass through the bedroom and attached office, just to be certain that no one was hiding there. The master bedroom could've come from a palace. The NVG didn't allow him to see color, but the furnishings here looked even more refined than the ones downstairs. They had to be hundreds of years old.

The office wasn't just for show. It looked as though the man used it extensively. The large desk had a messy spread of papers and data chips. Expensive paintings covered the walls and a few cases held knick-knacks. Mostly Egyptian stuff, Harry thought.

A spread of old looking parchment pages under glass took up one wall. The illustrations of plants and people looked medieval. The flora had to be a monk's flight of fancy. He was sure some of them weren't real.

Satisfied that they hadn't missed anyone, Harry headed back to the hall. It was time to collect the client and withdraw. He stopped outside the door closest to the master bedroom and knocked.

"Emily Schultz, your mother sent us. It's safe to come out. She said to tell you that she'd take you out with your friends Hannah and Cheryl as soon as you get back to the States. I believe cinnamon swirl ice cream is on the menu."

The door opened a moment later, revealing a young girl with dark hair dressed in a nightgown. Ten year-old Emily Schultz, the kidnapped girl. Her scumbag father had thought his money and influence could keep her

American mother from enforcing the custodial agreement that the U.S. courts had ordered. Not this time.

"Am I really going home?" she asked. Her voice was timid and soft.

"Yes," Harry said in a serious voice. "Dress fast. We only have a few minutes. Only take the important stuff. One bag."

One of the two women on his team ducked inside with the client. Two minutes later, they exited the way they'd snuck in. They piled into a plumbing van and left the scene at a sedate pace.

No need to draw attention. If you acted as though you belonged, the man on the street seldom questioned your right to be there. In the case of service people, they rarely even remembered what you looked like.

The trip to the coast went off without a hitch. No word of their invasion had made it out of the house, so no one had raised the alarm. Harry looked at his watch as they hustled the girl from the van to their borrowed boat. They still had maybe an hour before someone found all the unconscious people.

Unless they had completely crappy luck, they'd be back on the ship and into international waters before the search even moved beyond the general area around the villa. The man driving the boat would take them to their ship, return to shore, and get the plumbing van back to his shop before anyone got excited. He'd get a very large bonus for his part in the operation.

Harry didn't relax until they were several hundred miles in the clear. The news was all over the airwaves by then. Girl from rich family kidnapped, police looking everywhere for the villains. Good luck with that.

Only then did he turn on his satellite phone and call the girl's mother. She hadn't known when the snatch would take place, so she had to have been anxious for the last week. It was almost three in the morning on the East Coast.

"Hello?" Harry could hear mixed notes of fear and hope in the woman's voice.

"Miss Schultz? Harry Rogers. We have Emily and we're safely away."

"Oh, thank God!" He could hear the anguished relief in the woman's voice. "Can I talk to her? Is she okay?"

"She's perfectly fine. Here you go." He handed the phone to the little girl and stepped back to let them have their reunion.

Once they finished their long and tearful conversation, he took his phone back. The woman was still crying. "Thank you. Thank you so much."

"It's my pleasure. We'll have her back to you tomorrow evening. Try to get some rest."

He hung up with a sense of satisfaction, knowing that the woman wouldn't be able to sleep a wink. Another family reunited. Those were the best jobs.

That's when he noticed he had a voicemail from an all-too-familiar number. His father. Great. That man could ruin a wet dream.

Harry stepped onto the deck and looked out over the waves. The smell of the sea calmed him. It reminded him of a less complicated time when his family had taken long trips on the ocean. He must've been two or three. They'd hardly been a model family, but at least they'd been together.

He could ignore the message, but his father was resourceful and determined. One didn't build one of the most powerful companies on the planet by rolling over at the first setback. He'd get more and more irritating if Harry didn't call him back.

He sighed and listened to the message. His father's deep voice came out of the speaker.

"I'm sorry for disturbing you while you're at work, Harry. I hope you're enjoying the med. It's wonderful this time of year."

How had the man known where he was?

"Anyway, something has come up. I know that we don't have the greatest relationship, but an innocent woman is in grave danger. I'm willing to pay triple your usual rate, and you can attach a substantial surcharge for working for me. Please call me back as soon as you get this message."

The fees Liberty SOG—Special Operations Group—charged for the simplest operations were substantial. Private military groups took a lot of money to keep in specialized gear and weapons. And Harry paid his people very well indeed. They deserved every penny.

The amount of money his father was talking about was…substantial. Enough to tempt Harry, even against his better judgment.

He sighed. Might as well get this over with. He dialed the number, smiling a little at the time. At least he got to wake the bastard up at an inconsiderate hour.

* * *

THE PHONE beside the bed jarred Clayton Rogers from a sound sleep. Only a select few had his private number, or the code to make it ring through, so he knew it was his son before he checked the Caller ID.

He noted the hour with resigned amusement and answered the call. "Harry, it's good of you to get back to me so promptly. I hope your work bore fruit. Kidnapping children is a nasty business."

"And you know more than your share about nasty businesses, don't you?" his son said coolly. "Let's cut the pleasantries short. I'm not inclined to take your money. I know how you earned it."

His son's antipathy was no surprise. He really couldn't blame the boy. Clayton was honest enough to see his own failures. The things he'd done to climb to the top of his business were sickening, despicable, and occasionally horrific. And quite necessary. Something his son had never been able to understand.

Business in 2035 had very little in common with what it had been even two decades earlier. The largest international corporations were almost governments in their own right. Cutthroat didn't begin to describe some of the things they did to one another.

Rainforest—his company—was no exception. He'd like to believe that his behavior was less ugly than most of his compatriots, but that was only rationalizing. He did what he had to. The project was too important to fail.

"I strongly urge you to reconsider. If you walk away, it's likely that dozens of innocent people will disappear into hidden graves. Most of them are in no way associated with my business interests. These are the kind of people you help every day. On that I give you my word."

The long silence made him wonder if his word was no longer good enough. That day would eventually come.

"When the bill arrives, you'll pay it without a peep," Harry said. "Who are these people, where are they, and what pickle have they gotten themselves into?"

Clayton let out his breath slowly. He'd made it past the most difficult hurdle. Whatever Harry charged would be worth every cent and more. "They are a team of archaeologists excavating a Mayan ruin deep in the jungles of Guatemala. Communications there are quite spotty. For their own safety, they need to be brought out."

He could hear the surprise in his son's voice. "Archaeologists? Why in the world would people like that be on your payroll? You own the world's largest online store. Is Rainforest selling priceless relics now?"

"Only one of the people is associated with me. The rest are innocent bystanders."

"Who is this person and what do they do for you?"

"Her name is Jessica Cook. She's an engineer with specialties in space construction."

That silenced his son for a moment. "What is she doing at an archaeological dig in Guatemala?"

"I'm not precisely certain," Clayton admitted. "The man in charge of the site—a friend of hers—asked her to come look at something. Her office is at the Yucatan Spaceport, so it wasn't too much of an inconvenience, I suppose.

"I found out after she departed that your mother has taken an unhealthy interest in her. One of my spies in Kathleen's organization tells me that your mother has dispatched Nathan to collect her. And to make certain there are no unfortunate questions asked later."

His ex-wife was always on the lookout for chances to harm him or those around him. With cause, he admitted. Their marriage of convenience had become most inconvenient when he terminated it.

Scratch the CEO of any global corporation and you'll most likely find a high functioning sociopath. The ability to look past the harm people suffered during the course of making a company succeed was a prerequisite to doing business on that scale.

Kathleen Bennett had led her own company when he married her. One that had been in her family for generations. It had made up half of Rainforest when they merged. And he'd stripped it from her via a hostile takeover when they divorced.

The generous payout had done nothing to quench her burning rage at his outright theft of her family's company. Instead, it had given her the tools to wage war against him.

She'd started a new company, but something had broken inside her. She'd become a psychopath determined to hurt him in any way possible, no matter the cost, laws broken, or who she hurt doing so. She's become the poster girl for the apocryphal corporate monster.

And an almost cartoonish enemy. It wouldn't be unreasonable for most people to imagine Kathleen sat around rubbing her hands together while cackling madly and muttering "revenge!" to herself.

One day her insensible rage would bring her down. She'd do something so heinous that even her wealth couldn't save her. And he had to admit that she'd recovered her fortune quite well. She was worth almost as much as he was these days. Perhaps more.

The cruelest irony had been finding out she'd been pregnant with their second child after the split. He'd managed to gain sole custody of Harry, but she'd hung on to Nathan. He was almost as bad as she was now.

Harry and Nathan had clashed before, so his younger brother's involvement was actually a plus for Clayton. Nathan was one of Harry's buttons.

"Why didn't you say that up front?" Harry demanded. "That would've made this conversation go much more smoothly. As much as I despise you, those two are a completely different level of bad news.

"I'll need all the information you can give me about Jessica Cook, her friends, and the site. A secure upload to the Liberty SOG servers would be the simplest solution. I'll email you a link and a public encryption key. I have a child that I need to deliver. That will complicate the timing."

Clayton had planned around that contingency. "I have a ship in your general area. I can take the child off your hands and assure a safe and speedy delivery. It's something Rainforest prides itself on. Time is of the essence in this matter. Your brother is already on his way."

"Fine, but I hold you personally responsible. If the girl doesn't make it home safely, I'll come for that visit you've been pestering me about, but you won't enjoy it. Look for the email."

The call ended abruptly. Clayton returned the phone to its cradle and rubbed his face tiredly. Days like this made him wonder if his schemes were worth the pain they caused.

The only positive aspect to this situation was that he now had a way to bring his son into the plan. Only stage one, but possibly enough to whet Harry's appetite to learn more.

His son didn't know it, but Clayton had always intended to bring him in on his grand undertaking. In fact, his boy was a critical component of its eventual success. Even if he had to keep lying to his son until he'd ensnared him too deeply to extract himself.

Clayton glanced at the clock on his nightstand and rose. He had a lot of work to do if he wanted to salvage his undertaking and stymie his ex-wife.

## 2

J essica Cook removed her Astros cap long enough to wipe her face and reapply her insect repellent. The jungles of Guatemala were even hotter and more humid than she'd feared. What had she been thinking?

The trees towered over her, filled with life that called out to attract or warn off others that she would never see. The cover didn't stop the undergrowth, though. Someone had cut a path through the worst of it, but that wasn't saying much. And, God, the humidity! She was soaked in sweat.

Besides being far more uncomfortable than she'd counted on, this jaunt was taking her away from her job as the chief construction engineer for Liberty Station. They were coming up on some very important deadlines and she really should be preparing for them.

The rest of the world—those that even paid attention to such things— thought Liberty Station was going to be a space hotel for the uberwealthy. The truth behind that story was a lot more impressive. Clayton Rogers was building the first spaceship to take humans to Mars and beyond.

If the truth got out, plenty of people would try to stop them. The only players in space these days were the Indians and the Chinese. Both had Mars locked in their sights and were determined to be the first to put a human on the Red Planet. They'd lose that race when Liberty Station stole a march on them. Just one more reason to keep things quiet, since those governments might be able to stop them if they had enough warning.

The United States had given up on space, turning their attention to purely terrestrial problems. Oh, they'd tried to keep up appearances, but the

ISS2 space station project had imploded financially. Mister Rogers had bought the unfinished skeleton and they'd corrected its flaws and expanded on it.

They'd be the first global corporation to focus on the rest of the solar system, and the riches—both financial and scientific—awaiting them. With their technological lead, they'd have years to set up infrastructure that the rest of the world would be hard-pressed to match.

She stumbled a little and forced herself to focus on the here and now. A broken leg would slow her down even more than this side trip.

The boat had dropped her and her guides off that morning, but it had taken them all day to traverse just a few miles of thick jungle. The workers had it much harder than she did, though. They had boxes and bags of equipment and supplies to carry. The sight of them all moving in a long line reminded her of an old Tarzan movie. She could've used a pith helmet.

A stone column was the first indication they'd entered the Mayan ruins. With all the people behind her, she couldn't stop to examine it. Not that she could see much anyway. The thick vegetation hid it almost completely.

She began looking at the hills around them. The ones behind the caravan looked normal. The ones in front of them were more angular. They weren't hills at all. They were pyramids covered in jungle growth.

They'd arrived at the city.

The ghost of a road led them deeper into the long abandoned capitol of some forgotten Mayan kingdom. Her imagination filled in the missing details and she could see it as a bustling metropolis. Considering the Mayan's technological level, the city was a marvel.

She spotted a few young men and women with survey equipment on a small rise ahead. They waved as she and her party walked past them. Jess cheerfully waved back.

The caravan leader took them to the central camp in what must have once been a great courtyard. Tents stood in neat rows just past a large, dark hole in the ground. A small tumble of stone marked what she imagined had been a short wall surrounding it.

Doctor Abel Valdez stepped out from one of the tents and waved at her. "Jess! You made excellent time! Come! I must show you what we found."

Even though she ached to sit and rest, she wanted to see what had gotten her old friend so excited. And to find out what possible assistance an orbital engineer with degrees in mechanical and nuclear engineering, and several minors in space sciences, would be at an ancient ruin.

His enthusiasm was as infectious as she remembered from college. He'd almost convinced her to become an archaeologist before she'd dedicated her life to engineering. The past had called to him even as the stars seduced her toward space.

Jessica pulled him into a hug. "Abel! Take a breath! How are you? This place is amazing!"

His expression turned sheepish. "Better than good. I apologize. I should let you rest and recover from your trip."

"And miss this mysterious find of yours?" she asked with a smile. "No way. Maybe now you'll explain what the hell is so important that you couldn't tell me over the phone."

She'd been at the Yucatan Spaceport, so it had only been a matter of hours to fly to Guatemala. And then three days of rough travel involving overland driving, a boat she'd been certain would capsize, and a full day hiking through almost impenetrable jungle.

Abel grinned. "This is the most important find of this century and possibly any other. This city is probably from the late classical Mayan period, so around AD 700 to 900. I need your help in deciphering something critical."

She gave him a skeptical look. "I'm an engineer. What I remember about archaeology wouldn't fill a small notebook."

"It would be much easier to show you. I've kept details on this particular aspect of the dig quiet. If word gets out, it will draw the wrong kind of attention. You've studied astronomy and other esoteric space skills for your work in orbit. That is the kind of assistance I need."

Jess blinked in surprise. "Seriously? How can that possibly be useful?"

"Come inside and I will show you."

Abel led her to a formidable pyramid. Someone had cleared part of it and she could see the ancient stones as they climbed the steps to the top. He grabbed a pair of flashlights sitting with some equipment and took her inside. They'd strung lights, but there were still pools of darkness between the widely spaced bulbs.

He led her down through a confusing series of shafts and rooms. They moved too quickly for her to do more than glance at the stonework. Carvings worn with age covered some sections of the walls. She couldn't tell much about them. The stone beneath their feet was rubbed smooth by the passage of unnumbered feet. The almost oppressive weight of the ancient building above them made her crouch lower as they walked.

He finally reached a large chamber with a well in the center of the floor. Now every bit of stone contained images that tugged at her memory. She'd seen similar carvings in textbooks back in college. The room looked very important.

Oddly, they had passed no other people while getting here.

"Where is everyone?" she asked.

"Outside. I couldn't allow them to see the last chamber I found."

Jess saw that someone had put a wooden ladder inside the well when she stepped close. Rather than leading to water, it took them down to a chamber with four evenly spaced tunnels leading away into the earth.

Unlike the chamber above, this area was purely functional. None of the tunnels looked very stable, but one seemed particularly shaky. Someone had braced it with makeshift wooden beams. That was, of course, the direction Abel led her.

She eyed the ceiling warily. "That doesn't seem very safe."

"It's good enough for the moment," he said. "We'll bring in stouter timbers once we have the find fully documented. Word cannot be allowed to spread or looters will descend on this place like a biblical plague."

She ducked down and followed him through a twisting passage that led to another chamber. It was at least twice the size of the one above them. Rather than the rectangular shape she'd expected, it was circular. Except for the far wall, which was flat. The center of the room held another well. This one might even be real, as she could hear what sounded like water below.

The wall froze her in place. It held something impossible.

Though stylized, the inlay was obviously a map of the solar system. She remembered enough to know the Mayans didn't display their representations of the planets like this. They made sky bands showing the planets and representing the paths they followed overhead.

Yet the scene before her wouldn't be out of place in modern America. It clearly showed the sun as the center of the solar system. Something she wasn't certain the Mayans had known. Even the spacing between the planets looked approximately correct. Each world had a line of inlayed gold for its orbital path.

Abel gestured toward the wall unnecessarily. "You see why I contacted you? This cannot exist, yet it does. I need you to tell me if this is some kind of elaborate forgery. It seems to be as old as the ruin, but I can no longer trust my judgment."

Jess stepped closer and examined the jade insets representing the planets. They were about the right sizes, even for the worlds the Mayans shouldn't have known existed. "Correct me if I'm wrong, but they only knew about the visible planets, right?"

"That's correct," he confirmed. "They knew of Mercury, Venus, Mars, Jupiter, Saturn, and the moon. They might also have been aware of one or two of the largest asteroids. Ceres and possibly Vesta. That's it."

She pointed at the worlds outside Jupiter's orbit. "Yet here we have the outer planets. This shows the moons around them as little chips of jade. Even Pluto, Charon and Eris."

"And one even further out. A big one. I've read that scientists suspected that there were a few undiscovered bodies out there of significant size, but this one is almost as big as Earth. Quite the discovery, if true. How could the Mayan's know any of this?"

The archaeologist shrugged. "I have no idea. And that's not all. See this?" He pointed to another orbit, this one going around the sun inside Mercury and out beyond Eris. Its orbital path was inlayed with what looked like oxidized silver. "This looks like a comet. And here along its path? These markings are faint, but I think they're dates from the Mayan calendar."

The marks meant nothing to her, but she could look them up at some later point. "May I take pictures?"

"Of course, so long as you promise to keep them confidential."

"I don't imagine I'll need to talk to anyone about it. There's a very large database of heavenly bodies and their orbits. I can check it myself and use some computer time to see if these marks indicate a real time that matches any known orbits."

He nodded slowly. "Take your pictures and we can go back to camp. Dinner will be ready soon. We have much to discuss."

* * *

NATHAN BENNETT SCANNED the endless jungle outside the helicopter door. How could anyone find anything in this green hell? They could've flown over the target a half dozen times and been none the wiser.

His money had gotten them information that led to the river drop off, but none of the people he'd bribed had known where the ruins were located. They might be an easy day's walk or a week down some hidden trail. He had to keep looking, though, because Mommy Dearest wanted this woman.

Not that he cared, but the target was an important cog in his father's space hotel scheme. That idiocy seemed to matter to the old man, so his mother knew any disruption she could manage there would hurt him. And that's what she wanted most in the world: to hurt her ex-husband, no matter the cost.

He'd rolled his eyes and loaded a team on his private jet when she'd ordered him to do so. He couldn't imagine what use his mother would get from a space engineer. That made no sense at all.

Perhaps it was because she'd lost a lot of money and prestige when the US space program had collapsed. A decade ago, the liberal politicians in charge of the Federal government had wanted the money being "wasted" on the new ISS2 space station to go to public projects for the people who'd elected them.

The conservative minority had gone along so that some money could go to military spending. Unsurprisingly with the reduced budget, the project had come apart. Massive computer design failures crippled the control center when none of the software worked as promised. And his mother had already fired the people who could've walked the systems back to something workable to increase her profit margin.

In space, the station construction fell far behind schedule, even with the corners she'd cut, and the estimated costs rose precipitously. The government didn't do what his mother had expected, which was to pay through the nose to complete the work.

Instead, they terminated the contract. Lagrange Multinational—his mother's space company—had gone bankrupt, saddling her with massive debt and splashing egg all over her face.

The Russian government bought out all the international partners for pennies on the dollar, though he knew they didn't have the spare cash to complete the proposed station. They were far too busy subverting and invading the nations of the old Soviet Union while the US stood around uselessly waving its hands.

Not that Nathan cared. Whatever his mother wanted, she got. So long as she paid.

"Smoke at two o'clock," the pilot said over the intercom.

Nathan looked ahead of them and spotted it. Thin and grey, but undoubtedly smoke. "Find a place to set us down."

"I might be able to drop you in the river, but that's six or seven miles away. I haven't seen a single break in the canopy."

"Keep looking," Nathan snarled. "I'm not dropping into the water and hacking my way through the jungle. I need a place where you can pick us back up." Carrying an unwilling guest through this would be a nightmare.

His second in command, a bruiser named Jake Farley, jerked his chin toward the open door. "Why not drop in on top of them? We can rappel into their camp and get this over with."

Nathan gave him a steady look. "Because this isn't going down like the job in Syria. There's far less paperwork for me if we don't kill everyone that might recognize the helicopter or us."

"It's easier for me," Jake said indifferently.

"Right up until one of the local guards shoots you while you try to get untangled from a tree. We do this my way."

The man shrugged. "Whatever."

Nathan really needed to get some new blood on the team.

The pilot circled around the ruins at a distance. The jungle would dampen the sound of the helicopter rotors to a soft murmur. Technology couldn't completely eliminate the noise, but it was a lot better than it had been around the turn of the century. In his line of work, getting in and out quietly made the high cost of the equipment a no-brainer.

He finally caught a break about ten minutes later. A tree-covered hill rose above the canopy. The area it shaded from the sun had a relatively bare spot they could rappel into. He tapped the pilot on the shoulder and pointed. "We'll go in there. How long for you to get here when I call?"

"About ninety minutes. Add half an hour to get the bird ready."

"Bullshit. Keep the bird ready to roll. When I call, I want you in the air in ten minutes."

The pilot's acknowledgement was more than a bit surly, but Nathan knew the man would do what he'd told him. He'd seen firsthand the kind of pain Nathan could inflict on those who failed him.

It was already late in the day, so Nathan would get them settled in and wait out the darkness. Under other circumstances, he'd prefer to attack at night, but it would be far too easy to break legs and fall into holes stumbling through the wilds of Guatemala. Or be eaten by something. They'd strike out at dawn, locate the camp, and take the woman.

The pilot brought the helicopter to a hover over the bare patch and Nathan tossed his rope out the open door. He watched it fall to make sure it didn't kink. That could cause someone to lose their grip and fall right to the ground. That would be their problem, of course, but he didn't want to have less than a full team when he got to the camp.

Nathan checked his harness, took off his headphones, and stepped out onto the helicopter's skid tube. One last check below and he kicked off, using his braking hand to control the speed of his descent. He slowed to a crawl just above the ground and landed lightly on his feet.

It took only a moment to disconnect his D-ring and raise his weapon to cover the landing zone. He stepped away from the rope and watched as his people come in with mild satisfaction. All six of them made it to the ground safely.

They spread out to watch every approach to the LZ as the crew chief pulled the ropes back up. The helicopter turned and headed back for the airfield.

Nathan led the way into the jungle. It stank, and there must've been a million different creatures making suspicious noises in the gloom. He couldn't imagine why anyone would choose to live in a shithole like this.

The already faint light dropped off to almost nothing under the canopy. The way became congested with undergrowth so thick he had to put his rifle away and draw his machete.

This job was going to be a real pleasure. Thank God he'd fought hard for a bonus.

# 3

The rented boat dropped Harry and his team off at what he might charitably call a dock just after dawn. It only extended into the river far enough to allow a shallow-drafted craft to use it. That was just barely enough, but it beat swimming.

He showed the owner of the boat a small wad of American dollars. His Spanish was good enough to get his message across. "You come back when I call you and this is yours."

The skinny man shook his head. "Yes."

Harry gave him a steady look. "If you don't come when I call, I'll take back what I paid you up front, even if you've already spent it. Understand?"

The man swallowed hard. "I understand. I will do as you say."

"That will make me very happy. And when I'm happy, everyone else is happy, too."

The team hefted their packs and stepped onto the dock one at a time.

His sniper, Sandra Dean, watched the boat head back the way they'd come. "Did you really need to go all hardass on him, Harry? We look like mercenaries in an action movie. He's not crazy enough to double-cross us."

He grinned. "I'm living up to the image. If we need to get out of here in a hurry, we don't want him stopping for a beer." He eyed the trail and shouldered his pack. "Time to hit the road. I'd prefer to be long gone by the time my unlamented brother arrives."

\* \* \*

JESSICA STEPPED out of her tent and stared groggily at the cheerful people preparing breakfast. Actually, a glance at her watch showed they were getting ready for lunch. It was almost ten in the morning. She'd slept far longer than she'd intended.

Of course, she'd been up late studying all the pictures she'd taken yesterday. Not just of the amazing art deep in the pyramid, but of everything else inside the ancient building that they'd seen on the more sedate trip back out.

As far she could tell, only the one work was unusual. None of the other carvings, inlays, or paintings Abel had showed her after the big reveal held even a hint at the great secret buried deep inside the base of the ancient structure.

Abel said that the false well leading down to the secret level was unusual. The only reason he'd discovered it was that he'd tried to get a water sample and found stone instead. He'd taken some water from the real well in the secret room, but he was already certain it would be identical to the water in the well in the courtyard. He believed an underground river fed them both.

One of the graduate students waved. "Good morning! Would you like some lunch? The stew is almost ready."

Jess stretched her back and walked over to the young man. The day was already getting hot. "That sounds good. I hadn't intended to sleep so long. Where's Doctor Valdez?"

The young man gestured toward the pyramid. "Where else? Deep inside the secret chamber."

He laughed at the surprised expression on her face. "What? You thought no one knew about it? We snuck in the same night he told us not to go inside the pyramid. Well, it took us several nights to find the fake well. That was pretty clever. What do you think the wall means?"

"I think it means Doctor Valdez needs less inquisitive graduate students," she said sternly. "You need to keep this quiet."

The young man waved away her concern. "We've been with the doctor for years. His secret is safe with us."

"That's not really the point. If you talk about it, someone will overhear you." She gestured at the local workers all around the camp. "Do you think none of them understand English? You're almost certainly wrong. Some of them understand it well enough, even if they don't speak it.

"Others might be in the employ of Doctor Valdez's competitors. Under normal circumstances, that wouldn't be a major problem, but the wall changes everything. It might bring a horde of people determined to strip this find of everything of value to sell on the black market."

The graduate student stared at her with an expression that indicated he was waiting for her to deliver the punch line.

Jess shook her head. "You really don't get it, do you? People will kill for something like this. Forget you saw that thing and tell your friends to zip their mouths if they care about Doctor Valdez. And, yes, lunch sounds wonderful."

The bemused young man led her to the tent they'd set up for dining. She accepted a bowl and some water. The scent of the stew had her mouth watering before she took her first bite.

Whoever the cook was, they knew their business. It had enough spice to make it interesting without burning her mouth. She wolfed down her meal and went looking for seconds. She'd need to watch her diet or she'd get back to the spaceport with a few pounds to shed.

She washed her bowl and eating utensils, then went back to her tent to retrieve her camera and carry bag. After reading the graduate student the riot act, she probably shouldn't leave her sensitive notes laying around.

With her bag in hand, she headed into the pyramid.

NATHAN CHOSE an observation post near the summit of what looked like a hill, but was probably a Mayan ruin, watching the camp. There were more workers than he'd accounted for in his planning, but that wouldn't be a problem. Seven men armed with automatic weapons could intimidate an amazing number of people. Particularly if they made examples of a few loudmouths.

A flash of pale hair drew his eyes toward a woman walking across the central square. He focused his binoculars on her and quickly confirmed that she was the target. He'd chosen his hide with care so that the sun wouldn't reflect off the glass.

She was a real looker. Short, stacked, and curvy. Getting to know her was going to be a pleasure he'd savor for as long as he could.

He watched her head into one of the pyramids before he spoke softly into his headset. "Target confirmed. She just entered the pyramid on the north side of the square. It looks like they're getting ready for lunch, so we can catch them all at the table. Solidify a count of the people and stand fast for now. Note any other stragglers."

The team acknowledged one by one.

Nathan considered the tactical situation as he waited for them to serve the mid-day meal. The trip through the jungle had gone faster than he'd thought possible. In the daylight, they'd found game trails leading them in the general direction they needed to go. Now all he had to do was get the woman into custody.

He smiled at the thought of how she'd probably fight. Some women only resisted in the beginning, but he hoped this one might put up a prolonged struggle. Women with spirit were always more fun to break.

The workers finally came streaming to the dining tent. He watched the pyramid the woman had entered, waiting for her to join them. After half an hour, he decided that she wasn't coming. He'd have to go in after her. Which could be fun, too.

"She's not coming out," he said over the radio. "Move in on the workers and get them under control. No shooting unless they have guns. I don't want to warn the target that we're coming. Zip tie and gag everyone."

He backed away from the hide and climbed down the building where the workers couldn't see him. By the time he'd circled the rise, his people had everyone under the gun. His men wore balaclavas and their camouflage was of an old pattern still heavily used by every stripe of mercenary and guerrilla fighter in the area.

One of the men he'd chosen for this mission spoke the language like a native. He was doing all the talking. With only moderate luck, the Guatemalan National Civilian Police would lose his trail hunting for the wrong people.

Nathan tugged his mask over his face and strode out of the jungle. Four of his men split off to search the area looking for stragglers. There was always someone.

The roving teams found half a dozen workers at two sites and brought them back. There was still no sign of the woman emerging from the pyramid.

He motioned for two of his men to come with him and headed after her. The explorers had thoughtfully strung lights. That would make the job of finding them that much easier.

* * *

HARRY SLOWED his team as they started seeing signs of ruins. He didn't want to appear threatening, but he was cautious by nature. "Rex, scout the area."

"Roger." The scout slipped into the thick jungle and was invisible within seconds. They held their position waiting for word that they could proceed.

Rex ghosted out of the foliage three minutes later. "Hostiles have the camp locked down. I counted four with automatic weapons. They look like locals, but that might be to throw off the police."

Harry cursed under his breath. "Nathan beat us here. Dammit. Rex, go around to the right. Sandra, take the left. Get as close as you can. If they make the wrong move, take them down."

Sandra nodded. "Can do. Going tactical."

Everyone opened their packs and pulled out their weapons. Encrypted radios only from this point forward.

His people melted into the jungle while Harry made his way cautiously into the ruins. He'd opted to carry a heavy pack with an extra weapon. In this case, the tranquilizer rifle. With the right timing, he might be able to take out the hostiles. Or at least some of them.

He didn't feel any qualms about using lethal force on his brother's men. They were literally the scum of the earth. However, if his brother weren't out in the open, he'd prefer to keep him in the dark about their arrival.

Once he found a good place to observe, he slowly scanned the prisoners looking for Jessica Cook. He didn't see any women with blonde hair. The client was still in play. And that's how he thought of her. Screw his father. She was the one that mattered.

He focused his attention on the four men. Two of them watched the jungle while two intimidated the prisoners. The high-tech tranquilizer he used could drop a man in seconds, but with everyone so close together, someone would react. And when a man with an automatic weapon felt threatened, people died.

Well, he'd just have to distract them. He keyed his encrypted radio. "I need to get them looking in the wrong direction for a few seconds. Rex, make a noise. Something subtle, so they don't start shooting."

"Yeah, I'd like to avoid that," his friend said dryly. "If I can startle some birds, that'll probably be good enough. I'll give you a heads up before I do it."

"If I can take them quiet, we go that way," Harry said. "Sandra, if one looks like he's going to shoot a hostage, take him out."

"Copy. Call the targets as you engage."

"The one closest to me is home base. I'll start at first and make my way in for a home run."

"Copy."

A minute later, Rex called in. "I'm set."

Harry settled his sights on first base. "Go."

He didn't hear the noise, but he saw the birds take flight. First base, one of the mercenaries watching the jungle perked up. He turned his head and said something to his companions. Second base headed for Rex's location at a jog. Home base turned his attention in that direction, too. Third was looking Harry's way.

"Change in plan. Third, home, first and then second."

He lowered his aim to the man facing him and put a dart in his chest. The man staggered back a step and collapsed.

Harry was already moving his aim to home plate. The target must've heard something, because he pivoted toward the fallen man. He continued the turn all the way to the ground when Harry shot him.

First base called out a warning and ducked for cover. Unfortunately, for him, he didn't know where Harry was and his ass was exposed. Harry put a dart in it.

Second base sprinted for the jungle. Harry fired at him, but missed.

"Runner down," Rex said after a moment. "He was grabbing for a radio, but I don't think he got off a call."

"Tie him up and bring him back to the camp," Harry said. "Everyone, move in and keep a lookout for more hostiles."

Harry rose from the bushes and jogged into the large open area, scanning the buildings. He pulled out zip ties and secured the prisoners. He left searching them for weapons and other goodies to his team.

He chose a young woman who looked like she might be an archaeological student and cut her loose with his combat knife. He held a finger to his lips when she started to say something.

"Keep your voice down," he said softly. "How many others are there and where did they go?"

She pointed to one of the pyramids. "Three men went in there after Doctor Valdez and his guest. They're in the secret room at the bottom of a fake well, but those men will spot the ladder if they look hard enough."

Harry gestured toward the workers. "I want you to head down the path toward the dock. I'll send some of my people with you. Grab food and water, nothing else. Keep quiet or those men will come out and start shooting. You give the orders to the locals as I cut them loose."

He made his way from person to person, slicing their bonds as the woman whispered instructions to them.

That didn't keep him from sending orders to his people. "Rex, you and Leann secure the prisoners. Have some of the workmen carry them off with you. I don't want Nathan grabbing them on the way out. Move the civilians a mile off. We'll call when it's safe to come back."

"Copy."

"Allen and Paul, you're with me. Sandra and Mark, you keep watch from out here. If they come out with the client, use lethal force to stop them from taking her. Discourage them from going down the trail, too."

"Copy," his sniper said.

She'd do it without qualm, too. When she got in the zone, it became nothing more than a numbers game to her. Distance, wind speed, and elevation. If Nathan tried to escape with Jessica Cook, she'd stop him. Permanently.

He caught up with the woman coordinating the workers. "Do you have a map? How can I get down to the well fast?"

"Go to the center of the pyramid and down as far as you can. The well is at the bottom. It comes out into a chamber with four tunnels leading off. The one that looks almost collapsed is the one that leads to the secret room. The others meander around a while and go nowhere. Can you save them?"

She was putting on a brave face, but the woman was terrified. And for good reason.

"We'll do our best. Now get out of here."

He and his people kept watch on the pyramid until Rex and Leann herded the crowd of workers down the trail. Harry waited until he couldn't hear them anymore before heading into the pyramid.

It was time to save the woman of the hour.

# 4

Nathan was ready to pull his hair out. The damned place was a maze. The lights were no help at all. They went everywhere.

They'd stopped several times to listen and heard nothing. Or worse, they'd heard something and went looking only to come out somewhere else no closer to finding the woman.

Where the hell had she gone?

"Maybe you should've asked someone for a map," Jake said.

It took every ounce of Nathan's willpower to stop himself from shooting the smug bastard in the face.

"We must've missed something," he snarled. "There's some hidden passage somewhere."

He led them back down to the ornate well room deep in the center of the pyramid. The room had a string of lights going around the ceiling, but nowhere else. He glanced inside the well and saw a ladder a few feet down.

"Goddammit," he muttered. "They're down there. What could they possibly be looking for at the bottom of a well?"

He aimed his light down the hole and saw a stone floor. No water.

"Shit. These Mayans suck." He pointed to the second man. "Keep watch here. I don't want them stealing the ladder if they aren't down there. Jake, you're with me."

He slung his rifle and climbed cautiously down the ladder. Once he reached the floor, he looked around. Four tunnels. He noted scuffs in the dirt that indicated people had used all of them.

Once Jake was beside him with his weapon ready, Nathan turned off his light. None of the tunnels gave even a glimmer. He turned his light back on and listened closely, but there weren't any unusual sounds. They'd have to do this the hard way.

None of the tunnels looked exceptionally safe, but one looked markedly worse. He leaned close to Jake and spoke softly. He didn't whisper, because that carried further. "We go a little way down each of these. Come back after five minutes. Mark the path."

Jake took the tunnel directly across from the shaky one. Nathan wasn't surprised. It wouldn't be his first choice either. He selected the one to Jake's right and went in. This hunt was almost over.

* * *

HARRY FOLLOWED the woman's instructions slowly. He didn't want to give Nathan any warning. He slung his rifle and went with his pistol. It would be a lot more useful in these tight spaces.

He reached what looked like the final bit of corridor leading to the central well chamber and motioned for his men to slow down even more. One was backing him up while the other kept watch behind them. If they ran into any of Nathan's people, Harry wanted to take them out quietly, if he could.

That plan almost went out the window when he entered the chamber and someone knocked his pistol out of his hand. It clattered loudly across the floor, but Harry didn't go after it. He swung in close to his opponent instead, even though his hand hurt like hell. The bastard had used his rifle butt.

Harry grabbed the rifle with one hand and clamped down on the man's free wrist with the other. He yanked the two apart, which left him open for another attack, but prevented the mercenary from firing his weapon.

The bastard staggered to his left, directly toward the well. Harry tried to alter their course, but the man seemed determined to fall in.

Harry released him at the last moment, but the man grasped desperately at his equipment webbing as he tumbled over the low rim.

The fight had taken place in relative silence up to this point, with only grunts and growls between the two of them. That changed when they smashed the wooden ladder in the well to splinters.

Harry landed on top of the man when they slammed into the stone floor far below. Momentum sent him rolling into the far wall. He saw stars, but staggered to his feet. The light from above only cast a dim glow down here, but he didn't see any movement.

That wouldn't matter. Someone would come looking for the source of all that racket.

The man he'd fought with lay twisted in a way that could only mean he was dead. The ladder was in splintered chunks. He wouldn't be going up without assistance from above.

"You okay, boss?"

He glanced up long enough to see Allen looking down at him. "Better than the other guy. You have a rope?"

"Of course."

"Rig something to get me back out of here. And toss my pistol down."

A sound from the tunnel behind him made Harry turn. There was light coming toward him.

His pistol bounced off the dead man and clattered on the stone beside him. Harry grabbed it and moved to the side of the chamber, aiming toward the potential hostiles.

Two figures came out from the tunnel. Though their bright flashlights obscured them, Harry could tell they didn't have camouflage on. And one of them was a woman. He could tell when she let out a scream at the sight of the body.

Definitely not Nathan's people.

He opened his mouth to make some awkward introductions, but footsteps from the other direction warned him of an oncoming threat.

"Back into the tunnel," he snapped. "Unless you want to end up as dead as he is."

"Who the hell are you and what's going on?" a male voice demanded.

He didn't have time for this. "Move!" He advanced on them, causing them to retreat in the direction he wanted them to go. Harry made it to the tunnel entrance just as a man with an automatic weapon came into the chamber behind him.

The hostile opened fire as Harry shoved the woman back around the bend in the tunnel. She sprawled on her face, hopefully safe from the incoming rounds.

Harry returned fire to force the other man back. He doubted he hit the bastard, but the action bought him time to hunker down.

The other man emptied a full magazine into the tunnel. The shooter yelled into the ringing silence afterward. "Give us the woman and we might let you live."

"Pass," Harry said. "Give up now and you won't end up like your friend."

The other man laughed nastily. "Him? He was an asshole. No loss. I bet you think you got me where you want me. You probably have friends upstairs. So what? I got something for them."

Harry saw him dodge across the room and fired. Too late, as it turned out. The man threw something up the well and made it to the far side of the room safely.

A loud blast upstairs told Harry it had been a grenade.

Dirt and falling pebbles pelted him from the roof of the tunnel. He spun on his heel and tripped over something. A man lay on the floor, his eyes open and staring. The woman was giving him CPR, but from the amount of blood, Harry knew it wouldn't do him any good.

He scrambled to his feet, grabbed the woman's arm, and yanked her along in his wake. "He's gone! Run!"

She still had her flashlight in her hand, which allowed him to see ahead. There was a room around the next bend. They barely made it before the tunnel collapsed. A huge cloud of dirt and debris whooshed into the air, making him cough and shield his eyes.

A flash of light from the side gave him just enough warning to dodge and throw up his arm. The woman's flashlight hurt like hell, but better than if she'd caught him on the head like she'd intended.

"Whoa! I'm on your side!"

She took another swing at him, catching him in the shoulder. The light from her makeshift weapon made the room twist wildly. Her hair fell crazily across her face as she snarled at him. "You killed Abel!"

He caught her third swing and twisted the light out of her hands. He managed to turn his torso and catch her knee on his thigh.

"No! The people trying to kidnap you did. Your boss sent me to rescue you."

"I'll bet."

"He said to tell you that you're too important to Project Liberty to let them take you. The security passcode is kiwi."

She didn't look completely convinced, but she stopped trying to maim him. She wiped tears from her eyes and coughed. The dirt in the air was like being in a sandstorm. "Who the hell are you?" she demanded. "And why would anyone want me so badly that they'd kill a kind, gentle man like Abel?"

"That's a long story."

She gestured toward the collapsed tunnel. "We're not going anywhere soon."

"Hang on." He activated his radio. "Paul? Allen? Are you all right?"

"Harry?" Allen asked. The reception was poor, but comprehensible. "We're good. Are you okay? Part of the well room collapsed."

"Yeah, I'm seeing that up close and personal. I'm fine and I have Miss Cook with me. There's no way you're getting to us and the pyramid might be unstable. Get out now and organize a rescue."

The other man's tone sounded dubious. "Copy. We'll be back as soon as we can."

Harry turned to the woman now that he knew his people were safe. This was the first real look he'd gotten of her. The picture his father had given him didn't do her justice. She was beautiful. Even covered in dust, with her large eyes streaming tears. His greater height and weight didn't intimidate her at all.

"Miss Cook, my name is Harry Rogers. Your CEO hired me and my team to come after you when he found out his ex-wife had taken an interest in you."

She stared at him. "I've heard of you. The estranged son. Your feud with your father is legendary. Why would you ever work for him?"

He used her flashlight to examine the walls and ceiling for cracks. "That's an even longer story. The short version is because he's paying well and you're not one of his usual corporate douchebags."

"Thanks, I suppose. I'm just an engineer. Why in the world would his ex-wife be after me?"

"Because she's a vindictive bitch and a psychopath. If she can hurt my father, she will, even if it makes more sense to do something else. Were these cracks here before?"

He had his light focused on the wall. Large cracks ran down from the ceiling and the facing had fallen off. Glimmering bits of gemstones and gold twinkled in the debris.

"Oh, no!" Jess ran over to the wall, horrified. "It's gone! The artwork is gone."

"I'm sorry to hear that, but on the scale of our troubles, I think that ranks pretty low."

"That painting was the most important archaeological find in the last century," she almost snarled. "It was the crowning achievement of my friend's work. His life's work."

Harry held his hand out, palm forward. "Then I'm truly sorry." He reached past her and poked the cracked stone. It shifted easily and he could see darkness behind it. "This looks hollow. Maybe there's a passage behind it. We need to look without bringing the ceiling down on our heads."

Together, the two of them began gingerly pulling the stones out, revealing an open area beyond the wall. Perhaps their fate wasn't quite as sealed as he'd feared.

\* \* \*

NATHAN CAME BACK into the central chamber ready to shoot, but things were quiet. They weren't promising, though. The guard from above lay sprawled dead on the floor and the tunnel that had looked ready to collapse had done so.

Jake was working with his rope and a shard of the ladder. He was making a jury rigged grappling hook.

He grinned at Nathan. "Well, things could've gone worse. We're done here."

Nathan gave him a cold stare. "Tell me exactly what happened."

"Your asshole brother showed up. He killed that poor bastard, whatever his name was. We exchanged shots and he retreated down the tunnel. His people upstairs were a threat, so I tossed a grenade. Took them out."

He finished tying off the rope. "Looks like I took care of your brother, too. No need for thanks. I'll take cash."

Nathan's gut burned cold. "You absolute imbecile. What in the world made you think I wanted you to kill my brother?"

He shot Jake in the head.

"That's my job," he informed the newly created corpse.

The tunnel was well and truly gone. He hoped his brother could find another way out. It would gall Nathan for the rest of his life if he hadn't been the one to eliminate that self-righteous prick. The woman's death was a shame. A lost opportunity.

Fortunately, Mother had paid him up front. The loss of the success bonus would sting, but he could live without it. And he didn't have to pay Jake or that other dumb bastard.

At least he had another way out. The tunnel he'd explored had led him out beyond the massive building and toward the surface. It ended at a mostly concealed stone door that the Mayans had cleverly balanced. He'd opened it enough to see the jungle. He'd get out of here, gather the rest of his team, if they were still alive, and get to the extraction point. This mission was over.

He salvaged the weapons and radios from the dead men. They might prove useful.

Now it was time to get rid of any evidence. He opened his pack and pulled out several sticks of plastic explosive. He planted them around the chamber and into the three remaining tunnels. He rigged the wireless timer to blow them in twenty minutes.

Now he might be able to convince himself that he'd killed his stupid brother after all.

"See you on the other side, brother mine. After I send our father to join you in hell." He ran down the tunnel with a laugh.

## 5
---

J ess tried to keep her mind off the heavily armed man beside her, but it wasn't easy. How did she know he was really who he said he was? This could all be a trick. He might have been partners with the man that had killed Abel.

Yet, what choice did she have? The tunnel was gone. Hell. That by itself argued in his favor. What kind of idiot collapsed a ruin on himself to build a cover?

She was inclined to believe his story, simply because she could see the familial relationship between him and her boss. Admittedly, Harry was a taller and more ruggedly handsome version of his father. On any other day, his wide shoulders and hard body would warrant a closer look. Today, she just hoped they survived.

Reality dashed her optimism as soon as she grabbed the flashlight and took a good look at the area on the other side of the wall. It looked like some kind of tomb. One without another exit.

Jess's knowledge of Mayan burial chambers was sketchy at best, but this one looked important. Effigy figurines, polychrome pottery, masks, and mushroom figures packed the chamber. Other works of art, carved of jade and marble, sat around the chamber. She could also see a sarcophagus in the back.

"Do you see a way out?" the man asked. Harry Rogers. The man who'd renounced his own father.

"No. It looks like a burial chamber."

"Then we need to find another way clear."

She turned and gave him a look. "The way I see it, we have three options. We dig out the tunnel and hope it doesn't bury us, we go down the well, or we die. We can look in here and maybe we get lucky. If not, our best chance is the well."

He stared at it. "I don't have any breathing gear. We'll end up wet and dead."

"Maybe not. Abel seemed to think it's connected with the courtyard."

"Which way is that? If we go the wrong way, it will be just as deadly."

She pointed into the burial chamber. "That's a clue. I did some reading on the trip down here. The Mayans buried their dead facing either north or west. The pyramid is north of the courtyard. If you don't have a compass, we can make an educated guess and head toward the bottom of the sarcophagus."

He pulled an object off his belt. A compass. "The chamber is facing north-south. So we can try south. Come on."

"I'm not leaving without taking a few pictures. This site might be lost forever. Surely you can spare ten minutes."

By his expression, he didn't think so. She short-circuited his options and ducked through the opening. It was just wide enough for her, so he couldn't get in.

"We don't have time for this." His tone told her he wasn't used to other people arguing with him. Too bad.

She had to get what pictures she could. The art meant they'd buried someone special or unusual here. Perhaps a great astronomer. If she didn't document the site, Abel would never get the credit he deserved, and she couldn't tolerate that.

"I suggest you look for a good spot to tie off the rope while I take pictures. Please tell me you have a rope."

"Christ. How sturdy does that stone box look?"

She aimed her light at the sarcophagus. "It's stout. We can run a line around it. It should support our weight."

"Then take your pictures fast. The chances of the pyramid coming down on top of us increases every minute."

Jess stuck the flashlight into her pocket so that it illuminated the ceiling. She took pictures from the entrance, catching every angle to the room. Every time her flash strobed, she saw the glitter of gems and gold.

She wanted to get the layout before she tried to walk through the funerary offerings. She bent to get the statues and carvings in as much detail as she could. There were too many pieces and too little time to do them justice, but she tried to get a sampling.

Jess took some of the smaller pieces and slipped them into her pack. It was supposed to be waterproof, so she hoped everything made it through undamaged. Including her camera, which the manufacturer also claimed was waterproof.

Mayan carvings covered the stone slab lying across the top of the sarcophagus. The edges had markings that probably said something about the deceased. The top had more around the sides, but the central area was a scene. Well, a scene mixed with all kinds of ritual details.

A man seemed poised to leap off the top of a pyramid. Other men stood nearby, mostly kneeling. They all had the same kind of appearance with long hair and fairly primitive clothing.

The man in the center had some kind of harness over his bare chest, short hair, and an expression of beatific happiness. His arms were spread as though he were about to take flight.

She snapped pictures from every angle. It was magnificent.

"You about done in there? We really need to hit the road."

"Why? Hot date?"

"This place could come crashing down any second. The rocks and dirt are shifting."

She set her camera down on top of the sarcophagus. "I'm almost ready. Just one more thing to look at."

The heavy stone slid a few centimeters when she shoved it. Jess put her back into it and it opened almost a foot at the head. Time to grab a picture of the man of the hour.

What she saw inside froze her in place. The dried human husk was expected. His clothing was not. It wasn't primitive at all. It looked similar to the woven shirts men wore today. It had buttons. And what certainly looked like a name tag, though the lettering was unfamiliar to her.

"Harry," she said softly. "You need to come in here and help me right now."

He peered through the opening. "You look fine. Come on out."

Jess shook her head. "No, there's something really strange in the sarcophagus. A man with strange clothes. Modern clothes."

He looked suitably doubtful. "In a secret room at the bottom of a previously undiscovered Mayan pyramid? I read that book a few years ago. Pure fiction."

She stepped back to the opening and handed him her camera. "Then what is that?"

Harry stared at the image on the screen. "Is this some kind of joke?"

"Do I look like I'm laughing? Get in here and help me."

He hesitated a moment, cursed, and handed the camera back to her. "I sure as hell hope we don't live to regret this. Or not live at all."

The two of them widened the opening in just a few minutes. He took off his pack and forced himself through, leaving it beside the entrance.

He stepped carefully through the priceless art on the floor and played his flashlight into the sarcophagus. "Holy shit. It really is someone in modern clothes. Sort of."

She grabbed his hand when he started to reach into the sarcophagus. "Wait. It might look intact, but it'll probably turn to powder if you touch it. Help me move the lid aside so we can see the entire interior. If we can keep from breaking the lid, we might be able to cover him back up. They might be able to recover him later."

They managed to get the lid off and leaning against the side of the sarcophagus, revealing the corpse completely. He looked as dried out as an Egyptian mummy. His clothes seemed mostly intact and looked far too modern to be possible.

Jess started snapping pictures. His shirt was light in color. Perhaps it had once been white or tan. The name tag was over his right breast pocket. A real pocket. The letters didn't look at all familiar. The shirt had buttons that looked like some kind of plastic.

"How long has he been down here?" Harry asked. "The Mayans have been gone a long time, right?"

"Abel was sure this place was late classical, so AD 700 to 900. This site has been abandoned over a thousand years."

"Then where the hell did this yahoo come from?"

"I'm an orbital engineer, not an archaeologist. Or a science fiction author. Actually, this kind of seems more like a Dane Maddock adventure. If we survive, you can write a letter to David Wood and ask him how he'd set up this kind of story. I'd love to hear what Bones has to say about it."

The dead man's pants were more like shorts. Jess checked the fly, which caused the fabric to powder. It used buttons, too. She pocketed the one that came off in her hand. He wore low-slung shoes that didn't use laces. They looked like leather. A satchel sat just below his feet.

Harry looked at the man's shirt closely. "He has a patch of some kind on his shoulder."

It was too tight for her to see any details. His shoulder was only a few centimeters from the side of the sarcophagus. She put her camera into the space and took half a dozen pictures, changing the point of aim slightly each time.

"Are we about done?" Harry asked. "The hair on the back of my neck is standing up. Something's about to go down."

She prayed, opened her backpack wide, and slid the satchel into it. The thing came apart, but the contents were inside. She tossed her camera in, cinched the pack tight, and strapped it onto her back. "Ready. Let's get the lid back in place, get the rope tied off, and get out of here."

It took all her strength to lift her end, but they got the lid back in place. She sighed. They'd done it.

That's when a sharp shock sent dirt flying off the walls and made the ceiling groan.

"Time to go," Harry said. "Run."

She slid through the opening and watched the ceiling with growing horror. There were cracks and they were growing. "Do you have the rope ready?"

"Nope. Hold your breath."

He snatched up his pack and rifle, grabbed her in his arms, and hopped over the lip of the well.

She screamed as they fell into the darkness. The fall seemed to last an eternity, but it couldn't have been more than a few seconds. They slammed into the water and the force of the impact tore her from his arms.

Jess lost her flashlight, plunging her into pitch darkness as she floated in the cool water. She held her breath and let her head figure out which way was up. She exhaled and felt the air going up the side of her face. She righted herself and kicked for the surface.

The air tasted wonderful when she finally reached it. She took rapid, deep breaths.

Harry broke the surface to her left. "Jessica!" His voice echoed weirdly. "Over here."

Something splashed into the water beside her. Something big. She swam to the side as rocks from above fell into the water. The chamber had collapsed. The man and his secrets now rested under tons of rock and dirt.

The two of them came up against a wall of stone and she waited to see if the whole cavern caved in. The rocks finally stopped falling and they were still alive.

"Well," she said. "That was a little more exciting than I prefer. I don't suppose you managed to hang onto your light. Mine is at the bottom of the pool. It wasn't waterproof, either."

"Mine is." A bright light came on, pointed at the ceiling. She could see where the well pierced it. Or where it used to be. A massive boulder plugged it now. If that had fallen on them, they'd be dead.

Harry played his light around, revealing that they were in a natural cavern. "If there's a connection between the courtyard pool and this one, it's under water. Let me go look."

He pulled out his compass and they moved around until they were at the southernmost wall. "I'll be back in a minute."

She watched his light vanish into the depths with more than a hint of trepidation. What if there wasn't a way out?

That question had a simple answer. They'd die.

Jess sighed. It wasn't as though she had any control over what happened now. She had no choice but to wait in the dark and hope for good news.

* * *

HARRY DOVE, his light showing the wall as it plunged toward the bottom of the pool. He could see something glittering dully in the sand below him and to his right.

He made it all the way to the bottom quickly and easily. With all his gear, that was a forgone conclusion. He shed his rifle and pack next to a low opening in the wall. He could feel a sluggish current coming from it.

Then he looked into the passage. It wasn't too tight, but he didn't see it widening, either. It made a turn just at the limit of his light. He set his flashlight on the sand and undid his boots. He'd be able to swim easier without them. He tied the laces together so that he could carry them around his neck when the time came to go.

That took him to the limit of his air. He grabbed his light and headed back to the surface.

"Did you find anything?" She asked as soon as he broke the surface.

"A tunnel," he said as he caught his breath. "It looks natural. I left my gear down below and came back for more air. I'll get further that way."

"Do you think it leads to the courtyard pool?" She sounded half-hopeful and half-afraid.

"It goes in the right direction, so maybe. There's something that reflects light in the sand down there."

"Offerings, probably. Jade, I'll bet. They probably threw other things into the well as gifts to the gods, but they might not have lasted this long."

He was as oxygenated as he could get. "Be back, hopefully with good news."

Harry dove back down and veered toward the glinting object. It looked like polished stone, so it was probably jade. He tucked it into his pocket. That's when he spotted something near the wall. It gleamed like silver, but more dully.

The object wasn't big, so Harry stuck it in his pocket, too. Then he kicked his way into the passage. It led him around the turn and into a tighter area. He took a chance and swam into it. The tunnel was only three or four feet across at the narrowest point, but he thought it opened back up.

He turned off his flashlight and let the darkness enfold him. Yep, there was dim light from ahead. The two pools did connect. They might survive after all.

Harry turned his light back on, but it didn't work. Crap, the water must've gotten into it. This would be fun. He turned around and felt his way back. He kept a hand on the stone above him so that he'd know when to head up.

Once the roof turned into a wall, he went up. He was almost out of air when he broke the surface.

"Are you okay?" she asked. "What happened to your light?"

"The water got to it, I think. Rest assured, I'll be leaving a negative review about my experience on the Rainforest website. I went far enough to see light on the other end. I think we're good to go."

"But you're not totally sure? Great. We get to swim into a dark tunnel and hope it stays wide enough for us to make our way through. If not, we drown."

Grim, but true enough. "We can't tread water forever. I'll make the trip all the way and come back for you."

He could hear her breathing heavily in the dark. She sounded on the edge of panic. Her voice was steady, though.

"No. I'll go with you. We'll make it together or not at all. I'm a decent swimmer. How do we do this?"

"I'll take you down, grab my stuff, and lead you through. Hold onto my belt and follow my lead."

Once he was certain that she had a tight grip, he dove down, following the angle he'd used before. His hand felt the wall and he kicked his way to the sand.

He found his boots, slung them around his neck, grabbed his pack and rifle, and headed in. She kicked along behind him, but her grip on his harness was slowing him down.

It felt like an eternity before he felt the turn in the tunnel. He followed it around and into the narrowest area he'd explored. The grey glow of light ahead lured him on.

The brightness grew as he kicked his way forward, but the tunnel narrowed again. At least he could see it. This would be tight.

Harry tugged Jess forward and gestured for her to go first. If he couldn't get through, he'd only kill himself.

Once she was through, he shoved his gear to the other side and pulled himself into the narrow opening. He got stuck almost immediately. He struggled to push his way through, but didn't budge.

Jessica had stopped even though he'd motioned for her to go on. She grabbed his hand in hers, planted her feet on the rocks, and pulled. That gave him just enough leverage to tear free. She spun and launched herself into the growing light.

He grabbed his stuff and followed. His lungs screamed for air, so lunged for the surface. He made it. Barely.

The two of them gulped air and looked up. It was fifty feet to the roof of the cavern, then maybe twenty more to the opening. There was no way they were climbing those walls, either.

"You should've left me," he told her, "but thanks. You saved my life."

"So, we're even. And you're welcome. Now what? That's a long way up."

"We call for help."

His pistol was soaked, but the damned thing was almost indestructible. "Hold your hand out."

Harry locked the slide back, letting the chambered round fall into her hand. He held the pistol up to the light to make sure there was no dirt or mud in the barrel. That had the potential to blow the weapon up in his hand. The water wasn't doing it any good, but it would fire. Of that, he had no doubt.

Once he was sure it was clear, he took the round back from her, put it in his pocket, and let the slide chamber the next round.

"This will be loud. Plug your ears."

He aimed the pistol out of the well and fired three shots. The sound echoed off the walls, even louder than he'd expected.

"Are you calling for help or just catching dinner down there?" Rex shouted.

"I am kind of hungry," he said. "It's damned good to hear your voice."

"I thought you were gone, man. They blew up the whole pyramid. You got the civilians?"

"I have Miss Cook with me. Doctor Valdez didn't make it. Did the boys get out?"

"Just before the thing collapsed. I left Leann with the civilians and came hauling ass back."

A wave of relief rolled through him. "Thank God."

"Are either of you hurt?" Rex asked. "We've just about got a rope secure. I'll come down for you if I need to."

"We're fine. Rig one of the rappelling harnesses and we'll handle our end."

He looked at Jessica. "I assume you're fine with being hauled out of here."

"Hell, yes. The ride can't be any scarier than having a pyramid dropped on you."

"Probably not."

Harry holstered his pistol and waited for the harness. When it came swishing down, he strapped Jessica into it. "Just hold onto the rope and they'll get you out. Safe as houses."

"Thanks for coming for me."

"My pleasure. Haul away!"

They lifted her out of the well and quickly dropped the harness back down for him. Getting it on while treading water with his gear was a bit of a challenge, but he managed. "Pull!"

They lifted him into the bright sunlight. Ready hands yanked him over the rim of the well and he rolled over onto his back.

"Today has totally sucked. I'm charging my father extra."

Rex pulled him to his feet. "Let's get you into a tent to change into something dry. Sandra will help Miss Cook."

"I want eyes all around us. If some of them made it out of the pyramid, I want them found. Nathan is too damned selfish to blow himself up just to get me. He probably had another way out. Find him."

His people spread out as he lugged his waterlogged pack into the nearest tent. He'd be lucky if anything was dry. If not, he'd borrow something from Rex.

\* \* \*

Nathan watched them fish his brother out of the well with mixed emotions. It would've been nice to have Harry off the playing field, but he wanted to see his eyes when he killed him.

He had his crosshairs on his brother, but wasn't tempted to fire. He'd have too much trouble making it back to the LZ with Harry's team hunting him every foot of the way. If the copter crew was even ready when he called.

No, not the time to take chances. "I'll be seeing you soon, big brother," he said softly.

When the others began fanning out to search the general area, Nathan knew it was time to put some distance between him and them. He'd have to report a complete failure. They'd missed the target and his team was captured or dead.

Well, that was occasionally the price of doing business. They'd failed, so they could take the fall with the local authorities. They wouldn't talk. The money waiting for them when they got out ensured that.

Oh, well. He backed away from his hide and slung his rifle over his shoulder. He'd watch his brother for a while, and then call for a pickup when things calmed down. This was not over.

# 6

Thanks to her waterproof pack, Jess had dry clothes to change into. The female mercenary left her alone to change, saying she'd be outside if Jess needed anything.

What she needed was a stiff drink and some time to grieve for her lost friend. Time she suspected she wouldn't have. Not until they were safely out of this jungle.

She stripped off her wet clothes, twisted as much water out of them as she could, and packed them in a trash bag. They'd be nasty by the time she washed them, but that was a manageable problem. She then dried off and changed into the dry clothes she'd laid out.

The next thing she did was check her camera. It was dry and working, so she synced the pictures to her tablet, which was also intact. Thank God.

While that was happening, she eyed the contents of the dead man's satchel. It was mostly still together, but she needed to secure it better. They'd be traveling in a hurry and the fall into the water might have irretrievably damaged something already.

She saw several wrenches and a flat-bladed screwdriver similar to the one on her belt back at the spaceport. The tip was removable. There were other tips that looked as though they could fit on the screwdriver handle, but their purpose was murkier. They looked electronic, but there was no indication of a power source. Or what they might do.

She examined the screwdriver handle. The grip had a removable base that revealed a hollow. It held what certainly looked like a battery. It had strange writing on it, similar to the name tag on the mummy. No signs of corrosion, so there must not be an acidic component.

After all this time, the battery was certainly dead, but examining it in the lab might tell them the power level it was supposed to deliver.

At the bottom of her pack was a notebook. It was about the size of a diary and seemed intact. The cover looked like leather, but it wasn't cracked. The pages hadn't come apart either, so she risked touching her finger to their edges. No, it wasn't paper. It felt slick, like some kind of plastic.

Jess took a deep breath and opened the cover.

The first page had tight rows of handwriting in a language that she didn't recognize. Maybe it was a diary. The beginnings of some of the paragraphs were different, so that could mean dates. The inside cover had a few lines of text, maybe the man's name and how to return it to him if it was lost.

She took a chance and lifted the book out to lay it on the cot. She wanted pictures.

That's when she saw the tablet under it and stopped breathing. She set the book carefully down and picked up the device. The surface felt like glass, but that didn't mean much. It could be any number of materials.

The back was made of light metal and had a strange emblem centered on it. A tree of some kind with text in a circle around it. It shared some similarities with the Rainforest logo, but wasn't enough like it to feel creepy.

There were several recessed buttons, but she restrained herself from pressing them. The power supply had to be dead, but she didn't want to take any chances. She'd examine it more closely once she had it back in the lab.

It took her ten minutes to take multiple images of each page. The first third of the book only had text. The middle of the journal had a number of drawings as well. Some of plants that she wasn't familiar with, but also what looked like contour maps of terrain. One whole page had what was certainly a rough map of the Mayan city.

There were sketches of men and women she assumed to be Mayan. Not just the well-to-do, but workmen building a wall. Women tending to plants in a terraced garden. Even children playing some kind of game. The man had a good hand.

A second map seemed to show a path away from the city. There were notations in the strange language that probably meant distances or landmarks. The end of the trail had a heavy circle around it. More text beside that might indicate what was there, but she couldn't make heads or tails of the words.

Jess finished taking pictures, synced them, and put everything except her tablet back into the pack. She shouldered her bag and walked out of the tent. The woman was waiting. Another man was slowly turning, watching the jungle. The rest were gone.

"Is it safe out here in the open like this?" Jess asked. "If you think there are still some bad guys out there, maybe we should get under cover."

The woman shook her head. "We've already cleared the general area. We'll withdraw down the trail as soon as Harry is ready."

He stepped out of another tent as she said that. He was dressed in dry fatigues, but still had his wet pack on his back. And his weapons, of course.

She walked over to him. "What's your plan?"

"A couple of my people are looking to see if they can find any other bad guys, but I wouldn't hold my breath. Once they get back, we'll move toward the river and meet up with the workers. We'll call for the police when we get to the river."

Jess stepped closer to him and lowered her voice. "I took a few minutes to look over the artifacts. I found something you might want to see." She handed him her tablet with the map of the area on the screen.

He looked at it closely. "What's this?"

"A page from a book inside the satchel. I'm thinking it's a journal. This is the Mayan city here. This path leads somewhere the dead man thought was important. The police will be all over this area. We should see what's there before they accidentally destroy it. Or lead looters to it."

He gave her a stern look. "In case you forgot, there are people in the jungle that want to kidnap you. I don't think wandering around where they might get a second shot is the smartest thing to do."

"I know it's a risk, but this is important. Really important. Come on, surely even a man like you can see that the first extraterrestrial visitor and the things he brought with him need to be protected at all costs."

The corner of his mouth quirked up. "A man like me, huh? Perhaps it would surprise you to know I don't grunt when I walk or drag the backs of my hands on the ground. And we don't know this guy came from outer space."

Jess felt her face heat. "That wasn't what I meant." Actually, it had been exactly what she'd meant. It just wasn't polite to rub his face in it.

"There was a tablet computer in the satchel. Where else would someone with something like that come from? Atlantis? No. Humanity would've found some trace of a terrestrial civilization that advanced. This person came from space. With the condition of the body, he might not have been human."

Harry looked skeptical. "I've seen enough pictures of mummies to know that was a human being. An alien, even one that was bipedal, would almost certainly have some aspect of the face that was noticeably different. Unless, of course, you'd like to propose that humans were seeded all over the galaxy."

"I'm keeping my options open. Think of this from another angle. The artifacts we're recovering could lead to any number of breakthroughs. The technology would have to be very advanced." She thought of another angle. "It might even have military applications."

He shook his head slowly. "You really need to check your prejudices at the door, Miss Cook. I'm a warrior, not a warmonger. Perhaps you're right, though. If there were weapons or technology that could lead to a weapon, I'd rather not see it make its way into the world. There's already too much violence and killing for my taste."

Harry spent a minute examining the map. "I think the best course of action is to accompany the workers to the river. We can call for help from there. Then we'll set out for this place. If the scale is anything close to accurate, we might make it there by midday tomorrow. Maybe. What language are these comments in?"

"I'm not sure. I've never seen anything like it, but I'm not a language expert."

"Someone will figure it out. Come on. Let's get moving."

She watched him get his people into motion. They took down several of the tents and packed them. Probably so they'd have shelter overnight. That had her full approval.

While he organized things, she went back into the tent she'd come from and let the emotions she'd been holding back roll over her. Better to cry now than when she had an audience. Her friend was dead and that hurt. If she ever had an opportunity, the people behind Abel's death would pay.

* * *

Harry had the team ready to roll in ten minutes, but stopped when Sandra held up her hand. "Is something wrong?"

"The client is pulling herself together. Give her a few more minutes."

Not the time for it, but he could hardly blame her. He was sure the events of the day would give her nightmares for months.

He'd already cleaned and oiled his weapons, so he made one more pass around the camp. If they were going to be stuck in the jungle for a few days, he wanted to be sure that they had everything they needed.

They had enough water, but taking more would help if they had problems. The tents he'd commandeered would see them through until he arranged a pickup. The extra food and cooking utensils would make them a bit more comfortable.

When he had nothing else to do, he decided he owed his father a call. He reluctantly stepped away from the tents to get it over with.

"Harry," his father said when he answered. "Did everything go as planned?"

"Nothing ever goes as planned, but this went a little further off script than usual. Nathan and his team beat us here. We managed to get Miss Cook away from him, but his people killed the archaeologist leading the dig. At least one of Nathan's people died, as well. Both of them are buried under a collapsed pyramid."

"That is unfortunate news, but it could have been much worse. Well done. What's your extraction plan?"

Harry considered what he could say over an open line. Any unencrypted communication might have extra ears. "We're getting the workers to the river, but we're not evacuating with them. There are aspects of the situation that require our attention before we can get clear. We'll be here at least one more night."

The tone in his father's voice expressed his disapproval. "Miss Cook's safety is paramount. I'm certain that whatever issue you're concerned with can wait until she's safely away."

"I disagree, as does she. I'm not able to go over the specifics over an unsecured line, so you'll need to trust my professional judgment." He smiled at defying his father. The small pleasures in life were the sweetest.

"In any case," he continued, "I'll call when we're ready to evac. If you had a plane nearby and perhaps a helicopter capable of picking us up via cable from the jungle, that would make this go more quickly."

"I'm not happy with this turn of events and I expect a full briefing once you're clear. And, Harry? This better be more than just tweaking my nose or you'll enjoy our next meeting even less than you usually do."

The line went dead.

At least they understood one another. He cleared his throat outside the tent. "Miss Cook, it's time to go."

She came out, her eyes red, but her expression resolute. She shouldered her pack. "Ready."

He gave her a sharp nod. Her steadiness was admirable. Most civilians, male or female, would've come to pieces under the strain of the last few hours. Jessica Cook was made of sterner stuff.

They hefted their borrowed gear and moved down the path at a steady pace. The workers were only about a mile away with Leann. He took the time to brief them on the general events and to break the news that their boss was dead.

The students took it hard, but he got them moving again in short order when he told them that some of the bad guys had probably gotten away. They made it to the river faster than he expected. No doubt, everyone was eager to be away from this place.

Harry called the Guatemalan National Civilian Police. He kept the details to a minimum and feigned a bad connection before terminating the call. All they needed to know was that there'd been an incident with a fatality. They'd come in enough force to get the workers to safety.

Next, he spoke with the young woman now in charge of the workers. "You need to keep word of the secret room under wraps," he told her firmly. "The men that attacked you can't know about it or you'll all be in danger. You can't tell the police about it, either. Does anyone else know?"

"About the art? Just the other graduate students. I can't lie to the police."

He hadn't seen her standing there, but Miss Cook intervened. "Don't lie. Just don't mention it."

Harry gave her a quelling glance. "Word will get out if you speak of it. Your boss found something unprecedented down there. Unless you want to see this whole area stripped bare, stick to the basics. These men attacked you, they killed your boss in the pyramid, and they blew it up. You don't know why."

"I don't know why!" the woman almost shouted. "Those people almost killed us. Then you came in and saved us? Why? Who are you?"

Harry put on his least threatening expression. "We're Miss Cook's security team. Her boss should've sent us along with her, but there was a breakdown in communication. I'm certain that he'll give the police a full statement about us and provide access for the police to question us."

In a pig's eye. The old man would shut them down quick.

Miss Cook took the woman by the shoulders. "Do you really want the police to think you might have had some part, no matter how small, in Doctor Valdez's death? You'd be better off keeping quiet unless you like the idea of a few months in jail being questioned."

The woman's expression went from outrage to fearful.

Harry didn't like the idea of lying to the woman, but they couldn't tell her the truth. Miss Cook was surprisingly adept at managing the situation. She had hidden depths.

"Just keep things simple," Harry said soothingly. "Tell them the truth, just not all of it."

The woman nodded and walked over to her fellow graduate students. Time would tell if the scare kept them quiet.

"I'm a little surprised you told a whopper like that," he said softly.

"I'd tell a bigger lie if it meant safeguarding this secret," Miss Cook said. "I'm more concerned about what the prisoners will tell the police."

He looked over at the bound men shuffling along under Rex's guard. "They won't say a word. I'm sure the penalty of ratting out Nathan and my mother would be fatal. There's probably a financial sweetener to keep them quiet, too. And that reminds me, I need to send some money to the guy who was on the hook to pick us up. He still deserves to be paid."

They made the rest of the trip to the river in relative peace. Once they arrived at the dock, Harry trussed the prisoners up like prized turkeys and hitched them to handy trees. No way they'd get loose without assistance.

Surprisingly, it only took an hour before Harry heard a boat on the water. It came around the bend and he recognized the uniform the men wore. The Guatemalan National Civilian Police had arrived.

He tugged on Jessica's arm and the two of them backed into the lush vegetation. The rest of the team had spread out to keep watch for hostiles. They'd meet up at a predetermined rally point. Time to see what other secrets this jungle held.

## 7

---

J ess discovered that going through the jungle without a cleared path was significantly more difficult than walking down an open trail. Progress was slow and the insects were all over them. Time to give up that fantasy about exploring the wilds of Africa in a pith helmet.

The mosquitos were even move vicious in the deep jungle. The repellant seemed to be attracting them. She swatted them, but more came to take their place.

The mercenaries took turns hacking at the growth and politely declined her offers to assist. Instead, she followed Harry Rogers. She still knew virtually nothing about him, other than the rumors that she'd heard.

Those stories revolved around him and his father having a huge falling out when he was younger. Of him joining the US Army and becoming some kind of special operations officer. Him leaving the service to become a mercenary. Obviously, that last was true.

She still had no idea why someone that hated his father so deeply would get involved in rescuing her. It made no sense. Maybe she should ask.

"Hey," she said.

He glanced over his shoulder at her. "You need a break?"

"No. Why did you come for me?"

He smiled. "Because you needed rescuing and my father is paying heavily for the operation."

"You and he don't get along so well."

"That's something of an understatement. As far as I'm concerned, you're the client."

"It seems like I'm missing something important. You're a mercenary, right? Isn't this kind of job a little off the beaten path for you?"

He looked around at the trackless jungle surrounding them. "We're all a bit off the beaten path, but I get your meaning. No, I do this sort of thing for a living now. Rescuing people stuck in situations they have no way out of. We mainly recover kidnapped children held overseas by non-custodial parents."

Jess blinked. That wasn't what she'd expected at all. "So you're not mercenaries?"

"That's a matter of debate. Liberty SOG has people from the best US military units: SEALS, Delta Force, Marine Raiders, and others less well known. When the government decided to neuter the military, there were plenty of excellent candidates to choose from.

"We've done purely military operations, and honestly, we occasionally still do. But only if the moral reasons for doing so outweigh the trouble. Frankly, with all the problems in Europe, there's plenty of business that we don't need to hold our noses over."

She understood that well enough. It used to be that only the Middle East had issues with violent groups espousing virulent forms of Islam. Now Western Europe was fighting a cancer in its body. It wasn't politically correct to call them Islamic extremists, but honesty compelled her to say that was the right name.

The news organizations, with a few exceptions, and the government preferred to leave the religious part out. They said those people had nothing to do with Islam. That might even technically be true, but those people had no problem using Islam to justify terrible acts.

The European Union had opened their arms to an enormous number of refugees when the violence in the Middle East and Northern Africa spun out of control. War between Saudi Arabia and Iran quickly spread over the entire area around them.

Iran used nuclear weapons they weren't supposed to have on their enemies. Armed with US made defenses, the Saudis and Israel fended them off. Israel, of course, nuked Tehran and several other military strongholds inside Iran.

Others were less able to defend themselves and millions died.

That fractured Iran, but didn't stop the violence. It only shoved it underground. Groups like Al Qaeda and ISIS now openly recruited from, and infiltrated into, any country they could. With the general collapse of most governments in the Middle East, they saw their chance to create a Caliphate. Saudi Arabia and Israel were islands in a violent sea.

It wasn't looking so good for Europe, either. France was the worst off. Paris was more like Beirut these days. Roving gangs of militants kept the police penned into certain neighborhoods. Sharia law was the rule, not the exception. The French government was helpless and she suspected the militants would finalize their takeover before too much longer. How much longer until the rest of Europe caught the cancer, too?

The situation made her sad.

Frankly, she believed in the US government's viewpoint. Profiling was wrong. People should be judged by what they did, who they were, not what they looked like. You couldn't just label everyone of a specific ethnicity as something and rob them of their rights.

Only that open-mindedness hadn't worked out so well. Thankfully, she didn't have to fix the world. She'd be leaving it soon enough for Liberty Station.

Huh. His company had the same name as the project she headed. That couldn't be a coincidence. His father must've been making some point.

"Why call your company Liberty SOG? What does that mean?"

"Liberty is part of what we do. It plays into every aspect of our work. SOG stands for special operations group. Technically, we're a private military company. We have a number of teams spread out around the globe."

They arrived at a clearing. It looked like the team was setting up the tents for the evening. Good. Her legs felt like rubber.

She dropped her pack and sat on a fallen log after making sure nothing was waiting to bite her.

They had the tents up before the light faded. The guy named Rex built a very small fire and cooked some of the food from the dig. It tasted good after a long, terrible day. She turned in early and fell asleep before her head touched the sleeping bag.

\* \* \*

HARRY TOOK the last watch of the night while Sandra cooked breakfast. Frankly, he wished he could just declare Rex as the sole cook because he had the touch. Sandra made a much better sniper than a homemaker.

He let Jess sleep in. She'd insisted on him using her first name. Apparently, she thought saving her life entitled him to stop being so formal. That was fine with him.

Once the food was ready, he tapped her foot through the flap of the tent. She sat up abruptly and blinked at him. Her hair was poking out in every direction and she looked disoriented.

"What?" she asked. "Are we under attack?"

"Only if you consider Sandra's cooking a war crime. Breakfast is ready. We have a latrine set up to the south. Leann will provide overwatch while you take care of business."

He returned to the fire and did what he could to salvage breakfast. He handed Jess a plate when she came back. She'd brushed her hair and actually looked awake.

"Sorry I overslept. That's two days in a row." She took a bite of the food and made a face.

He almost smiled. Everyone did that. "Sorry about breakfast. It was Sandra's turn. She's says it builds character."

"That's okay. I'm happy to have it. How long do you figure it will take us to get to the site?"

Harry shrugged. "No telling. We'll be in the general area by lunchtime. Finding whatever is there might take days. Or never happen. Look around. There could be a city a hundred feet away and we'd never know."

She glanced around at the almost impenetrable jungle. "True. That would be very disappointing."

"If we don't find anything, I imagine my father will send someone else to look. So, all things being equal, I'd rather find it first."

"Competitive much?"

He took a few bites of something that might once have been eggs. "I make it a habit to never let my family get one over on me. Nathan almost captured you, so I have to make up for it by screwing things up for my father. It's complicated. Even if it takes a few days, I want to know what that site is before he does."

They broke camp half an hour later and resumed their trek. In the end, they didn't have to do a lot of searching. There was a big hill overlooking the general area. Sandra climbed a tree at the top to get a look.

"I have something to the northeast. A gap in the trees. It might indicate ruins."

All Harry could see was undergrowth. He waited for Sandra to climb back down and sent Rex off in the indicated direction. Odds were that he wouldn't find anything.

And, in fact, Rex didn't find any ruins. He did find something strange about the clearing. The gap was a perfectly circular clearing about a hundred feet across.

Even the undergrowth was missing. The limbs from the surrounding trees hid the spooky symmetry from the air, breaking up the curve. Bare ground was all that greeted them. Only a few dead limbs lay in the open.

Harry stopped at the edge, his finely honed subconscious screaming at him to back up. It thought he was about to be ambushed. He wasn't entirely certain it was wrong.

He glanced over at Jess. Her expression told him this wasn't what she'd expected, either.

"Can you tell me why there aren't any plants in there?" he asked.

She shook her head. "No. I've never heard of anything like this." She stepped out into the open before he could grab her and ran her hand over the ground. "It feels like regular dirt."

"Maybe you shouldn't be out there. What if it's some kind of poison?"

"One that works in a perfect circle? Doubtful. And even in poisoned areas, some plants are hardier than others. There's no natural reason for a clearing like this."

Harry couldn't think of one, either. "Spread out, everyone. If there's a group of people cleaning this spot, I don't want to be surprised if they come calling."

He stepped out beside Jess. "Why would someone clear a random spot in the jungle?"

"Because it isn't random. It means something to them. Let's give the ground in the middle a better look."

She marched to the center of the clearing resolutely while he followed behind her, his weapon up and scanning for threats. It felt like the trees were staring at him.

Jess squatted and ran her hand across the ground. "This feels different. More compacted." She opened her pack and dug inside, producing a small hand pick. "I grabbed this from the camp in case we needed to dig."

Within a few minutes, she had a section of the dirt dug up. It didn't go down far. Maybe 15 centimeters under the surface, she found stone.

"This isn't natural," she said. "See the tool marks? Someone put this here."

That made him shake his head. "Why cover something with stone and then bury it?"

"Because you want to protect whatever is under it. We might not be able to find out why the man marked this area by his book. We're not set up to dig up anything like this."

"How far out does it go?"

"Let's find out."

She moved a few feet over and dug into the ground. "More stone here. And this looks like a seam. Maybe there's a buried trapdoor."

Rex came out of the jungle as she started digging again. "I found a trail off to the east. There were some bare footprints. That might mean locals. It doesn't appear to have been used in the last week or so."

Harry stared off in that direction. "Post a watch. Tripwire protocol."

"Copy that. I'll put people out in the other directions, too. If we see anything, I'll warn you trouble is coming."

"Hey," Jess said. "I found a handle."

Harry examined it as Rex headed back out to set the perimeter watch. Sure enough, the stone slab had an area carved out so that someone could lift it. That wasn't to say that the two of them would be able to do so by themselves.

"Let's see how big the door is," he said.

It took them working in turns for half an hour to uncover the slab. It was a dozen feet across. That meant it was far too heavy for the two of them to budge. It must weigh tons. Still, it only had the one handhold.

He grasped the stone and pulled upward. The rock groaned and rose on his end. "It must have a counterbalance. That's pretty advanced. Did the Mayans know how to do something like that? And should it still be working?"

"Damned if I know." A flight of stairs descended into the darkness. They also looked like worked stone, but were carved and fitted together. It was obvious from the undisturbed dirt that no one had been down there in a long, long time.

He pondered their options and decided he wanted to know more. "Let's go take a look. Watch out for hidden death traps, Doctor Jones."

"Call me Indiana," Jess said with a grin. She pulled an appropriated flashlight from her pack and started carefully down the steps.

# 8

Jess proceeded down the steps with caution. Just because Harry had been joking when he mentioned Indiana Jones didn't mean there weren't traps for the unwary. She slid over to the right as far as possible. That way she wouldn't trigger something under the center of a step. Unless she was supposed to be on the left.

The stairs went a lot further down than she'd expected, spiraling gently to the right. Was that a Mayan feature? She wasn't sure. By the time she reached the bottom, she guessed they were at least fifty feet below ground level.

She expected a corridor, but found herself standing on the edge of a vaulted chamber. The walls looked like closely fitted stone. Heavier blocks made up the floor just in front of her, but that wasn't the most interesting thing in view.

"Holy crap!" Harry said as he stepped up beside her. "Is that a spaceship?"

Jess had to admit that it certainly looked like one. Its high tech lines were completely out of place in the ancient hiding place. As if the tablet she'd recovered weren't enough, this proved that the man in the burial chamber had come from space.

It stretched out about the length of a commuter bus, with wings that looked extendable. Much of its bulk was lost in the darkness. Her flashlight was totally inadequate to see the ship as a whole.

Something had mangled the front of the vehicle. The very lines of the frame seemed skewed. This ship had crash-landed.

Jess took a deep breath and turned off her wonder. It was time to be a space construction engineer. "Okay. We need to take some pictures of this thing and, if possible, get inside."

Harry seemed unconvinced. "We might have unhappy visitors before very long. My team is good, but we don't have enough people to stop a howling mob. We need to get a real security team to cover this area before we go all gaga over the spaceship." His expression soured. "Even if they are my father's people."

Jess shook her head. "Harry, this thing has been buried for a long, long time. I'm safe here. Go up and use your sat phone to call for help. Your people, his people, I don't care. This site must be protected."

He tugged a small box off his belt. It had an earpiece with a long cord, so it must've been a radio. "Put this on. I'll try to stay in range so you can yell if you run into trouble. And so that you can get word if we have guests."

After a moment's hesitation, he continued. "Have you ever shot a pistol?"

Deadly weapons weren't really her thing. "I've been to the range with friends a few times."

He shucked his pack and dug a holstered pistol out of it. "This belonged to one of the bad guys. Hang it on your belt. You probably won't need it, but if the crap hits the fan, I want you to be able to defend yourself."

She wasn't comfortable with the idea, but didn't turn him down. Yes, she'd been to the range, but it hadn't been the most comfortable experience. Guns were loud and scared her more than a little. She believed they caused more problems than they solved. He obviously had a different worldview.

Still, she was in the middle of the Guatemalan jungle with people trying to kill or kidnap her. It seemed like an appropriate precaution.

Jess listened to his short safety lecture carefully. If circumstances forced her to use the damned thing, she wanted to do it correctly. And, his warning to be certain what she was shooting at was only common sense. With her luck, she'd shoot at a bad guy and it would be him. No doubt, that was exactly what he was afraid of.

She slid the holstered weapon onto her belt and pocketed the spare magazine.

Once Harry was gone, she turned her full attention to the ship. She doubted it had made such a neat hole in the ground. That meant the Mayans had dug this area out, lowered the ship into it, and built the roof and stairs to conceal it.

That was a lot of work.

A rough estimate of the ship's weight convinced her they hadn't lowered it in. No primitive ropes would've been able to support it. Perhaps they'd dug out the hole, created a gentle slope, and used logs to ease it into place.

Jess dismissed that line of thought. Someone would figure it out. She needed to examine the vessel.

She circled the ship, taking pictures to document it. Once she had the ground level exterior covered, she made a closer pass. She didn't want to spend too much time on any one thing, but she couldn't stop examining the external fixtures.

Time had damaged so much. Metal left out in the air for long periods often decayed in ways many people didn't consider. Rust was only the most common kind of damage. It was a testament to its builders that this thing still existed at all.

The ship, of course, would never move under its own power again. The stresses would tear it apart. Yet the technology it contained could hurl them into the future with a number of leaps and bounds. Some of the exterior equipment was recognizable, most was not.

"You okay down there?"

Jess jumped at Harry's voice in her ear. She ordered her racing heart to slow down and searched for the button to transmit.

"I'm fine. Just taking pictures and looking at the equipment on the hull. Any sign of visitors?"

"Not yet, but I have Rex putting out some tripwires. We have some that will warn us silently if anyone is coming. I need to call my father, too. I really can't justify keeping you in a dangerous situation like this any longer. Dammit."

She could hear the frustration in his voice. She didn't understand the circumstances behind their relationship, but she sympathized. Her brothers occasionally sounded like that when complaining about her.

"Someone else was always going to take over this site," she said reasonably. "He'll guard it, but the Guatemalan government will find out soon enough. We're only temporary caretakers."

"Maybe I should've called them directly. Probably not. The corruption is so endemic down here that we wouldn't have any idea who'd take possession. How long will you be down there?"

"How long until the new protective force arrives and kicks us out?"

He laughed. "I should've guessed. Call me if you find anything dangerous or if you need any help."

"Will do."

Jess returned her attention to the ship. How could she get in?

\* \* \*

NATHAN WATCHED Harry from the safety of the hill. He couldn't see him directly, but the micro-drone he'd sent in transmitted the visual in maximum HD.

His brother's strange actions convinced him that he'd been right to take a risk and follow them.

What was he up to? Why come all the way out here to this hidden site? And how had they known it was even here?

Harry had left the workers to the police and came out to the middle of nowhere. They'd dug up some kind of stone slab and now the woman was underground. It was a mystery, and he hated mysteries. Someone always died, and it was rarely the self-righteous prick that deserved it.

With the forces opposing him, Nathan couldn't do anything but watch, but that was interesting enough. Something in the pyramid must've led them here. Or something the archaeologist had discovered. There was no telling.

Actually, he might be able to get an idea, but only if his idiot brother moved away from the hole in the ground. That meant Nathan needed to exercise patience. How boring.

He settled in to wait and watch. If the opportunity presented itself, he'd send the drone down the hole.

* * *

HARRY MULLED over what Jess had said and called his father with a sigh. Best to get this over with.

"Harry. Are you ready to tell me what this is all about?" his father asked when he answered.

"Not over an unsecured line, no. We're ready for a pickup, though. We'll also need a security force. There's something here that needs guarding."

"So call the police. That's not my problem."

Harry smiled humorlessly. "Oh, I think you'll want to send some people. You know how you're always raving about how good your word is? Well, this is the time to trust what I'm saying. You want a strong security force at the coordinates I'm sending you as soon as possible. You have an interest. You just don't know it yet."

His father was silent for a moment. "Very well. I can have a small team to your general area in about an hour. It will take at least two more to get a larger group of guards in place. Which is better?"

"Both. We're not in immediate danger, but that could change on very short notice. I'll send you the coordinates. There's a clearing large enough for landing a small helicopter, but rappelling in would be faster and safer. I'll talk with you again once I get Miss Cook in your hands."

He hung up before his father could respond.

Things could still go to hell in an hour, but they were making strides toward getting Jess to safety. He'd best go check up on her. Make sure she wasn't doing something dangerous. Of course, with strange technology, how would he know?

\* \* \*

CLAYTON CONSIDERED the phone in his hand for a moment. This kind of behavior wasn't typical for his oldest son. If Harry had something to say, he'd say it and damn the consequences. Whatever he was hiding, it must be important.

He'd already relocated to the Yucatan Spaceport, so he'd pick them up personally. He wouldn't go to this kind of trouble for just anyone, but this hinted at fast moving and important events. Events that he needed to know about as soon as possible.

His personal assistant looked up from his computer as Clayton came out of his makeshift office. "Yes, sir?"

"Hold all my calls and notify my pilot that I'm on the way. I want to be in the air as soon as I buckle in."

He didn't wait for a response. His man was more than capable of handling simple instructions.

\* \* \*

IT ONLY TOOK Jess a minute to find the way into the ship. Of course, that didn't mean she had a clue on how to open it. Or even the assurance that it was possible after all this time. It might be corroded shut. Or need power to function.

The hatch itself was about the size of a double doorway. More than big enough for a person, but small for cargo. The hatch failed to budge when she tugged on the handle, so she was pessimistic about her chances of getting inside.

"Coming down," Harry said over the radio. "Don't shoot me."

She glanced over at the stairway and saw his light. "You're good. This time."

"Thanks," he said dryly. "How's it going?"

"I'm trying to open a hatch with no success. Maybe you have a crowbar?"

"I have a wrecking tool, but let's hope you're not seriously thinking of destroying things."

Jess waited for him to arrive and gestured at the hatch. "This doesn't seem to have an exterior unlocking mechanism. The handle doesn't turn. It looks as though I should just have to slide it open, but it won't budge."

He played his bright light over the hatch. "Is it an airlock?"

"Probably. Even so, there has to be a way to open it from the outside."

Harry examined the area around the hatch. He pointed to a dimple on the hull to the left of the handle. "What's that?"

She examined it closely. "I'm not sure." It looked like a fold of metal in the hull. She pushed on it with her finger. It opened a little. "Good eye. Maybe it's some kind of keyhole. Too bad we don't have the key."

He frowned. "It's reminding me of something I found in the well." He set his pack on the floor and dug around inside it. After a few minutes searching, he produced a flat strip of metal about the size of a data chip. It gleamed with a sheen that told her it was made of something from the platinum group.

Jess took it from him. "You found this little thing in the water? I'm impressed. Definitely not something produced by the Mayans. Unfortunately, I'm certain that any power supply for the hatch is long dead. We can see if it fits, though."

The tip of the strip fit into the dimple and she slipped it in with a click. The hatch moved slowly to the right. She jumped back in shock.

Harry raised his rifle and covered the newly exposed area. "I think it still has power."

"Thanks, Captain Obvious. I'm pretty sure that we don't have to worry about live threats inside this thing, though."

"I wouldn't be so certain. If the hatch works, any internal defenses might work, too. That does kind of look like an airlock."

The ones on Liberty Station weren't very different. Some of the equipment inside looked like oxygen containers and spacesuits.

The suits looked more like coveralls than true vacuum gear. The fabric had rotted, of course, but she was already salivating over the construction techniques she might be able to learn from them.

At the far side of the compartment, the other hatch was open. Not surprising, as they were in a breathable atmosphere. She hopped into the airlock and aimed her light inside. A fine layer of dust covered everything.

The rear area looked more suited to cargo, but the forward section had bulky acceleration couches. The most forward of those had a wide, wrap around control console, similar in appearance to the tablet she'd recovered. The rear of the cargo area had an interior hatch. Two long bags lay on the floor of the cargo area.

Harry jumped in beside her and lowered his weapon so that it hung on his chest by a strap. "I suppose it does look fairly safe in here. Considering the condition of the exterior, things are in amazing condition. Our ride gets here in an hour, so you might want to pick up the pace."

"I'm not going anywhere until I give this a thorough look," she said firmly.

"Don't touch those."

Jess looked up from the long bag she'd been about to open. "Why not?"

"Because, unless I miss my guess, those are body bags. They don't look empty. Unless your plan is to dump some poor bastard's remains on the deck, you'd best steer clear of them."

She pulled her hand back. "Thanks. No, that wasn't on my list of things to do. These must be the man's crewmates."

He peered into the front of the craft. "The interior of this thing looks remarkably intact."

Jess tried the hatch at the rear of the cargo area and it opened without problem. The inside, as she'd expected, was stuffed full of equipment. Most of it was engines, she thought. They didn't look like anything she'd ever seen before. She wasted no time getting her camera into action.

"Do you think this is the power supply?"

She looked over at where Harry was pointing. A cube about ten centimeters across sat behind a clear panel. It glowed a soft blue. Jess took some pictures.

"Maybe. I can't imagine how any of this still works. Any kind of battery should be long dead. Also, there's no indication of reaction mass."

"Excuse me?"

"A spaceship gets thrust by igniting flammable fuels or heating something to high temperatures and letting it escape in the opposite direction from where they want to go. There's nothing like that on this ship. How did it fly?"

The mercenary shrugged. "Magic? Little blue elves? Black holes? Does it matter?"

"Yeah, kind of." She examined the cover over the cube. It didn't seem heavily shielded or all that secure. A simple latch kept it closed. It looked as though a tug was all it took to remove it.

Once she finished taking pictures of the engineering space, she led the way to the front of the cabin. She couldn't pilot a spaceship, but she knew acceleration couches. These could handle three or more gravities, she guessed.

The restraints looked heavy duty. It would've taken a very bad crash to kill someone strapped into one. She was willing to wager that the people in those bags hadn't died in these couches.

Gingerly, she sat in front of what she guessed was the pilot's console. The curved panel in front of her was dark and covered with dust. She swiped her hand across it. That cleared a swath of the surface and caused it to light up. Another curved panel at window level lit up, too, showing the room outside. Since it was pitch dark in reality, there must've been some kind of enhancement taking place.

"Holy crap," Harry muttered. "That looks like something out of a movie."

It sure did. The controls were incomprehensible to her, but she recognized the writing as similar to the script from the book. She kept her hands far away from the glowing icons and graphs, afraid she'd activate the engines if she touched anything.

Jess looked up at Harry. "Call your father again. Tell him to speed things up."

* * *

NATHAN RAN the drone down the stairs as far as he dared. Communications were getting spotty and he didn't want to lose control of it. That's when he saw what looked like the bottom of the stairs.

He gnawed his lip. To chance it or not? If he lost the drone, they'd probably find it. That wouldn't be good. Still, he needed to know what they were doing.

Deciding to risk it, he nudged the drone deeper into the underground area. It still had communication with the controller unit when he reached the bottom, but only just. He didn't dare go any further than the bottom of the stairs.

The room was darker than the pit of Hades. Where were they? In some other part of an underground maze? He flipped the visual to mixed mode. Two bodies appeared in the infrared spectrum. One of them was sitting and the other was looking over the first one's shoulder. They were somewhat indistinct. There was a significant barrier between the drone and them.

He activated the small UV spotlight. For a moment, he didn't understand what he was seeing. Then he almost dropped the controller.

That couldn't be right. Was that some kind of aircraft? In the bottom of a Mayan tomb?

Nathan stared at the image for several moments, not really comprehending what he was seeing. Where had that thing come from? Who'd put it there? Why were his idiot brother and that bimbo looking around inside it when they should've been getting the hell out of here?

With a shake of his head, he decided that he'd better pull the drone out before someone came down the stairs behind it. He goosed it straight up when he reached open air.

His timing was good. One of Harry's men ran from the trees and down the underground stairs moments later. He looked a little panicked. Curious, he scanned around the area.

His brother's mercenaries were still out there, but they weren't alone anymore. Dozens of people were creeping in from the east. Nathan smiled. His brother was about to be ambushed. Oh, this was going to be good. He wished he'd brought popcorn.

## 9

"**P**ossible hostiles inbound," Rex said over the radio. "Estimate thirty plus."

Harry cursed and keyed his microphone. "Copy. I want visual confirmation. Pull back to the prepared positions."

He turned to Jess. "Get ready to leave at a moment's notice, but stay down here. If these are locals, we should be able to drive them off."

"And if they're more of your brother's men?" she asked.

"Then we're in serious trouble. Hang tight and don't do anything until I call for you to come out. If someone else comes down, shoot them."

"That's a bit hasty."

"You can comfort yourself with the thought that you'll probably miss."

Jess gave him a steady look. "That's not comforting."

He headed toward the hatch. "Keep your head down."

It only took a minute to run up the steps and meet up with Rex. "Status?"

"I'd say they're locals. They're using the terrain very well, but they don't move like trained fighters. If so, that means no body armor and probably no heavy weapons. We should be able to turn them around without killing the lot of them."

"Unless this is a religious site. We both know that changes things."

Rex's expression soured. "Yeah. Let's hope they aren't as fanatical as those buggers in the sandbox. I figure we have about ten minutes before they think they're close enough to attack."

Harry went to the position they'd dug for him. He didn't like having his people scattered on all sides of the clearing, but he'd had no way of knowing which direction an enemy would come from. They'd consolidate quickly if things went into the crapper.

"Liberty Six, Long Gun." It was Sandra.

"Go Long Gun."

"I have eyes on the intruders. They look like locals. No armor. Some guns. Some machetes. They're sending scouts toward the clearing. Orders?"

"Do not engage unless they make the first move. I'd prefer we scare them off."

"Copy. Shoot to defecate."

He smiled. "Orders confirmed."

Harry settled in to wait.

\* \* \*

NATHAN WATCHED the primitives come closer and considered his options. He grinned and brought the drone's explosive package online. If he used it just right, he might be able to screw his brother over. It wouldn't stop him in the end, but he owed the bastard.

He sent the drone slowly down.

\* \* \*

JESS FINISHED TAKING pictures of everything she thought was interesting. The pilot's console had gone dark again, so she brought it to life once more and took detailed close ups. Maybe one of the mission pilots could help her make sense of the icons and graphs.

She'd just finished when a sharp explosion went off somewhere above her. The ship didn't move, so it couldn't have been too bad. She stood there listening, dreading. If the ceiling collapsed, it would probably crush the ship and her.

Something small bounced off the hull. She waited in dread, but that was it.

Once she was relatively certain that she wasn't going to die, she ventured to the hatch and looked out. Her light showed she was in trouble again. Rocks covered the stairs leading up. Perfect. She scanned the ceiling with her light and it looked intact. Jess hoped it stayed that way.

"Harry," she said over the radio. "Can you hear me?"

No response.

She ran her hand over her face. Now what?

\* \* \*

THE UNEXPECTED EXPLOSION made Harry throw himself down. There wasn't any follow up gunfire, so he peeked over the log behind him. It had come from somewhere back toward the clearing.

Shit.

He ran back as fast as he could. The trapdoor had fallen into the stairwell. He skidded to a halt and stared at the damage with dismay. Only a small opening remained. The entrance had collapsed.

Harry keyed his radio. "Jess, are you okay? Jess?"

No response. The ceiling was obviously intact, so she was probably safe. As long as he could get her out before her air went bad. Or the roof really did collapse.

Where had the explosion come from? Did the locals have a mortar? He doubted it. He'd have heard the round on the way in and the damage would've been significantly worse. This was a surgical strike.

If it wasn't the locals, odds were it was Nathan. His father's men hadn't arrived. He'd have heard the helicopter. That little bastard was still around here somewhere.

"Liberty Team, this is Liberty Six," he said over the radio. "Be advised we have advanced hostiles in the area. If you see someone, light them up. Long Gun, what is the status of the locals?"

"Holding position and conferring," Sandra said. "I don't think they liked the sound of that explosion. Some of them seem to be circling around, maybe to get a look from the other side of the clearing."

"Keep the main group in sight. I'm going after the client."

"Scout to Liberty Six, you need to charge extra."

As if he wouldn't make his father pay through the nose for everything. "I will. Go find that bastard, Rex. Bring me his head."

"Copy that."

The opening looked wide enough for Harry to wiggle into. Hopefully the slab wouldn't shift and crush him.

\* \* \*

JESS LOOKED at the rock pile with dismay. It completely cut off the stairs and there was no telling how much rubble was there. If she started digging, it would continue to fall out. All she had were her hands, anyway.

A few minutes later, the sound of stone scraping stone startled her. That wasn't falling rock. It came from the other side of the chamber from the collapsed stairway.

The sound was too steady to be natural. It was as though someone was dragging a rock across the floor every few seconds. She jogged to the side of the spacecraft and aimed her light over at the wall.

Part of it was open a little. It slid a few centimeters more as she watched. Its jerky movement gave her the idea that it was almost jammed. She couldn't see inside it, but it had to be some kind of hidden entrance. That meant there was a way out.

And that someone was sneaking in, probably to do bad things to her.

What should she do? Hide in the ship? If she closed the hatch, she'd probably be safe for the time being. And trapped. If she stayed outside the ship, they'd see her.

She could try to bluff them with the gun, but that seemed stupid. What would she do if they called her on it? Give up, most likely. She didn't see herself getting into a gunfight.

Jess decided stealth was her best course of action. She ran back into the ship, ducked into the engineering space, and chewed her lip. Taking a deep breath, she opened the cover shielding the glowing cube and yanked it out.

Nothing terrible happened. Hopefully, she wasn't getting soaked in lethal radiation. She couldn't leave this for them to find. She stuffed it into her pack.

She raced back out of the ship and yanked the key from the lock. The hatch slowly slid shut. The cube must not be its only power source. It didn't budge when she tugged on it.

Most people were right handed and they tended to go around things on their dominant side. She slid to the other side of the ship and turned off her light.

The door scraped along for another minute and stopped. She knew her eyes would reflect any light they carried, so she looked at the ceiling. There was one source of light moving toward the other side of the ship.

So far, so good.

Once she judged that they were rounding the ship, she started around her side. With the bulk of the vessel between them, they'd be none the wiser as long as she didn't give herself away.

The reflections of their light were just strong enough for her to see the door. Refusing to run, she walked toward it as quietly as she could.

The door opened onto a dirty chamber scarcely three feet across. A passage led straight up from there with holes cut into the rock for climbing. Dim light filtered in from somewhere above.

She considered closing the door, but even if she could move it, she might be trapping those people down here to die. She'd just have to take the chance that they wouldn't come up and catch her in the act of escaping.

Jess made it about two thirds of the way up when someone shouted below her. A glance down showed someone climbing rapidly toward her while a second person shined a bright light upward.

Time to pick up the pace.

She threw caution to the wind and raced toward the surface. If she fell now, they'd kill or capture her, so she jammed her boots into the holes as deeply as she could.

Which, in hindsight, might have been a mistake. Her foot got stuck just shy of the surface.

Jess cursed and wiggled her foot. When she felt it give, she yanked hard. Her boot came loose, and so did the stone. It fell straight down and smashed into the man behind her. Much screaming ensued.

"Sorry," she said as she pulled herself up to the surface. Hopefully it didn't kill either of them.

She came out into the dim light filtering through the trees and jumped to her feet. It looked as though they'd rolled a rock out of the way to gain access to the passage.

"Well, well. It looks like I get a second chance after all. There must be a god."

Jess whirled and stared at the man in camouflage leaning against a tree. He had a pistol held loosely in his hand. "Come along quietly and I won't have to use this. Resist and my idiot brother can carry your corpse home in a body bag."

* * *

Harry was still trying to widen the hole enough to wedge himself inside when shots rang out to the west. A lot of shots. He sprang to his feet and headed for the tree line at a jog.

"Shots fired," Rex said. "Somewhere back toward the clearing."

"Who's engaged?" Harry asked.

A chorus of negatives came back.

He looked around the tree he'd chosen for cover. "Enough of this crap. Pop smoke and drive our visitors back. Rex, you and I will find the source of those shots."

It had sounded like a pistol. Someone had let off at least a dozen shots in short order. He wondered what the hell they'd been shooting at.

A sound off to his right caught his attention as he eased into the undergrowth. Someone was hauling ass. He headed in that direction, stopping occasionally to listen.

He knew he'd focused on the movement a little too closely when the tree beside him took a bullet that sent splinters into his face. He dropped and rolled, looking for his attacker.

"You think you can sneak up on me, shithead? Wrong answer!" The voice was obviously a very stressed out Jess.

"Do you kiss your mother with that mouth?"

* * *

"Harry?" She stared toward to source of the voice, trying to ignore the ringing in her ears.

"I'm going to stand up," he said. "Don't shoot me."

He rose cautiously out of the undergrowth. "You want to put that thing away?"

She stared at the pistol for a second and then lowered it to her side. "Sorry. It was your brother. He ambushed me."

"It looks like that didn't work out so well for him. Where the hell did you come from? I was about to dig my way in."

She gestured behind her. "There's a secret tunnel back there. There were two guys in the chamber and I dropped a rock on them."

Harry shook his head in amused disbelief. "Aren't you the resourceful one?" He took her pistol from her, checked it, and held out his hand. "You're almost dry. Give me the other magazine."

She handed it to him as Rex came through the trees at a run. He hefted his rifle and scanned the area, making her feel a whole lot better.

Harry swapped out the magazines and slid the pistol into her holster. "Are you hit? Turn around."

"No. He missed me. He said he was your brother. He shot at me and I drove him off."

"So you said. Where's this hole down?"

Jess felt like she was in shock. Her vision was all weird and tight, and she couldn't seem to think straight. She took a deep breath, focused, and led him into the trees.

He grabbed her arm when they spotted two men hobbling away. One was supporting the other. "No need to shoot at people who're retreating. Just let them go."

"I wouldn't have shot them," she said indignantly. At least she hoped not. She'd been reaching for her pistol when he grabbed her.

The man supporting what looked like a teen saw them and hobbled faster. In moments, they were gone in the trees.

Rex came into the small clearing. "I found a few blood drops, so I think he took a round. You want me to chase him down?" He inclined his head toward Jess. "Good shooting."

Harry grunted. "No. We can't afford to let him ambush one of us alone. Help me close this off. We'll post a guard and make sure the new people know about it. I don't want that asshole slipping in there to blow anything up. Pardon the language."

She smiled. "I said something like that a few minutes ago. How long before the ringing stops? That gun is loud."

Jess cocked her head. She heard something in the distance. It was the distinctive sound of a helicopter. "We have more company."

The two men rolled the rock back over the opening. "Rex, stay here."

He led her back to the clearing. A helicopter was hovering overhead and men in Rainforest security uniforms were rappelling down.

"Thank God," Harry said. "We'll let them get deployed and then I'll fill their team leader in. Once they're good, we'll hoist you up and get the hell out of this damned jungle."

She felt relieved. "That's the best thing I've heard since this sorry trip started."

## 10

———

Once the security team was in place, Harry quickly briefed the Rainforest team leader as the helicopter searched the area looking for signs of Nathan. There wasn't much chance of spotting him, but it was worth a try.

He dialed his father's private number as soon as he finished the briefing.

"Are you on your way out?" his father asked.

"Almost. Nathan showed back up. We drove him off and we're about to take to the air. You'll want a total lockdown of the two sites, particularly this one."

The line was quiet for a moment. "I'll call my friends in the Guatemalan government. With the generous application of some bribes, I should be able to gain control of the Mayan site. At least in the short term. It will take significantly more money to extend that into the long term and I'll need a compelling reason for doing so."

"You'll want to talk to Miss Cook about that as soon as she gets back to the spaceport. I believe you'll find her reasoning and evidence compelling."

"Speaking to her is my highest priority. There's a chartered plane waiting for all of you at a private airport nearby. It will fly you directly to the Yucatan Spaceport as soon as the helicopter delivers you."

Jess walked over to Harry. "Are you talking to Mister Rogers? Give me the phone."

He handed it over. "Don't go into any detail over an unsecured line."

She put the phone to her ear. "Good evening, sir. Jessica Cook here. I need to meet with you as soon as possible. This information has some bearing on the project and it's literally earthshattering."

After a moment of listening, she continued. "Yes, sir. It's that important. Thank you."

Harry took the phone from her. "We'll be there sometime tonight." He disconnected without waiting for a response.

"You're not looking forward to seeing him," she said.

He allowed the corner of his mouth to quirk up. "You're very perceptive. No. He and I haven't seen eye to eye for a very long time. But that's me. He's your boss. God save you."

"What happened? Your split with him, his split with his ex-wife and his other son, and your not-so-subtle war with your brother. That's a bit dysfunctional."

"It's also a bit personal."

"We've saved one another's lives. We're like blood brothers now. Blood siblings? Something like that. We're supposed to bond."

Harry laughed in spite of himself. She was a bold one.

"Let's just say that the two of us didn't see the world the same way. My mother is like him, only worse. As for my brother, he's a homicidal maniac that I'll take out of play one day very soon."

She nodded seriously. "I can't argue with that."

"And what about you?" he asked. "I didn't think there were many orbital engineers left after the collapse of the American space program. Nobody is building anything anymore. Well, except for the Indians and the Chinese. Who'd have expected those two to get into a race to Mars? It's kind of sad, really."

"Once the government liquidated NASA and sold off all their assets, those kinds of jobs pretty much went away," Jess said. "The Russians bought the skeleton of the ISS2 station from the other partners and sold it to a private firm. It's not common knowledge, but if you dig through all the shell companies, Rainforest is where they all lead. And that's how I come into the story."

He frowned. "What the hell does a global seller of everything need with a space station? Aren't drones fast enough?"

"We're always looking for new ways to deliver things more quickly. You'd be surprised how fast a package dropped from orbit can get to your house."

"Nice."

A grin lit up her face. "I use that at parties. Would you believe we're turning it into a space hotel?"

"Actually, I might. I heard my father talking about something like that a few times when I was growing up. How could you make a profit? The construction costs must be ruinous. Even with the skeleton already in place when you bought it."

"That wasn't any help, cost-wise. I did an inspection after we purchased it and there were flaws in a number of critical struts and supports. Your mother's company cut some very serious corners. The thing would've probably come apart when they spun her up. It certainly wouldn't have lasted the entire planned lifecycle."

He felt his eyebrows rise. "You've been in space? Impressive."

"I know, right? I've been up there six times."

"And this thing can turn a profit?"

"I'm just the construction boss. You'd need to talk to someone on the business side for that."

The helicopter circled back around and dropped lines for them. The crew chief handed out earplugs and hauled them one at a time.

On the flight to the airport, he thought about his father's plans. The idea of building a hotel in space was ludicrous. He must've spent billions on the project. No way he'd make that money back with paying guests. There must be a different angle.

Harry hadn't figured out any answers by the time the helicopter landed. It was after dark. They walked over to a private hangar.

The interior was lit up brighter than day. A sleek private jet with the Rainforest logo on the tail waited for them. A woman in an immaculate light green uniform stood at the foot of the fold-down stairs.

"Good evening," she said. "I'm Alicia and I'll be your attendant tonight. If you and your party will board, we'll take off immediately, Mister Rogers."

The faint smirk on her lips told him she was one of the shrinking minority of people that had seen the old television program. At least she hadn't felt the need to sing the damned song.

He let his people board while some men opened the hangar door. A small tug backed in and attached a tow bar to the front wheel of the aircraft.

The interior of the plane smelled like money. Leather and dark wood everywhere. Wide seats that looked more inviting than his bed. His father knew how to live.

That's when he saw him come out from a door at the rear of the cabin. The Devil had come to Guatemala in person.

* * *

CLAYTON LOOKED his son over with a critical eye. "You look like hell, boy."

His son's expression hardened. "Let's see how you look when someone drops a pyramid on you. I didn't expect to see you so quickly."

"Obviously not. Everyone, get your gear put away and Alicia will serve dinner and drinks while we fly out of this hellhole."

He stepped up to the cockpit as everyone found places for their gear. The pilot looked back at him questioningly.

"What did the tower say when you didn't file a flight plan?" Clayton asked.

"The same thing they said when I didn't give them a tail number. Thanks for the money. I'll fly us out on a course that doesn't lead to Mexico. I'll turn when we're safely away."

Clayton nodded. "Excellent. Carry on."

He returned to his seat and openly studied his son. Which no doubt led to the steam he could almost see rising from the boy's ears. Harry had never been the best at concealing his emotions. Especially the hostile ones. Perhaps that was a plus in his line of work.

Alicia made the rounds and had everyone secured by the time the pilot started the engines. They'd only landed a short while ago, so the warm up time was minimal. They took off and rose into the night sky without incident. Once they leveled off, Alicia took orders for food and drink.

Clayton gestured for Miss Cook and his son to join him at the rear of the craft. He had an office there that would give them privacy to probe what had sent the levelheaded engineer into a tailspin. He couldn't imagine how she intended to link an ancient Mayan ruin to Project Liberty, so it was undoubtedly going to be a surprise.

Because he knew that sitting behind the desk would only make matters worse with Harry, he arranged all the seats in the open area in front of it. He'd already eaten, so he sipped a fine double malt whisky as the others put some food in their bellies.

Once the intensity of their hunger diminished, he spoke. "Miss Cook, I'm delighted to see you alive and well. I heard your friend didn't make it. Please accept my deepest condolences. I regret that my ex-wife and son perpetrated this vicious attack. If I may be so bold, what did you find that warrants my immediate attention?"

She opened her bag, which she hadn't stored, and pulled out a moderately expensive looking digital camera. "Do you have a screen controller?"

He gestured to his desk. "Please have a seat and load them up on the wall screen."

She removed the memory chip from the camera and inserted it into a slot on his desk. The wall screen came to life a few moments later. There were a number of images. Some of jungle, some of ruins, a few of people, and many of chambers indoors. The interior of the pyramid, he assumed.

He pointed at a picture of a man standing beside a pyramid. Presumably the one that had collapsed. He was young, Hispanic, and grinning widely. "That must be your friend."

Her face sagged a little. "I took that the day before everything went to hell. He was on top of the world. I suppose that's a lesson in how wrong we can be."

"I'm not certain that's the lesson I'd take away from this terrible situation. Perhaps that the world is more dangerous than we expect. To always remain vigilant."

"I doubt that would've helped him. He found a chamber hidden deep inside the pyramid. It had some art that is literally game changing. Though it's not the reason I asked you to come, it's a good place to start."

She selected an image and zoomed in. The art and inlay of polished stone was impressive. It took him a moment to realize what was wrong with it. It showed the outer planets.

"That can't be right," he said after a moment. "This has to be faked."

She shook her head. "We found something later that indicates otherwise in the strongest terms possible. One more thing to note. There's something marked here that comes from the outer system to the inner. An extinct comet, most likely."

"There are dates in Mayan script beside it at several points. We should be able to figure out its orbit based on that. Also, it shows a large body in the outer system that we don't know about."

"That is extraordinary," he admitted. "Now I understand why your friend sought you out. This is indeed the find of the century. How could the ancient Mayans possibly be aware of the outer planets? They had no telescopes, if memory serves."

"Allow me to show you what else we found in the pyramid."

The next picture showed the devastation that used to be the Mayan artwork.

"What a loss," he murmured. "This happened when the pyramid collapsed?"

"No, it came apart when a grenade caused the tunnel leading up to this point to cave in. We thought the cracks in the wall might lead to a hidden tunnel, so we opened it up."

"Is that how you escaped?"

"No," Harry said. "We had to jump down the well in that room and search for a passage to the one in the courtyard. We were lucky."

He considered the two of them. "Exceedingly so. I'm not certain that I would play the lottery going forward, if I were you. You may have used your allotted share of good luck."

"Actually, I think the lottery is a good analogy," Miss Cook said.

She skipped ahead and showed him what was behind the wall. The burial chamber astounded him.

"Amazing," he said.

She showed picture after picture until they opened the sarcophagus. He stared at the impossible image on the screen. "This cannot be correct."

"It was there," Harry said bluntly. "I saw everything from the moment we opened the tomb. The wall was old. Really old. This wasn't planted."

The lie his eyes told him warred with his bedrock certainty that his son's word was good. If he said it was true, it was true. He watched as she scrolled through the pictures. The clothing was definitely anachronistic. Similar to modern clothes, but not in every way.

The pockets, buttons, and name tag stood out. And the patch on the man's shoulder. The angle wasn't very good, but it looked like a tree surrounded by text. Well, by gibberish in text form. Not something that anyone found in an ancient tomb should be wearing.

Clayton stared at them. "What the hell does this mean?"

"It means a lot more than you think," Miss Cook said. "Let me show you what we found at the second site."

The image changed and he slowly stood as he realized what he was seeing. "Is that…"

"It's a spaceship," she confirmed. "One that's been buried in the jungle for about a thousand years."

* * *

JESS WATCHED her boss's expression with satisfaction. He got it. He knew what this find meant.

"The man in the pyramid undoubtedly came from this ship," she said. "Harry found the key to opening it in the well once we escaped the collapsing pyramid. I saved what I could from the burial chamber, but we need to recover the body and go over everything that survived the collapse with a fine toothed comb. We also need to recover Abel's body. His family deserves to have him back."

The elder Mister Rogers nodded. "Of course. I've already called a few people, but I'll start working every contact I have to get complete control of both sites. We'll need to have everything you recovered gone over very carefully and protect it from deterioration. I'll arrange for some restoration specialists to preserve everything. Those artifacts are literally priceless."

Clayton looked at her with a very serious expression. "Do you realize the scope of what you've found here? The immensity of it? The value of this find is incalculable."

"Even before we found the ship, I knew," she said. "Even the Mayans knew. Look at the lid of the sarcophagus. See how they have him as though he were about to take flight? He came from above and they knew it."

The older man stared at the image. "It certainly seems that way. I realize you have many duties awaiting your time on Project Liberty, but we need to debrief you in detail."

Harry cleared his throat. "Perhaps you've forgotten, but this isn't your find. It's hers. As in she owns everything in that pack."

Mister Rogers paused. "A valid point. Thank you for the reminder. Miss Cook, if you'll allow me to bring some experts in to conserve and examine the artifacts you've recovered, I believe that it might be worth a great deal to me. And you."

"And to Harry," she said. "He was there every moment of this exploration."

The younger Rogers shook his head. "I was under contract to rescue you. I have no claim to anything in that chamber or the data you found."

"You risked your life to get this. I say you do."

"And I say I don't."

Clayton Rogers made calming gestures with his hands. "I'm sure the two of you can work that out at your leisure."

His son's jaw shot out. "She'll want to contact an attorney she trusts to review whatever you offer. You're a shark and I won't let you gobble her up."

"I bet your military group has an attorney," Jess said. "If you were my partner in this, you could loan him to me."

Harry gave her a look. "Maybe. I'm going back out front. Don't let him bully you into signing anything. I'll give my lawyer a call tomorrow and arrange for her to review your contract." He shifted his gaze to his father. "I might have to take a small share just to keep you honest. Don't cross me."

She stared at the door after he'd departed. "Is he always this mule headed?"

"My son is many things, including stubborn. He's also honorable to a damned fault. My advice is to listen to him. This find is valuable. Very valuable. Well worth killing for or cheating someone out of their share."

"Would you do that?" she asked as she retrieved her memory chip.

He steepled his fingers. "I've done things in business that would horrify you, I'm certain. I could swear my intentions are honorable, but that should fool neither of us. I'll strike as good a bargain as I can while still being fair."

He leaned back in his chair. "We'll talk tomorrow. Please, take your bag and stow it near your seat. I want you to have sole custody of it until we settle the details of what this means."

She made her way back up to the front of the plane and sat down beside Harry. "I'm not sure what to do next."

"Get some sleep," he advised. "Tomorrow is going to be a long one. Also, make sure and count your fingers once you shake on this deal."

He stuck a pillow behind his head and quickly went to sleep.

She ordered a stiff drink and it wasn't long before she joined him.

# 11

Harry slept like crap. He'd run through collapsing tunnels chasing Jess for what seemed like hours. He woke when the plane touched down, more exhausted than when he'd dozed off.

His people gathered their gear and deplaned once the pilot shut the engines down. To his annoyance, Jess seemed rested and ready to take on the world.

The view of the Yucatan Spaceport was rather limited in the middle of the night. He couldn't see any of the launch towers. Hills blocked the no-doubt inspirational view.

His father directed them to cars that would take them to the hotel. They'd sleep again and join him for a late breakfast. Jess sat beside Harry in the one he piled into.

"So, how careful do I need to be?" she asked. "He might be your father, but he's my boss. I don't want to overly antagonize him."

It took a moment for Harry to squelch his instinctive response that Clayton Rogers couldn't be trusted. That was his bias speaking. "Have a lawyer look everything over before you sign it. Mine, yours, or someone else you trust. Bargain hard. My father will slip something past you if he can. Once you both sign on the dotted lines, though, he'll honor the agreement.

"And by that, I mean what's spelled out in black and white. Oral agreements don't count. Read the fine print and look for things he can twist. This is worth a lot of money and he plays hardball when it comes to stuff like that."

She nodded slowly. "I'm not really interested in the money. I want to follow the mystery."

Harry snorted. "Don't tell him that. He'll value what you found more highly if he has to pay for it. Show him that while you might've been born on a Tuesday, it wasn't last week."

"You're funny. Give me the name of your lawyer so I can have someone check her out."

He gave her the woman's name and number. "Tell her I sent you and that the work is highly classified. She'll keep it under her hat."

"You seem to trust very few people. How can you be sure about her?"

"I rescued her son from Eastern Europe about five years ago. She's as loyal as any human can be."

Jess's expression softened. "You're like a knight in camo. I'm not kidding."

Harry shook his head. "Don't make me into something I'm not. I've done as many bad things as anyone else. War sucks."

They pulled up to a brightly lit hotel. It was almost four in the morning, so things were quiet. Someone expedited the check in and had them in their rooms a few minutes later.

Harry put his pack in the closet, locked the door, and put a chair under the knob. He didn't like sleeping in places he didn't control.

His pistol sat on the toilet seat while he took a quick shower. It went on his nightstand when he face planted.

It only seemed as though a few minutes had passed when someone started pounding on the door. One glance at the clock showed it was only seven. "Go away."

"You'll miss breakfast," Jess yelled through the door. "They might have blueberries."

"Is that your criteria for a high end breakfast?" He rolled out of bed. "Give me a few minutes to get dressed."

"You want the clothes in the hall?"

"Hand them through."

It only took a moment to pull the chair back and crack the door. She stood in the hall looking well rested. She wore a pale blue blouse, a dark skirt, and shoes without heels. If he didn't know better, he'd never have suspected she'd been on an adventure in the Guatemalan jungle yesterday. She had her pack over her shoulder.

"I had no idea you were shy," she said with a grin.

"I could be naked over here."

She raised an eyebrow. "Are you? What if ninjas attacked?"

"Then I'd kill them naked."

"I'd pay good money to see that."

Harry grabbed the clothes and headed for the bathroom. He closed the door most of the way, took care of business, and washed his hands and face. "How can you be so chipper? You were awake as long as I was."

"I thought you military types got up early every day so you could run ten miles and do an obstacle course."

"That doesn't mean we have to like it. You learn to sleep when you can."

"That's rough. I'm a morning person."

"Figures. Nobody's perfect."

He dressed, combed his hair, and started shaving. "I dreamed about that damned spaceship last night. I can't believe it, even after having seen it with my own eyes."

"I'm in the same boat," she said. "The scope of this find is mindboggling. Advanced humans long before the Europeans discovered the American continents. Where did they come from? Space? That seems almost inconceivable."

"Why not time travel?"

"Let's stick to reasonable possibilities."

He grabbed his boots and headed back into the bedroom. She was sitting on the edge of his bed. "Why? Because advanced humans from outer space is a more likely alternative than time travel? You said that ship didn't use reaction mass. Maybe it's a time travel ship."

She opened her mouth to say something and stopped. "I guess I shouldn't dismiss the idea out of hand. I should let the evidence tell me what's possible. How much do you think a find like this is worth?"

"A lot of money. It's proof that others visited our world and educated some of us to work for them."

He smiled at her surprised expression. "I read science fiction. I get this has implications with aliens. That's big stuff. And, if word of it gets out, everyone and their third cousins will be after the technology. It means weapons, star drives, and possibly any number of other things. I'd be real careful who you mention this to."

"Aliens might be a jump. We've only found evidence that humans were involved."

"Since there's no indication of a high technology center on Earth a thousand years ago, the tech had to come from elsewhere. That means aliens. Unless you believe in Atlantis."

She rolled her eyes. "At this point, I'm not ruling it out, but I don't think so. Plato almost certainly used the fictitious island allegorically. Even he said the events he supposedly chronicled took place something like 9,000 years before his time. But, with this find, it makes me wonder if he was being literal. This just boggles my mind. I want to see where this leads."

"Me, too," Harry admitted. "If anywhere. I figure other signs of this are long gone."

"Except in space. The only place we've been to in person is the moon. NASA wanted to go to an asteroid a couple of decades ago, but that never happened. They killed the idea of returning to the moon and gave lip service to manned missions to the asteroids and Mars, but they never did anything more than blow hot air. That was the end of American leadership in space. Hell, recent events were the end of America going into space at all."

Harry snorted. "I had a ringside seat when my mother did her part to put NASA out of business. Corporate greed and governmental incompetence at its worst. Now China and India are locked in a race to Mars"

"Yeah, both of them are a few months away from leaving orbit, but the ships are complete. The planets just need to line up."

He nodded toward her bag. "That might just change things. Maybe make my father pony up some cash to get a mission out to that comet."

She gave him an odd look. "Could be. We need to get moving if we want to eat."

They stopped talking about the find once they got onto the elevator with other people. Jess changed the subject adroitly. "What will your people be doing while we talk? Shouldn't they be out saving the world?"

"If they're smart, they're sleeping in. Depending on what I hear this morning, I'll either send them back to the US or keep them here."

The doors slid open and everyone hustled out. A rotund man in a suit came from behind the desk when he saw them. "Mister Rogers, Miss Cook. I'm Thomas Quincy, the hotel manager. I hope you had a pleasant night. The elder Mister Rogers has arranged breakfast in a private conference room. If you'll come with me, I'll see you there."

Jess took the man's offered hand with a smile. "It was perfect, thank you. Tell me, do you have blueberries?"

"Of course."

She grinned. "Excellent."

He turned to Harry. "Do you have any specific breakfast requests, Mister Rogers?"

"No, I'm pretty pedestrian in my tastes. I'll want some good coffee, though, and lots of it."

"I'll make that happen. This way, please."

Harry followed the two of them and watched Jess almost skipping along. Blueberries. He might never understand her at all.

\* \* \*

JESS WALKED to the conference room with the manager. Two large men in dark suits eyed them with disfavor, but opened the door. The elder Rogers was already there, sipping on coffee and talking with two women in lab coats. All three looked over as she and Harry made their way in. The manager did not accompany them and the guards closed the door.

Clayton Rogers rose from his seat. "Miss Cook, Harry. Meet Doctors Paulette Young and Rachel Powell. They are two of the most experienced professionals on the planet at restoring and protecting delicate artifacts. If you have no objections, they will remove everything you found from the pack and begin the preservation process. They are independent contractors and will answer to you unless we come to an agreement."

Jess slid the backpack over to the women. "Us. Harry is part of this."

She watched Harry look to the ceiling, probably praying for strength. "That again? I told you, I was under contract to rescue you. I'm a hired gun. One who has finished his work, by the way. I expect to be on my way shortly."

Harry's father pursed his lips. "It's true that you were there at my behest. However, I've consulted with my attorneys and they tell me that the find is unrelated to the work I hired you to do. Which I have paid you for, by the way, with a significant bonus."

The mercenary's eyes widened for a moment, and then narrowed. "You don't give anything away for free. What are you up to, old man?"

"Why don't you eat your breakfast while we discuss that? We've shielded this room from monitoring of any kind. No transmissions in or out. The good doctors have signed strict non-disclosure agreements and my people will search them closely when they leave their laboratory. If we can come to an understanding, the items will be under heavy guard and 24/7 observation by the most paranoid security people I employ."

Jess watched the interplay between the two men with interest. Harry's antipathy couldn't be plainer, yet his father accepted it as though it was normal. Dysfunctional didn't begin to describe their relationship.

At her nod, the women took possession of the pack and one of the guards from outside escorted them down the hall.

"And how do we order breakfast if we can't call out?" Jess asked once they were gone.

"The old fashioned way." He slid a pen and pad of paper over to her. "Write whatever you want on that. When we have everyone's order, we hand it to the paranoid men outside. They send it to the kitchen and examine what they bring back. The coffee is in the carafe. It's quite good."

She raised an eyebrow. "And how do I know what I can order without a menu?"

The older man smiled. "You tell them what you want and they figure it out. The sky is the limit. Do you want caviar and champagne for breakfast? Something even more esoteric? Make it so."

That set her back for a moment. "I'm a woman with fairly simple tastes, so I don't expect to break your bank account."

"As long as you have blueberries, she'll be happy," Harry said with an amused glance at her.

"Then you're in luck," Clayton said. "I had some with breakfast yesterday. Now, to address your earlier comments, I'm not giving anything away. From my point of view, it doesn't matter how the two of you split my offer. Or even if you do. Your objection needs to go to her. Frankly, I hope you stand your ground. That would simplify matters a great deal."

Harry stiffened and his demeanor shifted. "I'll bet it would. Well, maybe it's better that I keep an eye on what you're up to. Not only for her sake, but to keep you from misusing this find."

"Let's eat before you become even grumpier."

Jess suppressed a smile as she wrote out her breakfast order. Her boss had just played his son. She could see the satisfied gleam in his eye. As sharp as Harry was, he had baggage.

And, to be honest, so did she. Mister Rogers was her employer. A wealthy man in a position of great power over her life. She'd best keep that front and center as they talked. She had a fine line to walk while guarding her interests.

Jess gave Harry a pleading look. "I hope you reconsider. No offense to your father, but I've worked for him for years. I'm not sure I'd push a hard enough bargain."

The younger man nodded. "Maybe. For you." He started writing an order for himself.

While he focused on that task, she looked at his father. He inclined his head slightly with a hint of a smile. He'd seen through her plea.

Once Harry slipped their orders under the door, the elder Rogers leaned back in his chair. "The doctors are aware that these items are of an indeterminate age and unknown origin. They'll be working exclusively on this project for at least the next year, with options to extend that by two one-year periods. They know nothing of the ship and it's probably best we keep it that way for now.

"As there was no choice, they are aware that some or all of the items in that pack may be of extraterrestrial origin. They're being exceptionally well compensated for their isolation and discretion."

She took a deep breath and picked her purse up from where she'd set it on the floor. "There's something else that I think I'm more qualified to look over." She took the cube out and set it on the table along with the key to the spaceship.

Harry gave her a disapproving look.

"You took that and didn't tell me? What if the ship had blown up?"

"I couldn't leave it down there. What if the ceiling had collapsed? Again."

The older man gave her a searching look. "What is that, and why is it glowing?"

"I think it's a power supply," she said. "I'll need to get it into an engineering lab to work on it, but based on the fact it still had enough charge to power the crashed ship after a thousand years, I think it's pretty damned important."

"So, it's a battery?"

"I think it's a power generator of some kind. Given that there was no indication the ship used reaction mass, it had to require a significant amount of power to move. I'll need to do a lot of testing to figure out how it works."

Her boss took a sip of his coffee. "That will be a priority, I'm sure. The potential applications are enormous. I'd say they might be useful in our current endeavor, but I think the project is too far along."

"You can never have too much energy," she said.

"True enough. I see several paths going forward. First is the pyramid. I've volunteered Rainforest's services to the Guatemalan government in recovering Doctor Valdez's body from the ruins. That will take some time, of course, and may not generate any recoverable artifacts.

"The second site with the spaceship is self-evident. The third possible recovery site is the astronomical body you found reference to. If it was important enough to note, it may have some interesting ruins of its own."

Harry frowned. "How will you search there? A probe? That's going to be difficult and take a while, especially if it's not near Earth."

His father steepled his fingers. "You might not be aware of it, but I purchased the ISS2 space station from the Russians and have begun converting it into a hotel. That's actually a deep cover story. We've added a concealed propulsion section, beefed up the superstructure, and built it substantially larger than the original planners envisioned. Liberty Station will be the first ship to Mars. It's also capable of making a trip to other portions of the solar system. Even the outer system."

Harry's eyes widened and he looked at Jess. "You knew this?"

She smiled. "It would be hard to design and direct the construction of a spaceship without knowing that part. I couldn't tell you because the project is classified.

"We're getting the last of the supplies loaded now. We also need to get the engines ready. We saved that part for the end, because if word gets out, there might be enough outcry to cause Mister Rogers some trouble."

The older man grunted. "It's nuclear, so every environmentalist crackpot on the planet will burst into flames. As if the universe doesn't already have enormous amounts of radioactive material. Idiots."

Jess poured herself some coffee. "I'm sure that any number of governments would disapprove, too. It doesn't use weapons grade material, of course, but they might worry that it's a weapon held over their heads. Once the reactor is loaded and the fuel secured, the project can't be stopped short of using force."

Harry could see how that might get people all excited. "Where's the material coming from? The US? That might be difficult."

"The source of the material is a closely guarded secret," the elder Rodgers said, "but I'm willing to share it with you. The reactor core is an experimental prototype your mother has been developing in France. I plan to steal it. And, if we can come to an agreement, I'd like you to help my security forces make that happen. Your people are even better at that sort of thing than they are."

"We might be able to work out a deal," Harry said. "I owe Mother some payback. Isn't that leaving things up to chance? What if you don't get your hands on it?"

"They have a demonstration for her major investors scheduled for this week. The invitations are already out. We'll hit them before they have a chance to realize anyone else even knows it exists. Obtaining the fuel is rather more straightforward."

* * *

CLAYTON WATCHED his son out of the corner of his eye as they ate and chatted. The woman was a moderating influence on him. Normally by this point, Harry would be snarling.

She was clever, too. She'd seen his reverse psychology for what it was and used herself as a lever to get Harry on board. He'd reward that behavior with a good final deal. If she were the tie he needed to bind his son to the plan, he'd use her and make certain she had no cause to complain.

Harry took a bite of his pancakes. "So, now I know what you want to do. Go to Mars. Why?"

Clayton sipped his coffee. "Actually, while the ship can go to Mars quite speedily, that isn't its primary purpose. It'll find a suitable asteroid, set up a mining outpost, and then beat everyone else to Mars.

"With the resources harvested in space, we should be able to fund additional construction and use the raw materials as a means to do so. Liberty Station is intended to be a self-sustaining home to explore the solar system."

"The ship has a lot of room in the torus," Jess said. "That's what we call a habitat ring that generates artificial gravity via centrifugal force.

"We've designed and built multiple sets of mining and refining equipment, so we can leave teams on at least three asteroids. With the right kinds of raw material, it could be quite lucrative in a short period of time."

His son mulled that for a moment. "What about that wandering asteroid? Any idea where in the solar system it is now?"

Clayton inclined his head. "A fairly good one, actually. The dates on the painting gave us a timeline to trace it. If they're accurate, it's just about to pass Earth on the outbound leg of its eternal journey. The experts concur that it's most likely an extinct comet, by the way."

He considered them as they took in his words. It wasn't quite time to push for closing the deal, but he already knew he'd offer more than Jessica Cook expected. And he'd come through, too. The potential of this find could put his plans ahead by decades. He might even live to see them come to fruition. When it came to the potential of this deal, the sky was quite literally the limit.

## 12

K athleen Bennett stared at the trembling man on the other side of her desk. She eyed the distances and gestured for the guards to drag him back a few steps. Burmese Teak was naturally resistant to moisture, but she didn't want to chance getting any blood on the golden wood. The desk was worth far more than the wretch in front of it.

The slight man quivered in barely restrained terror. Only the two guards gripping his arms kept him from falling to the floor and pleading for his life. Again.

She shook her head. "You disappoint me, Vincent. Exactly how did you expect this to play out? Did you think your other employer would whisk you away once you'd done his dirty work? That was foolish. Once he had what he wanted, you became a liability he could safely dispose of.

"I realize you information technology people are insulated from the real world, but this goes a few steps into blindly stupid. You stole from me. I certainly hope you enjoyed the extra money while you could, because it won't do you any good now."

Vincent Curtis, the former assistant director of her IT department, swallowed noisily. "There's been some kind of horrible mistake, Mrs. Bennett. I would never betray you."

She smiled like a shark. She knew so because she'd perfected that expression in a mirror. "Don't insult my intelligence. You copied files from the classified database. You didn't quite manage to erase the entire trail of evidence, though. Sloppy. You'd best be forthcoming, because your punishment will reflect your cooperation. Or lack thereof."

He started in on another round of denials, but she stopped him with a raised hand. "If you don't tell me, Donald will break something you value. Who were you working for and what programs did you access?"

"No one, Mrs. Bennett. I was just—"

"Donald, if you please."

Her chief of security grabbed the man's hand and bent one of his fingers back with an audible snap. Vincent screamed and thrashed in the guards' arms.

The door opened and Nathan sauntered in. Her son raised an eyebrow at the scene and dropped into one of the comfortable chairs with more panache than grace. He winced a little at the landing. "What did this one do, Mother? Steal your parking space?"

She sighed. Her son's timing was execrable, as usual. "Donald, please take Vincent back to your office and determine the particulars of the security breach. Vincent, I advise you to cooperate. If you satisfy Mister Reynolds before I arrive, I'll let you live. You won't enjoy it, but that beats an unmarked grave. And remember, the longer you take, the more broken bones you'll have to suffer through."

The security team dragged the blubbering fool out of her office. Kathleen focused her attention on her son. "It took you long enough to get back. This was supposed to be a simple kidnapping. Do you have any idea how much of a scene you've caused? You destroyed an entire Mayan pyramid and you allowed your idiot brother to capture your entire team. On reflection, Harry isn't the stupidest of my children."

His face reddened. "I had no idea he would be there and I didn't blow up the pyramid. That was the moron I hired. He paid for it."

She shook her head. "You still don't get it. Take poor unfortunate Vincent as an example. He stole classified data from me, but I hired him. The ultimate responsibility for this situation falls on me. I don't make the mistake of trusting the wrong people often, but when I do, I don't blame them for their failures. I blame myself."

"So that's why you're sparing his life? I thought that was uncommonly generous of you."

"Don't be stupid. He condemned himself the moment he conspired against me. Donald will let him babble on until he's certain that he's gotten every bit of useful information and then take the poor bastard off to his private torture chamber. I'll never see Vincent again and good riddance."

"You hire some real winners, Mother. You're living up to your nickname. Has anyone accidentally called you Cruella to your face recently?"

She ignored his jab and walked over to her bar. She'd earned a drink. "Donald delivers everything I could ask for in a security chief. He keeps the riffraff out and the employees in line. His personal quirks are none of my business.

"You, on the other hand, disappoint me. You can't even carry out the simplest of tasks without creating an international incident. The police have your team in custody."

Nathan smirked. "They won't talk. I have a very generous bonus for situations like these. They'll keep their mouths shut and retire when they get out of prison."

"They won't be getting out," she said flatly. "I've already made arrangements. There will be a riot. Your people will not survive it."

Her son sat up abruptly. "You can't do that! If word gets out that my word isn't any good, then I won't be able to—"

"To sweep your failures under the rug? No, I imagine not. Too bad. My security is worth more to me than your reputation is to you. Frankly, your performance has been so questionable recently that I'd liquidate you if you weren't my son."

His smirk returned. "I'd watch that kind of talk if you want those grandchildren you occasionally pine after. And there's more to this situation than you're aware of."

She turned toward the wide windows and stared out over the company grounds. Modern buildings surrounded by exquisitely manicured lawns and parks lay before her. Hundreds of people in her employ walked around like little ants.

This was her kingdom. All she surveyed was hers. She controlled every aspect of anything that happened here. Her word was law. That always shot a thrill up her spine.

She sipped her gin and glanced over at her son. "What am I unaware of? The fact the woman I sent you after escaped with your brother? One of my spies saw them arrive at the Yucatan Spaceport early this morning in the company of your father. They're all closeted in a secure hotel discussing God only knows what."

"I know what." Nathan pulled a data chip from his pocket and tossed it onto her desk. "You'll never believe what they found."

She loaded up the video and stared at it as it played, her drink stopped halfway to her mouth.

When it finished, she stared coldly at her son. "What kind of garbage is this? As excuses for your failures go, this is a whole new level of ridiculous."

"That's just it. It's real. I tried to capture the woman again when she came out of the second area, but she proved to be more resourceful than I expected." He shifted in his seat and winced again.

Kathleen considered her son for a long minute. "If I find out you're lying to me, you'll envy poor Vincent."

"I'm not worried."

"Then I need to call Donald. I think the files Vincent stole went to Clayton. If so, I want to be certain that we get the true and complete story as quickly as possible."

She took another sip of her drink. "Don't unpack your bags. Gather a competent group of associates and go down to Mexico. I want you to capture the woman when she reveals herself. She will eventually."

Kathleen leaned forward. "Listen closely. You may detain your brother if circumstances allow, but you may not kill him or the woman. If one of your people makes another 'mistake', you'll suffer for it."

She gave him a cold look. "And as for grandchildren, you'd best remember how well some of my genetics projects are proceeding. I can take care of your progeny without you, if need be."

* * *

CLAYTON CONSIDERED JESSICA COOK. He finally had her alone. His son had excused himself to check on his people.

"Harry has no doubt cautioned you to scrutinize every word I say and every angle of the deal we're about to discuss. I urge you to do the same. What I'm about to propose is complicated by our already existing employment relationship. One I do not want to disrupt. Still, we need to discuss matters at a high level so that we can come to an understanding before we proceed. Agreed?"

She took a deep breath and nodded. "No offense, but I will have his attorney look over the papers and I'll discuss the framework with someone I went to college with that does corporate work."

"An excellent idea," Clayton said. "One thing, though. Are you certain you can trust the second individual? I've had Harry's attorney vetted quite thoroughly. We cannot allow this information to go public."

"I've never shared a secret with my friend that would be a challenge to his morals, but I trust him implicitly."

Clayton smiled. Her trust in her friends was adorable. "I can discreetly arrange a test through an intermediary, if you like. I'll make him a very generous offer if he reveals something he shouldn't. If he accepts, then no one will ever hear about it from me, but we will know. If he rebuffs my advances, then he's reliable enough to go over the framework."

"Forgive me, but what's to keep you from making up a story that he's unreliable to keep me from seeking his advice."

His smile widened. "That's a wise question to ask. My associates will record the conversations. While that still leaves me some methods that could taint the results, I think any failure on your friend's part should be clear enough. We need to trust one another to some degree for this to work."

She gave him a name that he jotted down. He slipped the piece of paper into his jacket. By dinner, he should have a comprehensive dossier on the man.

"What do you have in mind going forward?" she asked. "It may be months or years before we have even the most basic grasp of what this technology means."

"Spoken like an engineer. There are no certainties in business, only opportunities. You risk money on the chance to make even more money. Sometimes you win. Sometimes you lose. Every venture is a roll of the dice. It's my job to evaluate the possibilities and make an offer consummate with what I think the reward might be when counterbalanced with the risk of failure."

She shook her head. "No. It's your job to make the most profitable offer. That's why people negotiate, to get the best deal they can. I'm not a negotiator like you. I have no idea how much something like this is worth."

"In this case, circumstances dictate that the best deal isn't the one that earns me the most money."

Miss Cook turned a little in her chair and frowned. "You lost me."

Clayton allowed himself a small laugh. "Contrary to what my son believes, money isn't the altar at which I worship. It's a means to an end. Some things are worth doing, even at a loss. Project Liberty for example. Though, to be fair, I eventually expect to see a return on that, too."

She inclined her head, conceding the point. "Project Liberty is worthwhile even if it never makes back the investment."

"And there lies the basis of an agreement between us," he said. "I could make you a very generous financial offer, but I have a better idea. You're an integral part of the project. One I don't want to risk losing. What I propose is giving you a stake in Project Liberty."

That made her sit bolt upright. "Are you joking?"

"Absolutely not. Think of everything you found as the tip of an iceberg. Where did this man come from? What kind of civilization would it take to make those devices? What examples of this technology still exist, where might they be, and what could they teach us?"

She shook her head. "We have no way of knowing. There might not be anything left of them."

"Or there might be something incredible on that comet. Whoever they were, they didn't show themselves lightly. There has been no contact, other than this one instance over the course of recorded history. We might never know why, but it seems to me that this man was somehow cut off from his fellows."

"You make it sound like he didn't come from Earth at all. He certainly seemed human."

Clayton rose from his chair and stretched. "I suspect he was. That doesn't mean that he came from Earth in the way you're imagining. Someone, or something, trained him. Educated him. Whoever they were, they didn't want humans in general to know about them."

"Harry said something similar." She scowled at him. "We have no proof to back that up. Those are just theories."

"Ones I have every confidence that we can find more evidence to support, if we look in the right places. We have a trail of breadcrumbs that could lead us to the biggest discovery in human history."

"Aliens?"

"Aliens. Someone took humans and raised them to a technological pinnacle in advance of our own achievements more than a thousand years ago. Something like that would leave signs. So, where are they? I say they came from the stars. Perhaps only to visit. Perhaps they stayed a longer time and some calamity took them down. I hope to find out.

"In any case, that's the value I see behind this find. With luck, we might find examples of technology that would allow us to create ships capable of visiting other stars. That's Project Liberty writ large. Are you ready to hear my offer?"

"Shouldn't we wait for Harry to get back?"

"I'm not asking that you accept anything this very second. I just want you to understand how seriously I'm taking this. I'm offering you a thirty percent stake in Project Liberty."

She blinked at him for a moment. "That's ridiculous."

He felt the corners of his mouth rise. "Very well. Make it forty percent and Harry can have the extra ten. That's my limit, though. I insist on maintaining operational control of this project."

Her lips firmed into a thin line. "That's not what I meant. With the amount of money you've poured into this project, that's a tremendous sum. Tens of billions of dollars."

"If you take the research and side projects into account," he said, "Project Liberty has cost me most of my personal fortune. Almost one hundred billion dollars. You didn't know that I was broke? Well, one must keep up appearances. If the project fails, I go down with it. When my enemies finally grasp how deeply invested I am, they'll swarm like carrion birds. Only success will save me."

She visibly gathered her wits. "But the return on your investment will be in the trillions. Personal wealth unimaginable to anyone alive. Even you, I suspect."

"Beyond a certain point, it's really only keeping score. That said, there's something magical about skunking your opponents so badly that they realize they were never in your league to begin with."

He stood and straightened his jacket. "Consider my offer. Thirty percent ownership of Project Liberty, or whatever I decide to rename it to because of this find, for you and ten percent for my son. Don't worry about what he brings to the table. He's quite resourceful. And very soon, unless I miss my guess, we'll be fending off military incursions. He's quite capable of taking the lead in that area."

She smiled. "And you get to pull him back into your life again. Is my cooperation in that area part of our bargain?"

"I'd make it so, if I thought I needed to. You see him for who he is. In fact, you maneuvered him into accepting part of the deal. Well done, by the way. And much appreciated."

Miss Cook stood. "Now what? You need to check my guy and I need a contract to submit to Harry's lawyer. And, since we're going to be partners, you should call me Jess."

He extended his hand. "Clayton, then. I can't tell you how eagerly I'm looking forward to working even more closely with you." He gestured toward the door. "You should go give my son the good news. You'll want to get the yelling out of the way before dinner. It's bad for the digestion."

# 13

It took a few hours, but Harry had spoken to all his teams. If he knew his shithead brother, there'd be an attempt at payback. He'd expedited the missions he could and delayed those that hadn't kicked off.

Liberty SOG employed half a dozen full-time strike teams. He knew enough reliable semi-retired pros to put another half dozen teams in action with a few days' notice. He summoned those he could to join him here.

Once he had things in motion, he called Rex in for a private chat. The scout had changed into a pair of jeans and a mind-numbingly bright Hawaiian shirt. He lounged back with one leg over the arm of his chair, chewing on something that looked like grass.

Harry shook his head. "Seriously?"

Rex grinned. "You know the deal. Blend in. Have you seen the tourists on the commercial side of the spaceport? Who knew seeing cargo launches to the space hotel would bring in so many retired Floridians."

"Apparently you did. I hope you enjoyed the break, because it looks like we have a new job."

The scout's grin dropped away and he sat up. "That was quick. Where next? Libya? The Black Sea? Disney World?"

"As if we'd ever be lucky enough to get Disney World. I'd love to see Jeremy try to crack their security."

"Give him a chance and he'll make you proud. What's up?"

Harry considered how much he could tell his friend. He trusted Rex with his life and had done so for years. Still, he didn't know how much of this fantastical story he'd believe if he hadn't seen it with his own eyes.

"I can't tell you everything," Harry said. "For now, treat this as a classified mission brief. We found something in the pyramid and something even bigger at the second site. Things I can't fully explain either to you, but they're seriously important."

"Like a supervillain's lair? I've always wondered where they hid those things."

"Just about that unexpected. The bottom line is that it's something worth killing over. I've made preliminary arrangements with my father to work in tandem with his people on certain aspects of something he calls Project Liberty."

"Hey! That's our name! Did he steal it?"

"Probably. In any case, our interests are aligned in this matter."

Rex's eyes widened. "With your father? That's some serious shit. Does it have something to do with that asshole brother of yours?"

"Not really, but he might make another appearance looking for Jess."

The scout smiled. "Jess, is it? You know, I hear shared danger makes for hot sex."

He gave his friend a stern glare. "And lousy long-term relationships. Focus. I've summoned all available teams, including those on standby. We'll work with my father's security forces, but we don't take orders from them without my say so."

"I'm totally focused. She's hot. Besides, blokes like us don't live long enough to have long-term relationships. As for the teams, that's a lot of people. Why do we need so many shooters?"

"That's classified, too. The basic outline is a heist. Something large and valuable. While I'm not normally prone to grand theft, my mother was the one pulling Nathan's strings, so I'll make an exception. My father's security people have been working on a plan for some time. We'll integrate with them to make it happen, hopefully with me in overall command. This is going down in less than a week and once it does, I expect all hell to break loose."

A knock at the door interrupted them. Allen stuck his head in. "Sorry for the interruption, Harry. You have a call from that lady we rescued."

Harry stood. "I'll be right there. Rex, get the team together and briefed. I don't trust my father and I want to be ready to move at a moment's notice. As far as I'm concerned, Jessica Cook is still our client. Get a two person guard detail ready for her."

"On it."

He followed Allen back to the sitting room and picked up the phone. "Rogers."

"Harry, it's Jess. We need to talk about something that came up in the meeting after you left. Do you have a few minutes?"

"Sure." He gave her the team's suite number and hung up when she ended the call.

* * *

HARRY OPENED the door when Jess knocked. He'd changed into khakis and a dark shirt.

She took a moment to admire the view. "You clean up nice. Now you look like a secret agent."

He smiled. "I'm sure that isn't quite the case, but thanks. We searched the rooms for listening devices. All clear, and one of my people is here 24/7. Let's go and have that talk."

Harry led her back to the room they were using for conferences and closed the door. "I haven't told them anything about what we found. I'll eventually need to, but I'd rather do it once I know what's really going on."

Jess sat and crossed one leg over the other. "I'm seriously considering taking your father up on his offer. Not that it's any of my business, but what happened between the two of you?"

"We don't have enough time to explore that. Suffice it to say, he's not the humanitarian of the year. He's done things that hurt people. Saying he's good in comparison to the other corporate oligarchs isn't saying much. He's a mile better than my mother, but he's still a son of a bitch. Be very careful of any offer he makes you."

"We discussed the framework of a deal already. No agreement or anything, just an idea of what he's looking at paying. An offer that includes you."

His expression soured. "That fails to fill me with joy. I'm not quite sure how this happened."

"Maybe you just wanted to keep him from taking advantage of me. In any case, he's offering an interest in Project Liberty."

"The mission to Mars? Honestly, I'm still not really seeing the return in something like that. How much money could mining in space bring in?"

She decided it was time to pull the curtain back a little. Harry's father was offering a stake in the project, so he deserved to know what that meant.

"Let me lay it out for you. The most common asteroid is a C-Type. That stands for carbonaceous, by the way. Those make up something like 75% of all asteroids. The outer part of the asteroid belt and beyond may have an even higher percentage of them. That's the critical takeaway from this. They're extremely common.

"While the specific breakdown of each asteroid is different, even within a narrow classification like this, we can make some basic assumptions about them. First, the average density is between 2.9 and 3.5 grams per cubic centimeter. About forty percent of the density of iron, give or take. You with me so far?"

Harry tried not to smile. "Barely. I'm not an engineer, Miss Scott."

"A gratuitous Star Trek reference. Nice, but my Scottish accent stinks. Anyway, let's assume a median of that density and a decent size asteroid. Say 1,000 meters, or maybe a bit larger for the math. 1,050 meters at that density would be about two billion metric tons of material. There are roughly a thousand asteroids of that size in near Earth orbit by current estimates. Again, once someone is out there looking for them, they will almost certainly end up finding more."

He nodded. "Okay, I'll grant that's a lot of material. It would cost a mint to mine it, wouldn't it? Also, you'd need to get the ore back to Earth. That seems like a limiting factor to me."

"It is. Iron makes up a bit more than twenty percent of the total material. 440 million metric tons. The cost of extracting the raw ore here on Earth varies, but it usually sells for around $50 a metric ton. That makes the iron on the one asteroid worth twenty-two billion dollars. That, of course, doesn't count how much it would cost to ship it into orbit for use in space, which is a lot more expensive."

"That's a lot of money," Harry admitted. "You're not talking about bringing it back to Earth? Isn't that where the market is?"

"I'll get to that. That one element is literally only the tip of the iceberg. Let's talk platinum. They'll be able to pull about 2,000 metric tons of that out of the asteroid. That'll be worth about 80 billion dollars. And there are many other valuable minerals. It only makes economic sense to ship the most profitable back to Earth. We can use the rest much more efficiently in space."

He considered that for a moment. "It looks like you're thinking big."

"We are. On average, each metric ton of raw material will bring in about $1,500. A few decades ago, that number would've been somewhat lower, but scarce minerals are getting even harder to find.

"So, let's roll this up. One asteroid. Two billion metric tons. Three trillion dollars. It would be more if we selected an asteroid even heavier in platinum group metals. It might approach twice the value.

"As I said, we'd only ship the most valuable elements to Earth for sale. We'd use most in space to create infrastructure and habitats. This would fuel the spread of humanity to every part of the solar system. It would free humanity from the bonds of Earth. Hence, Project Liberty."

Harry was quiet for a while. "Ambitious. How long would it take to mine something like that?"

"When the prospective mine is fully operational, which might take a few years, we figure it can process between 50 and 100 million metric tons per year. So, that one asteroid would take 20 to 40 years to fully mine. And the best part is everything is useful. No waste.

"The majority of the output could go right into setting up other mining sites and habitats. There's a significant amount of water tied up in these kinds of asteroids too. That means air, water, and fuel. Life for people in space."

He took even longer to digest that. Jess sat back and let him think about it at his own speed.

"Okay, I know why a normal person might think this is a good idea, but what does my father get out of this? Control of humanity? Something else? He doesn't do charity."

"You'd have to ask him. I assume he's doing this because it's in his own long-term interest. It'll make him the wealthiest man who ever lived. Anyway, that's enough detail for you to understand the scope of the project. Your father is offering me a thirty percent stake in Project Liberty. You'd get ten percent."

"Wow. That's a lot of money. He has to have something else up his sleeve. Make sure you get the contract examined closely."

"I will. As long as the details check out, I'm going to accept the offer. Even a minority stake in something like this would give me so much more input going forward."

Harry gave her a skeptical look. "I hope it works out the way you expect. I need to go confer with my father's security people. If he can't get the engine for this thing, the project is deader than the guy in the pyramid."

# 14

Getting onto the spaceport wasn't as difficult as Nathan had feared. It wasn't on total lockdown. His new team had an ally inside that helped get them into the area around the hotel, though he'd said he couldn't get them inside.

Nathan wasn't convinced that was true. With the right motivation, the man could probably come up with a way.

First, though, he'd listen to what the man had learned. He sat behind his borrowed desk and adjusted his backside to ease the discomfort. The woman's shot had only grazed him, but it hurt and it was his ass. The bitch would pay for that when he caught her.

His mother's spy wasn't much to look at, scrawny and short. The bones of his dark face stood out as though someone had starved him for a month. Not even the pricy suit he wore could make up for the air of starvation that seemed to hang over him.

Nathan's temporary headquarters were inside an unused office with a view of the hotel. One of his men had found a spot on the roof to use as a sniper hide, though that really wasn't anyone's idea of a good plan. The odds of successfully extracting were slim if every security guard was on alert.

Two of his people flanked the man as he sat gingerly in front of Nathan. Their silent presence kept the man a little on edge, just as Nathan intended. The sweat on the man's forehead was a pleasant addition to the proceedings.

With a studied, cold expression, Nathan gestured for the man to speak. "Tell me everything you've learned about the mercenary and the woman he came in with. Leave nothing out."

The man's smile was fleeting and perfunctory. "Of course, sir. They came in early yesterday morning with Mister Rogers. The hotel is in lockdown. We moved all the guests to other accommodations. The elder Mister Rogers and Miss Cook were in a secured conference room all morning and part of the afternoon.

"The owner's son spent a short while there, but retired to a suite occupied by his companions before lunch. I was unable to gain access to the conference room, but I did manage to spy on some of the other occupants as they left."

He slid a data chip across to Nathan, who handed it off to one of his people. The man booted a tablet and loaded the video. It showed a guard escorting two women. The women wore lab coats and carried a pack as though it contained something very fragile. The clip lasted less than ten seconds.

Nathan wasn't impressed. "That's all you have? Who are they? What's in the pack?" He, of course, already knew more than he'd said, but the little bugger needed some extra motivation.

The sweat on the man's face grew heavier. "I'm sorry, sir. I don't know. Security around Mister Rogers is exceptionally tight, and the two women are isolated. I did manage to get a list of the equipment they brought with them, though. It's also on the chip."

The mercenary found the file and opened it. Nathan scanned the list. It looked as though they might be setting up a clean room, though some of the equipment just didn't make sense for something like that. He'd need to have a technogeek look at the list.

"And when did my brother leave?"

"He's still here, sir. Mister Rogers indicated that they would remain for at least several days and possibly much longer. It appears that the two of them have some type of arrangement. One of my associates is procuring some equipment and clothing for them. It's being charged to Rainforest."

That made no sense at all. Nathan knew his brother hated their father as much as he did, though for all the wrong reasons. He wasn't sure what had convinced Harry to rescue the woman, but he certainly wouldn't be doing long-term work for their father.

Nathan leaned forward and smiled coldly. "I want you to get something into their rooms. I'll give you a device to plant."

The little bastard had the gall to shake his head. "They aren't allowing anyone into the rooms. Not even maids to clean up. As far as I can determine, someone is always present there. It just isn't possible."

"I'm not interested in excuses. I want results. You will make that happen. I'll leave it to you to fill in the 'or else' part."

The frightened man nodded. "I'll try."

"You better do more than try, little man. Get him out of here."

Once his men had roughly escorted the weasel out, Nathan pulled out his phone and dialed his mother's private number.

"This better not be bad news," she said after a single ring.

"I'm sending you a video of two unknown women. They seem to be part of whatever scheme father has cooked up."

"How so?"

"I expect their identities might provide a clue. I also have a list of equipment and a mystery."

"Don't drag this out, Nathan. What mystery?"

"The one where dear Harry and your ex-husband are working closely together."

The connection was quiet for a minute. He could imagine his mother wracking her brain for the cause of such an unlikely alliance.

"Get me some answers." She hung up without another word.

\* \* \*

JESS EYED the two guards that Harry had sprung on her with disfavor. They seemed unmoved. Sandra Dean didn't look all that intimidating, but Jess knew she was a very capable sniper and all around badass. Allen Ellison towered over both women, muscled and tough.

Yet he deferred to Sandra, which told Jess all she needed to know about which was the more dangerous of the two.

Both wore the same kind of camouflage uniform that they'd worn in the jungle, a liberty bell patch with the numeral 1 on their left shoulders. Instead of allowing them to blend in, it made them stand out. As did the pistols on their hips and the automatic weapons that hung in front of their chests.

"Don't you think this is a little over the top?" Jess asked Sandra. "We're in the middle of a hotel under heavy guard. There's no one here but us."

The wiry woman shrugged. "That's assuming we can trust the security, which I don't. If I think one of them is making a move on you, I'll cap him." She smiled sweetly at the uncomfortable looking man in a suit that trailed them. He'd easily overheard every word.

"That's harsh." Jess thought Harry was being overprotective, but she couldn't blame him. His brother had almost gotten her twice. The memory of drawing her borrowed pistol and shooting the hell out of the jungle trying to hit that bastard would haunt her for a while.

Which reminded her. "I need your advice," she said to Sandra. "I appreciated Harry loaning me the pistol, but I'm not going to cart something like that around on my hip. Can you recommend something smaller that I can carry in my purse?"

"Mexico is pretty restrictive on weapons unless you have a permit. Especially concealed. If they'd have caught us in the jungle, I'm sure Guatemala would've locked us up, too. You'll need your boss to make some calls."

The Rainforest security guy took the hint and called someone on his radio. After a brief conversation, he looked back at Jess. "My boss knows someone who can expedite a permit. He's making some calls."

"Thanks."

Sandra darted her eyes toward the ladies room they were just passing. Jess didn't need to go, but she took the hint and angled over toward it. "I'll just be a couple of minutes."

The mercenary woman followed her in without a word to her companion.

Jess frowned a little. "Are you going to follow me into the ladies room every time I have to go?"

"Duh. It's a great ambush spot. The bad guys can literally catch you with your pants down."

Sandra cleared the bathroom stalls. One had an occupant. The mercenary banged on the door. "Security. Wrap it up and move along."

"I'm busy," a woman said acerbically. "You'll just have to wait."

"If you're not done in sixty seconds, I'm coming in to help you with that." She keyed her radio. "One extra in the bathroom. Stand by."

The woman in the stall sighed and finished quickly. She washed her hands and glared at Sandra as she exited.

The mercenary was apparently immune to embarrassment. She finished searching the stall and called the all clear to Allen.

"Now, let's go over a few ground rules," she told Jess. "First, you don't pull this gun unless you really need to. Allen and I are here to provide security. If there's trouble, you do exactly what we tell you to do, which will not be to shoot at anyone. Clear?"

Jess nodded. "I only used the pistol last time because I didn't have a choice."

"I heard. You got a piece of him, right?"

"Rex found a little blood, so I think so. It must not have been anything important."

"That's good. It'd have been better if you shot the bastard in the head, but take what you can get. I've heard stories about cops and thugs emptying their pistols at one other while standing a few feet apart where they missed every shot. Adrenalin screws up your perception, so you have to train hard to overcome it.

"Rule two, if you draw your weapon, shoot to kill. Do not shoot to wound. That never ends well. If you need a salve for your conscience, surprisingly few people die from gunshot wounds unless the shooter is really good or lucky. Odds are that anyone you cap will make it to the hospital and survive the experience. Don't give the enemy any advantage. Clear?"

"Yes. Don't draw unless I have to, only draw if I intend to kill someone, and then shoot to kill." Her stomach roiled a little at the cold-bloodedness. A few days ago, she'd never have considered anything like this. Her worldview was changing in ways she didn't really like.

Sandra looked her in the eyes for a moment, and then nodded. "Good enough." She unclipped her rifle and set it on the counter. She then tugged her shirt up, revealing a black bra with a pistol butt poking out from beneath it.

"Seriously?" Jess asked. "You have a gun attached to your bra?"

The mercenary grinned. "Last place you'd expect to see one, right? The holster snaps around the center between my tits. Guys never see past them to what they're hiding. Boobs of death."

Sandra unsnapped the holstered weapon and gestured for Jess to lift her blouse.

"You're more stacked than I am, which is a good thing for keeping something like this hidden," Sandra said as she attached it to Jess's bra. "This keeps the pistol under your breasts horizontally so that you can lift your shirt and draw. The gun comes free with a good tug. You'll want to practice with the weapon unloaded. I want you to be able to draw from a dead sleep."

"You want me to go to bed armed?"

"No, but you need to get the muscle memory in there. In a crisis, you'll do what you've trained to do. You want your first response to be the right one, especially when someone is trying to kill you."

Once the holster was in place, Sandra pulled the pistol free and unloaded it. It looked very much like the one Harry had loaned her, though a little smaller.

"This is a Glock subcompact 9mm," Sandra said. "The one you had in the jungle is its big brother. You have ten rounds in the magazine and one in the pipe. I have a spare magazine that can go in your purse. Twenty-one rounds total. Most confrontations take place inside of ten feet and are over in seconds. That should be enough ammo.

"We'll be training you more on how to use this later, but it should make you feel safe enough for the moment. You'll be self-conscious for a while, but no one will see it under your blouse. Hell, they might not even find it during a pat down if they cop a feel. Pretend it isn't there. If this isn't to your taste, we can go shopping for a different kind of holster or gun later."

"I don't want to take your stuff. I need to buy my own."

Sandra shrugged. "You can buy me some new toys later. A girl can't have too many hand cannons. Remind me to show you my .50 BMG single shot pistol."

"BMG?"

"Big Mutherfracking Gun."

Jess shook her head. She'd never understand some people.

They walked through loading and unloading the pistol safely. Then Sandra put it in the holster unloaded, Jess slid her blouse down, and she practiced drawing it a few times. The pistol came free surprisingly cleanly, though it did feel odd exposing herself a little to get at it. She supposed the distraction was a plus.

She examined herself closely in the mirror. She didn't see the gun at all.

"It's not exactly the most comfortable thing, but I suppose I'll get used to it."

Sandra clapped Jess on the shoulder and handed her a spare magazine from her belt. "A gun is supposed to be comforting, not comfortable. You need to hit the can?"

Jess shook her head and put the magazine into the side pocket of her purse. She could get to it quickly and it wouldn't be popping out if she needed her brush. "I'm good. They've got to be wondering what we're doing in here."

"Guys have no clue what women do in the bathroom. They might be impatient, but they'll never guess the truth. Come on."

They came out of the restroom and Jess headed down the hall with the group at her heels. "Sorry I took so long. I'd like to go see the restoration specialists."

The Rainforest guard stepped ahead of them. "The doctors are in a suite on the sixth floor. This way, please."

# 15

Harry walked into the head of his father's security forces' office with a chip on his shoulder and two armed guards at his back. His father's, not his.

The man across the desk from him eyed Harry for a few seconds. "Wally, close the door on your way out."

The guard in question, who looked like a boxer that had taken a few too many shots to the nose, looked at Harry uncertainly. "You sure?"

"I'll yell if I need you," the man's boss said.

Harry waited for the two men to leave and stood next to the bookcase, ignoring the chair set out in front of the desk. He wasn't going to play these head games. He'd play his own.

The selection of books looked professional, most relating to the security industry. The ones that didn't fit that meme were thrillers of one kind or another.

He allowed the silence to go on. That, too, was a power game. People abhorred silence. They wanted to fill it. Patience and keeping your mouth shut often gave one an advantage. He'd wait for hours, if need be.

As he'd expected, the other man spoke first.

"I'm John Cradock, Mister Roger's head of security. I want to start this meeting off by making it clear that I'm in command of the operations around here. I don't give a shit if my boss is your dad or not. You got that?"

Harry took one of the thrillers off the shelf and read the back cover. A military thriller. Snipers and terrorists. Sandra might like to read it for laughs. He slid it into his pocket, turned toward the desk, and basked in the glow of the man's dismay at his petty theft.

"And, for my part," Harry said, "I don't give a shit that you don't give a shit. My father can go to hell and you can escort him there. That said, someone I do care about needs this heist to go off without a hitch. Unless you have a lot more experience than I expect at this kind of thing, I'm going to be calling the shots."

The way the man was glaring, it was a wonder that the books behind Harry didn't burst into flames. "That isn't going to happen."

"Then we're done here. You can explain to your boss why I'm pulling out and he can flap in the wind. Or we can work out a mutually agreeable plan. I have years of experience getting into places that I'm not meant to be and taking things that other people don't want to give up. People, mostly, but we guard the ones we love the best."

Cradock ran his hand through his hair. "Shit. I don't know you and I'm the one responsible for this mission. If it fails, I'm going down for it."

"Then let's make sure that doesn't happen. We'll go over your plans and I'll make suggestions. I'll have almost a dozen spec ops teams here in two days, every one of them with experience being on the sharp end. Surely you and I can come up with a plan to use them effectively once we've gotten past this pissing contest."

"Shit. Fine." He pounded on the keyboard with his thick fingers and a street map came up on the screen across from the desk.

"This is the satellite view of the target. It's an industrial park on the outskirts of Paris. BenCorp owns the entire park. Why they built in that cesspool, I'll never know. The outer buildings are empty. The central building is where they designed and built the reactor.

"I imagine they'll bring in other tenants after the secret project is complete. Or maybe things will go so bad that they'll abandon it. Some parts of Paris seem to be on fire 24/7 these days."

The map showed how isolated the target was. Fences topped with razor wire surrounded the facility. Based on the markings, guard teams heavily patrolled the grounds. The public wouldn't get within a thousand feet of the research facility. Not even the terrorists virtually running Paris these days.

"Where are the guard posts?"

"There are a dozen along the perimeter and roving patrols all over the place. Random times and patterns. Dogs, bomb-sniffing robots, and automatic weapons. They're ready to repel the strongest attack force."

Harry nodded. "But you've found a weak spot."

"Right." Cradock added a layer to the image. "Sewers. BenCorp has them wired, but we've spent the last six months hacking the security protocols. We'll be able to bypass the alarms and slip inside their perimeter when the time comes. The tunnels have a spur that services the target building. We'll be inside it with no one the wiser."

"If you believe that, you're an idiot."

Cradock bared his teeth. "You don't know me and you don't know how carefully we probed this thing. It's a real weak spot."

"It's a trap. My mother is like a spider. She likes people to think they've gotten one over on her, right up until the bear trap snaps shut on their hand. There's no way she'd leave something basic like that unprotected."

"I just said it was protected. We've spoofed all the security monitors. I had a team probe the sewers all the way to the basement of the target building."

"I'm sure you did. And when your teams come in force, something you never saw coming would blow the shit out of you. I have a genius at security on my team. Let him go over what you have. If he agrees that my mother is slipping into dementia, fine and good. If not, you don't lose dozens of men."

"Fine," Cradock said unwillingly. "Call him down. Use the desk phone. Cell traffic is blocked."

It only took a moment to call Jeremy Gonzales. Harry returned his attention to the security man when he finished explaining the situation. "Is that where the fuel is, too?"

Cradock shook his head. "No. Mister Rogers has a factory in Northern Africa. They made deuterium-tritium pellets there for years. They have a large stockpile in storage. Unfortunately, the government collapsed and a warlord has taken over the area. He's probably not aware of what he has under his nose, but there are militants all over the facility. They think it's something they can use to make nuclear bombs."

Harry chuckled. "As if anyone sane would allow that to happen after Tel Aviv. Israel turned most of Iran into glowing craters. Good riddance. You're right. That's a solvable problem. We can focus on the tough nut first."

\* \* \*

NATHAN PAUSED the porn on his tablet and answered the call on his encrypted cell. "Mother."

"The women in your video are experts at restoring and safeguarding ancient artifacts. The kind of thing one finds in a Mayan pyramid. Or, I suppose, in an ancient spacecraft."

"Not exactly helpful. Your man on the inside isn't able to get a bug into Harry's room and I've seen no sign that he or the engineer are coming out any time soon. We're just sitting here spinning our wheels."

"Perhaps not. I've heard that Harry is calling in his special operations strike teams. Some are on the way down to the spaceport right now. Your window to make any gains is short."

Nathan sat up abruptly. "He's calling in his shooters? How many of them?"

"How the hell should I know? All of them, as far as I can tell."

"Shit. Once they lock the hotel down with that kind of force, we won't be able to do a damned thing. We need to go after them right now."

"Exactly my thought," his mother said. "Except they're not the most important thing in that building. If you can catch them, great. What I really want are the artifacts. I'm working with my people in Guatemala to take the sites away from Clayton, but he's spent a prodigious amount of money. It won't be easy, if it's possible at all. We need to know what they're looking at and get samples of it."

Nathan nodded thoughtfully. "We'll go in just as the sun goes down. The other teams will be close to landing and their guard will be more relaxed. He only has one team here and they're probably not guarding the artifacts. In and out. We'll need to evade the security response long enough to escape the area, though."

His mother smiled. The small picture didn't do her justice. "I know just the right kind of distraction to give you the time you need. Call my man and get this rolling."

\* \* \*

THE DOCTORS HAD SET up their lab in a large conference room. Jess didn't recognize most of the equipment, but imagined they used it to stop the deterioration of delicate artifacts. The two women had their heads together over the book.

They looked up as Jess and her entourage entered. Security was tight. There were two Rainforest guards outside and two inside, all in body armor and armed with automatic weapons. Clayton Rogers was taking security very seriously.

Jess's guard detail peeled off and took up spots against the wall opposite the Rainforest security team.

"How are things going?" Jess asked.

Paulette Young gestured toward the book. "This is amazing. The pages are made from a material somewhat like plastic, but almost as flexible as paper. It's obviously much more durable. The pen used an ink that bonded with the pages. It's quite ingenious. I hope the pen turns up."

"What about the writing itself? Has anyone looked into what language it might be?"

"We haven't had any luck identifying it yet. It's written from left to right and isn't similar to any lettering that I'm familiar with. Rachel scanned it in and we have a search of our offline database running now."

Rachel Powel gestured toward a computer. "We have samples of every known language on file. If it's been used on Earth, we'll find it."

"What about the tools?"

"They seem to be made of the same material. We took a sample and sent it off to the lab. The tools don't seem to have lost their tensile strength over the centuries. The only object that seems to have broken down is the satchel and even it has held together surprisingly well. I'm not sure there's much for us to preserve, other than that."

"There are other...objects being brought in. You'll probably need more space."

The scientist nodded. "Mister Rogers said that he has a lab building that will be ready for us tomorrow morning. It will be more isolated and not disrupt the hotel."

A flash of light outside caught Jess's attention. It was getting dark, so the flare was quite visible. Was a cargo shuttle launching off schedule?

She'd taken one step toward the window when Sandra tackled her like a linebacker and covered her with her body. The larger Allen was right behind the sniper and planted himself between the two scientists with his back to the flash.

The large windows blew out in a maelstrom of broken glass. A massive explosion roared in the distance. A few shards nicked Jess's exposed arm and the sting of pain was surreal.

Her head rang with the aftereffects of the explosion. It was worse than when she'd fired the gun in the jungle.

Dazed, she almost fell over when Sandra yanked her to her feet. "Time to go," the mercenary said. "Allen, clear the hall. We're going back to the suite." She keyed her radio. "Liberty Base, Long Gun. Condition Gamma. We're returning via the stairs on the south side of the building."

Jess didn't have much of a choice. The woman almost dragged her back to the hall. Allen had his weapon up and covered the Rainforest guards as the three of them withdrew.

She didn't think they were much of a threat. They'd been looking right at the windows when they exploded. The two interior guards were down, clutching their bloody faces. The guards from outside were staring at the destruction in shock.

The Rainforest guard assigned to them must've ducked. He had a long gash on the back of his hand, but was otherwise okay.

"Wait," Jess said. "This had to have been an accident. Something exploded at one of the launch pads."

Sandra didn't seem to care. "That's someone else's problem. I'm getting you back where I can protect you."

"What about the scientists and the priceless artifacts? We need to keep them safe."

"They aren't my responsibility."

"Bring them with us. At least grab the book."

"The other guards can see them to safety. Let's go." She dragged Jess down the hall. Allen sprinted ahead to clear the stairs.

The big mercenary had just disappeared when Sandra jerked to a halt and collapsed. Jess had just enough time to turn and see the grinning Rainforest security man pull his stun gun back from Sandra's neck.

"Don't make me hurt you," he said as an automatic weapon started firing in the stairwell. "Mister Bennett wants you in one piece."

## 16

Harry sprinted out of the Rainforest security center and appropriated one of their vehicles. He cut off a car full of tourists and floored the gas. He figured he'd be back at the hotel in less than three minutes.

"Liberty Base, Liberty Six. Client status?" He had a lot of experience multitasking in combat, but swerving to miss idiots in traffic was new.

"Shots fired upstairs. The protective detail is not responding."

"Retrieve the client."

"Copy."

He cut across a field and made directly for the hotel. Jess didn't have seconds to spare.

* * *

NATHAN STEPPED over the body in the stairwell. Another mercenary, a woman, lay sprawled on the hall carpet. The Rainforest guard on his mother's payroll stood behind the woman who'd shot him in the jungle. He held a stun gun to her neck.

"Well, well. What an unexpected surprise!" Nathan said with a chuckle. He gestured for his team to continue past him. "Hit the lab. Take anything of use and kill everyone. Leave my father's gift on the table."

The woman trembled, deliciously terrified. It warmed his heart.

"Have you searched her for weapons?" he asked. "She has hidden depths."

The man pinned the woman face first into the wall and started patting her down. His reach was limited with the stun gun planted on her neck.

"Idiot," Nathan said. "Keep her still while I check her."

He started at her ankles and felt his way up. She squirmed when he roughly checked her privates. "Get used to that. I'll be examining you much more closely."

"Bastard. I'm going to kill you."

Nathan laughed. "If only you knew how many women have said that to me over the years. It's almost an endearment at this point."

He made a point of fondling her breasts as he finished patting her down. They were his favorite part of a woman and hers were magnificent. Gunfire erupted down the hall. It ended quickly and his team called back in that the room was secure.

"She mentioned a book," the guard said. "She made it sound like that was the most important thing in the room."

"Why didn't you say that earlier, moron?" Nathan updated his team. They quickly reported that they had it.

The woman glared at him. "Harry won't let you get out of this building alive."

Nathan grinned nastily. "My brother will be very late to the party. And if you think his people will rescue you, well, you're in for a very disappointing day."

The floor jumped and the stairwell door swung open a little. The booby trap he'd left below had found some customers.

He glanced at his watch. "Time to make our way to the roof. Move it along, people."

* * *

JESS KNEW that time was running out. If the bastard got her out of the building, she'd never escape. Right now, she only had him and the turncoat guard to deal with. She needed to do something while she could.

The guard had relaxed a little now that the heavily armed team had arrived. The damned stun gun wasn't on her neck anymore. That gave her a small window of opportunity.

Nathan had his attention focused down the hall waiting for his people to leave the preservation room. Jess had to make her move now.

She jammed her hand under her blouse and pulled the pistol free. The guard gaped, probably having no idea what she was doing.

He recognized the pistol, though. She stepped away from him even further, wanting to keep him from grabbing her gun. He was still drawing his weapon when she had hers lined up on his head and pulled the trigger.

The results of that shot would feature prominently in her nightmares for years to come, if she survived.

She turned her attention to Harry's brother. He had body armor and an automatic weapon. One that was swiveling in her direction.

Jess threw herself into the stairwell just as he opened fire. The doorframe disintegrated, spraying her with splinters of wood.

Allen Ellison lay sprawled on his back in a pool of blood. He didn't look like he was breathing and his eyes stared sightlessly at the ceiling. His weapon still hung around his neck.

She set her pistol on the floor, grabbed the rifle, and waited. If Nathan just came around the corner...

At the first sign of movement, Jess yanked the trigger. She quickly lost control of the automatic weapon. The barrel rose unexpectedly, but she forced it back down on target. The man's burst went harmlessly to the side as he slid down the wall, leaving a trail of blood. Her gun locked open surprisingly quickly.

It wasn't Nathan. Dammit.

Jess listened to the shouts down the hall as she grabbed her pistol and retreated up the stairs to the next landing. If they came this way, she'd give them something to regret.

\* \* \*

HARRY WAS ALMOST to the hotel when his windshield shattered. He'd just hit a big bump in the ground, so the bullet aimed at him blew out the dashboard instead.

He couldn't stay in the sniper's kill zone, so he floored the SUV and started swerving. The main entrance to the hotel was right there.

More bullets hit his vehicle, but missed him. He entered the area where passengers unloaded at what some might kindly call an unsafe speed and went right through the big glass doors.

He stood on the brakes and stopped just short of the front desk. He jumped out and ran past the shell-shocked staff to the stairs. Automatic weapons fire came from above.

He passed what looked like an exploded booby trap on the third floor landing. The lifeless bodies of a number of Rainforest security guards lay around it. He reached the hotspot and found his team already in place. Two of them were working on Allen, but it looked bad. Two more had just dragged Sandra in. A dead hostile lay sprawled just inside the hallway.

Jess stood on the stairs above them, a pistol in her hand, looking as though she were going into shock. "They went after the preservation room," she said. "They used a stun gun on Sandra."

The man working on Allen shook his head. Dammit.

"Rex, grab Sandra and get Jess clear. Everyone else is with me."

"Your brother said he was leaving a gift in the room," Jess said over her shoulder as Rex hustled her down the stairs. "Be careful!"

A Rainforest security man lay dead a few feet down the hall, his head shattered. The team moved as a unit past him to the open door. Three—no four—dead men lay scatted around the room. There was no sign of the two scientists.

There was also no sign of the alien gear recovered from the tomb, at least not in plain sight. And he didn't have time to go looking for it.

A small stack of plastic explosives sat in the middle of the central table. A helpful timer indicated there was less than two minutes remaining before the device exploded. Not enough time to exit the building.

That was enough explosives to bring the hotel down. The device almost certainly had some kind of anti-tamper protection, too.

Harry pondered his range of options. The bomb's sensors would know if he moved it, but there was some play. Otherwise, even minor shaking would set the thing off.

"Hold it steady. Lift it just a little."

Two of his people held the bomb while he cut the straps securing the explosives. He held his breath and slid the lower packages to the side. The ones on the edges of the top layer also fell away. Leann tossed them out the broken window.

That reduced the scope of the explosion enough to spare the building. Maybe. At his gesture, they set the bomb down carefully and ran like hell.

* * *

REX HUSTLED Jess out the side door of the hotel just as a helicopter took off from the roof. It had medical markings. She saw Nathan through the open door. He waved at her.

She was tempted to take a shot at him, but she knew she wouldn't hit anything.

Dammit.

Less than a minute later, the side of the hotel blew out. Debris showered around them even as Rex dragged her behind a parked minivan. Something heavy landed on the vehicle, crushing the roof.

She screamed. Who wouldn't?

When the rain of debris finally stopped, she stared at the devastation. The hotel was mostly intact. It had a huge divot in the side and it was on fire, though. Steel and concrete littered the parking area. Every car alarm within a mile seemed to be going off. The stench of the explosives made her nose itch. And her ears were ringing even louder.

She turned to Rex. "Is Harry okay? Did he get out?"

The big man nodded grimly. "He made it down a few floors. It sounds like they're okay."

"I saw the mercenaries. They flew off the roof in a medical helicopter."

"They won't get far, but it'll probably be enough to slip away. Dammit. That's twice that assclown tried to kill some of us, and this time he did it."

His eyes shifted toward the hotel. "At least we took one of them out."

"Two," she said as she watched fire engines pull up to the hotel. "One of the Rainforest people was a traitor. He zapped Sandra. I shot him. Then I used Allen's weapon to kill the mercenary in the hall."

He blinked in surprise, but said nothing.

She knelt beside the sniper and was happy to see signs that Sandra was waking up. Since slapping her cheek seemed like a very bad idea, Jess just waited.

The other woman sat up abruptly, reaching for her weapons. Jess held the rifle down. "Whoa! The fight is over."

Sandra blinked and felt the back of her neck. "What happened?"

"You know where you warned me that trouble could sneak up when I least expected it? It did. Allen didn't make it. I'm sorry."

The sniper said something particularly foul. "Help me up. Rex, what's the situation?"

He filled her in while they watched the building. Jess was happy to see other people streaming out of the damaged structure, including the two scientists from the preservation lab. They must've gotten the hell out of there right after the explosion at the launch pad.

Jess didn't relax until she saw Harry and his remaining teammates come out. Then she allowed herself to cry in a mixture of relief, terror, and horror.

\* \* \*

HARRY HELD Jess when the reaction set in. He wanted to ask her exactly what had happened, but this wasn't the time. He stayed with her until he saw his father climb out of an SUV. Harry passed the wrung out engineer to Sandra and headed over.

His father looked at the building. "This was Nathan, wasn't it?"

"Yes. He made off with some of the artifacts, but not the scientists. Or Jess. He killed a bunch of your guards, too. One of my people died in the stairwell, but it looks like he dropped one of the enemy and allowed Jess to escape. Rex said he flew off the roof in a medivac helicopter. What did he blow up?"

"The fueling station for pad 3. He killed some of the staff. Security said the helicopter landed outside the fence and they climbed into some vans. They're gone. The police are scouring the city, but it wouldn't surprise me if Nathan had some cops in his pocket. I'll put out a massive reward for their arrest, but don't hold your breath."

Harry considered the hotel while he thought. The fire was spreading quickly. It might be a loss.

"Nathan knew," he said after a moment. "He must've gotten a look inside that second chamber and saw the ship. The race is on now. What next?"

His father turned toward him, his expression as cold and hostile as Harry had ever seen. "We make them pay. If we want to stop Kathleen from derailing our plans completely, we need to act quickly.

"I know corporate contracts are supposed to be almost incomprehensible with legalese, but we don't have time for that luxury. If I write out a short deal swapping an ownership stake for access to the items already provided and anything recovered in the future, will you accept my word that it will be good? You can send it to your attorney for confirmation."

"On one condition. Mother has obviously compromised your organization. I want to be in charge of all security operations for Project Liberty. That includes the upcoming missions because your guy is fighting me on it."

"Done," his father said immediately. "Once your mother gets a chance to think this through, she'll realize what we're doing. You need to move the Paris timetable up."

Harry shook his head. "Your guy's plan feels like a trap. There's something going on there. We need more information about the facility and what they really have planned."

His father considered that. "I have a man in your mother's IT department. He was supposed to get me the final plans on this and a number of other secret projects, but he's gone quiet. She must've picked him up. If he got the data, it would be very helpful to retrieve it. And it would hurt her badly."

Harry smiled coldly. "Get me what you have and I'll see about returning Nathan's visit."

# 17

J ess turned down the doctor's offer of something to calm her nerves. She needed her wits about her. Mister Rogers had presented her with a ridiculously short contract that matched what they'd discussed in astonishingly plain language.

Harry had already run it past his lawyer and she'd found no issues. The company would own the finds—past, present, and future—and profit from them. The ownership was unambiguous and Jess would have her say in the new company, Humanity Unlimited.

Clayton was the chief executive officer, she would be the chief operating officer, and Harry would be the chief of security for the organization. Each would share the profits according to their stake.

Harry had said he'd sign it if she did. Time to do her own check. She looked up the number for her college friend and dialed.

"Dawson and Treadwell, Aaron speaking. How can I help you today?"

"Aaron, this is Jess Cook. How's it going?"

"Jess! I was just thinking about you the other day! Things are great. I made partner last year. Are you still building bridges while dreaming of space stations?"

She smiled at the joy in his voice. Aaron had always been a happy one.

"Actually, I'm working in space. In fact, I wanted to see if I could beg a favor about that."

"You need me to come up and turn a wrench? Bad call. My wife won't let me do home repairs due to liability concerns."

Jess queued up the contract on her tablet. "I made a find that the owner thinks is worth a lot of money. He made me an offer and I need someone I can trust to look it over."

"Sure. Do you have my email address? Send it and I'll take a look. I can probably have an answer for you in a couple of days."

Jess sent the contract. "Things are moving pretty quickly on this end. If you could just take a peek, I'd appreciate it."

"Contracts are nothing to skim," he said seriously. "The devil is in the details. One little word in the boilerplate can change the whole...Wait a second. This isn't complete. It's only one page."

"That's it."

The silence on the other end of the line dragged on as her friend read. "This is pretty plainly stated. You cede control of the listed artifacts to the company, as well as those discovered in the future, and you get an ownership stake in the sole entity that will profit from them: Humanity Unlimited. This list of items you found seems pretty pedestrian. Wrenches, a book, and... wait. A crashed spaceship? Is this a joke?"

Sometimes, it seemed like it. One on her. "Nope, completely serious, though I need you to keep the details confidential. I'll send the general assets list for the company, too."

Once he had it, he continued. "This says the company owns a spaceship constructed from the ISS2 skeleton. It lists tens of billions in assets. And you're getting an outright stake of thirty percent? Jess, I've never seen a contract so straightforward. I don't see any gotchas."

"That's what I needed to know. Remember, keep it under your hat and watch the news over the next few weeks. I owe you one."

Jess hung up and signed the contract. She sent a copy to Clayton, Harry, and herself.

They'd relocated to the spaceport proper. To say that security was heavy was an understatement. Several of Harry's special operations teams had arrived and all of them seemed to be keeping an eye on her. And the building they were in, to be fair.

Sandra was back on her feet and mad as a wet cat. For her, that meant brooding silence. The rest of the original team was off doing other tasks. The room Jess and Sandra were in had four men standing guard, armed for war. Four more stood in the hall outside.

"Sandra, I'm sorry about Allen."

The other woman looked up with cold, hard eyes. "Me, too. He was a good man. It's not your fault. It's mine. I let that traitor get behind me and almost lost you, too."

The sniper visibly shook herself. "Sorry. My mind is already on payback. That'll come in time. Allen took them out and got you free. That's what matters."

"Actually, no. I wish he had." She gave Sandra a rundown of what had happened.

The other woman's eyes widened as she listened. "Oh, God. I'm sorry you had to do that. To see that."

Jess shrugged. "I didn't have a choice. They had it coming, but I'm going to have some bad nights. I just know it."

"You need to talk to someone," the sniper said firmly. "If not today, then soon. PTSD isn't a joke and you don't want to let something like that take over your life. I don't know if you're religious or not, but you might see someone there, too."

"I will. When I have time. Harry's figuring out what we're doing next. I need to be part of that."

"Then what the hell are we doing sitting here? Let's go."

Sandra stood and keyed her radio. "Scotty is on the move."

"Scotty? Seriously?"

"Harry suggested it. You want a different call sign? Pitch it to me and I'll see what I can do. It's like a nickname, though. Sometimes you don't get to pick the one you like."

"That sucks."

Several of the mercenaries stayed at the office while the rest formed up around Jess and Sandra. The Rainforest guards wisely got out of the way when they saw them coming.

Harry was in a conference room in the basement of the security building with one of his guys and several Rainforest types. He had a satellite view of what looked like a college campus up on the screen. He paused what he was saying when she came in. "Jess, I hope you're feeling better."

"I'm riding the tiger." She picked out the most senior looking Rainforest guy and held out her hand. "Jessica Cook."

"John Cradock, chief of Rainforest security operations."

Part of her felt sorry for him, but the rest wanted to slap him for hiring traitors. "I'm sorry you lost some people."

He grunted as though someone had punched him in the stomach. "I'm sorry one of them turned on you. That's on me."

The large man gestured to the screen. "We're planning on returning the favor. Mister Rogers—the elder—told me about the change in organizational structure. The younger Mister Rogers is in command of these operations going forward. As a minority stakeholder, you'll have input, too."

Harry gestured toward the chair beside him. "Have a seat and I'll fill you in."

Jess sat down while the mercenaries took up places against the wall. "Did you sign the contract? I signed mine just before I came down."

"Not yet." He pulled out his tablet. "Let's get that out of the way so this is official. Done. It's off to my father. God help me."

He pointed to the screen. "That's BenCorp headquarters in the US. My mother's flagship company."

She leaned forward and examined it closely. "Is this a retaliatory raid? Do we have time for that?"

"We always have time for payback. In this case, though, it actually has some relevance." He touched the controls and brought up the image of a skinny man. "Meet Vincent Cruz. He used to work for my mother as the assistant IT manager of BenCorp."

"Used to?"

Harry nodded. "Right up until the moment she found out he was spying for my father. Now he's almost certainly a prisoner. He was supposedly in the process of stealing a trove of classified information that he never had a chance to turn over, including detailed plans for the facility where they built the reactor. We need them, so we need him."

Jess could only imagine the trouble the man was in. "He must've stood to gain a lot of money to cross people like Kathleen Bennett. She doesn't even know me and yet she's tried to kill me several times. How can I help?"

"Honestly, you can't," Cradock said. "This is a straightforward security operation. Having you along would be a major distraction. With the damage here at the port, it might be best if you worked on getting ready to launch the fuel and reactor once we get them."

She agreed with the basic sentiment. The last thing she wanted was another gunfight. "Do we have the fuel?"

"Not yet, but we will. The militants won't be able to hold onto the facility. I'm taking care of that operation while Harry gets the data on the Paris facility. Then he'll lead his people there to get the reactor."

"It'll need to go into orbit as soon as we get it back here," Harry said. "We don't want to give them a chance to strike back before we can boost it."

Jess considered the two assaults and their timing. "With one pad out of operation, we can only do launches on two. We could fuel one of the lifters and carry it over to pad three. When the reactor arrives, we'll load it and fire it off. I figure maybe an hour, if we're on the bounce. You'll need me in Paris."

Harry didn't look pleased at that news. "Why?"

"Because it's a nuclear reactor. You need a skilled engineer in case they've made it operational. Based on what I've seen of the design, we could move it locally even while it's running, but flying it in that configuration is out of the question.

"Worst case, we'd need to power it down, disassemble it, and fly it out a few days later. That would require a secluded area that no one could find for three days. Hopefully, it won't come to that."

"It better not," Harry said. "The French will lock the country down as soon as they know its missing. We need to get clear before they realize what we took."

"The laws of physics and thermodynamics are outside my control," she said. "I also need to be at the factory in Africa, once you have it locked down."

"That's not happening," Harry said bluntly. "The area is overrun by fanatics. The fuel extraction will almost certainly be under fire."

She shrugged. "Then you probably won't get the fuel."

Harry and Cradock glanced at one another. "And why is that?" the Rainforest security man ventured.

"Because it's locked down in an area where the militants aren't looking for it. Only a few people were ever on the access list. They died when the militants took over the factory. The computers are isolated, so it's too late to add anyone else. I'm on the list already."

"Crap," Harry said. "Give me a minute to think about this."

Her tablet chimed. She looked at the incoming message. "Your father just signed the contract. We're committed now."

"Yea." The young mercenary's tone indicated anything but excitement. "You can go, but you're not going in until they've suppressed the enemy. You land, open up the storage area, and get the hell back out of there. The security teams will extract the fuel. You got that? I want you in and gone before the militants can strike back."

"No argument from me. I'm tired of getting shot at."

"And Sandra takes a team in with you. If she says it's too hot, she'll abort your portion of the mission. You got that, Sandra?"

"Orders received," the sniper said.

Jess was both relieved and annoyed by the exchange. Somehow, she suspected her life would never go quite the way she expected from this point forward.

* * *

ONCE JESS and her team had left, Cradock gave Harry a searching look. "Are you sure that's the best idea? We need her for the reactor."

"Then make sure the facility is locked down. Hit it with everything you have, clean it out fast, and get clear."

Harry stood. "My people and I need to get moving. I need you to get us out of here without advertising it. My mother obviously has eyes on what we're doing. I don't want her to know we're coming."

"How about you make a big show of boarding some cargo planes bound for the Middle East?"

"And then what?"

The security guy grinned. "Then we play a shell game. Swap them out for other planes going to the US for high tech equipment. We just lost a fueling station. We need those parts."

Harry liked the plan. It played into the events his mother had caused.

"So long as no one knows, we can work with that. Military equipment is more difficult to get into the US, so we'll need some help on that end. France, too."

"I'll work something out," Cradock said. "The US is the more difficult of the two. You can buy heavy weapons on almost any street corner in Paris these days."

"Okay." Harry stood. "Let's get this in motion."

# 18

Clayton spent the next several hours getting things in order. Harry was heading to the US, his other teams were diverting to Paris, and Jessica Cook was on her way to the factory in Northern Africa.

Her mission would kick off first. The ruckus might give Harry an opening to get into the BenCorp facilities. Clayton had a few more people on his payroll that could provide some kind of cover, but the less they took for granted, the better.

Where were they keeping his spy and where was the pilfered data? Hopefully, the man had secreted it somewhere they could get to it. They wouldn't know that until they had him.

His ex-wife's chief of security was a real sweetheart. Rumors swirled around the man's penchant for torturing people. If he had Cruz, odds were good the man was in whatever dungeon the sadist had constructed.

And that just might be the right place to look first. Kathleen was a terrible person, but he doubted she let her security chief torture people in her office building. The man probably had a private facility for his personal amusements. One where the screaming wouldn't disturb the neighbors.

Clayton smiled. Time to see if he could locate it.

\* \* \*

Kathleen Bennett examined the book closely. The cover looked like leather, but it wasn't natural. It had a slickness that spoke to something artificial. The pages were definitely synthetic. The lettering didn't look like anything she'd ever seen before.

The tools were a combination of modern and other. They didn't look like any alloy she was familiar with, but that would come out in the lab report.

It wasn't much. She'd expected significantly more from a direct intervention. Dammit. They had a spaceship in the jungle. Surely, they had more than this to examine.

She glared at her son. "This can't be everything."

He shrugged. "It's all they had in their makeshift lab. Your man in the hotel said that the permanent facility wasn't ready yet."

"Why would Clayton call Harry's people in? Not for guarding the spaceship. They've buried the site in Rainforest security people. What are we missing?"

"Maybe the mystery is right under your nose, Mother. He's on a spaceport, paying Harry to protect a space engineer. Perhaps the secret is in orbit right over our heads."

She made a derisive noise. "The space hotel? Don't be any more of an idiot than you have to be. He's welcome to pour money down the drain on that project."

"Are you certain it's what you think it is? The old bastard is sharp enough with the rest of his business ventures. Could the space hotel be a cover for something else?"

She considered that. "A weapon's platform? There's no way. All of the leading nations are keeping an eye on nukes. The little power plant he has up there is barely strong enough to keep the lights on.

"Besides, I paid to have the construction monitored from a telescope in Hawaii. They watched it for months. There's no place to hide missiles."

"You asked the question," he said. "If my answer doesn't satisfy you, perhaps you should look elsewhere."

"Go figure out where your brother is," she snarled. "If he's going to get even, I want to know where to double the guard."

She dismissed her son from her mind as soon as he was out the door and picked up the phone. She'd rouse her staff and figure out if anything was going on in orbit, just in case.

*　*　*

GETTING into the US proved to be anticlimactic. The plane flying Harry and his people in landed in Texas and the inspector never even looked inside. It lifted off and was in Chicago two hours before the sun rose.

They'd spent the entire trip gathering intel and rejecting plans. The security chief, Donald Reynolds, lived in company housing to one side of the facility. His home was large and somewhat separated from the rest, but it was inside the perimeter.

The man himself had an unsavory reputation and a criminal record. His rap sheet looked like the guidebook to a serial killer. Animal torture and mutilation, assault of the elderly, and the police suspected he'd had a hand in the disappearance of a high school classmate.

Those run-ins with the law stopped once BenCorp hired him. Apparently he'd found someone willing to use his talents and provide a cover for his hobbies. He wished he could say that surprised him, but it didn't.

The team exited the plane once it landed at a smaller airport near Chicago and piled into an unmarked van. It took them to a disused warehouse about half a mile from the target. Two men who didn't give their names were waiting for them.

The larger one, a black man with closely trimmed hair and a diamond stud in one ear, gestured toward a number of boxes stacked neatly on the floor. "You'll find weapons and electronics there. The plane will be ready to take off the moment you get back to the airfield. Good hunting."

Harry helped his people unpack the boxes. The selection was a little sparse on the weapons front, but more than he'd expected to have available in the US. The police would freak if they had any idea of what was in the warehouse. He made sure everyone had burner cells just in case.

Jeremy Gonzales went over the electronics. "This is good stuff. Top of the line. If we can get past the perimeter fence, I can get into the house."

"And how do we slip past the live guards and electronic security?"

"With these." Jeremy held up some jumpsuits. "They minimize IR radiation. I can get us through the exterior fences. We time the patrols and slip in right after one passes. The monitors will see something, but probably mark it as an artifact of the team that just went by."

"And if they don't?"

The Hispanic man grinned. "Then we better not take our sweet time. The guards will circle back and check the area again. By then, we'd better be gone."

Harry liked the audacity of the plan. "That's entry. Next up, we need to breach the target residence. You can bet that he'll have top of the line intrusion detection. Once inside, we have to locate Cruz and get him out. Preferably without making a big scene. We still have to retrieve the data, if possible. Then we exit stage left, possibly with everyone on alert and hunting us."

Rex hefted a rifle with a grenade launcher. "That's where I come in. I can make a ruckus in a different area and draw their attention. If you need me, then they're already aware of you. It won't matter if I blow something up."

Harry examined the communications gear. It was similar to what he normally used. Encrypted burst transmissions. Anyone hearing it would think it was static. Unless, of course, they had the very best equipment and were on the lookout for strange signals.

"Okay. Gear up and we'll make entry in thirty minutes. We need to be in the target house by dawn. We'll plan on exterior guards and a very short window of opportunity. Keep communication to a minimum."

* * *

Jess slept through the flight to Northern Africa. She blearily stared out the window as the aircraft touched down. She was almost awake by the time they pulled up to a hangar. Two other large aircraft sat nearby.

Cradock's people exited first and many went inside the hangar. One of them gave a high sign.

Sandra started down the stairs. "That's the all clear. Let's get in there and get this show on the road."

People crowded the hangar, all of them dressed in desert camouflage and heavily armed. Cradock's people were gearing up from open crates.

The senior security man gestured for Jess to join him at a table. Several other young security types stood around. The map in front of them showed the manufacturing plant.

"Where's the fuel stored?" Sandra asked.

She pointed to one of the barracks. "Under here. The cover story was that the building had bad pipes. They kept it locked during the plant's operational run. The rear wall butts up against the plant where the finished product came out. Trusted personnel moved the fuel into the secure facility and shipped out water in its place."

One of the younger men spoke up. "Why the switch? Why not really ship the fuel back to Mexico when it was finished?"

Jess had asked that very question when she'd found out what they were doing. "The station everyone expected doesn't need this kind of fuel. If they'd shipped it back then, there was a significantly higher chance of someone seeing something they shouldn't.

"The cover story for this plant is that it was creating heavy water for research. Enough was on hand to verify the contents shipped to the test site in Italy. The first few barrels actually held heavy water. The rest came from a tap. No one ever checked past what they saw."

Sandra grunted. "Clever. Only the government here fell and this became a lawless state. Now a warlord runs things. He probably looked the facility over and decided that he didn't need something like that. Besides, a little common sense would tell someone that heavy water is pretty useless by itself.

"Which explains the militants taking over. Common sense isn't their strong suit. Do we have any idea how many hostiles we're talking about?"

"We sent a drone over the area an hour ago. IR shows a good number of people scattered throughout the buildings. Including the target."

"What's the plan?"

Sandra leaned over the map. "We have helicopters inbound to pick us up. The militants have sentries out, but our scouts will take them down as soon as we're on approach. We'll drop in right on top of them. A few rockets into each of the other buildings will take out the majority of the hostiles.

"Our main team clears the barracks while the rest of the buildings burn. After they call the all clear, Jess comes in to open the vault. We verify the fuel is present and she evacuates while we start loading the bins into cargo helicopters. Total mission time should be less than half an hour.

"And then we get her out of country before anyone starts getting nervous. We've got a private jet fueled and ready to go in another hangar. We'll will return straight here and head to France."

The rest of the mission planning went quickly. The helicopters arrived and the armed strike teams were on their way. The helicopter Jess rode in with Sandra's group headed in the same direction, but more slowly.

Her chopper was an older cargo model fitted with door guns. Jess had flown similar craft a number of times. Earning her pilot's license was a proud moment for her and flying was fun, as well as being useful in getting equipment to remote areas.

The helicopter crested a low hill and she saw the fuel facility burning. They landed without any fanfare and the mercenaries hustled her into the barracks.

The whole area smelled of gunpowder, fire, and death. A number of bodies lay scattered about. They all seemed to be men. Based on the number of weapons laying around, they'd fought back. Armed security people had a number of women and children crowded into a corner of the barracks. They were crying and screaming, of course.

Jess had limited sympathy for them. She'd seen plenty of video where men just like their husbands and fathers had done inhuman things. These people were here because they'd thought they could build a weapon. That made them fair game.

The bathroom was foul. She gagged from the stench, but forced herself to the showers. Someone had ripped the tile down in one area, probably so they could sell the pipes.

She pointed to a blank cinder block wall. "This has to come down. There's a lift behind it."

They pulled back and a few charges shattered the wall. The lift behind it was operational and took a group of them down to the lower level. A massive vault just outside the lift door yielded to her palm print.

Bins filled the storeroom. Jess opened one and examined the fuel pellets. They were sealed and looked good.

"All of these need to go. Without the factory, we won't be making any more fuel in the foreseeable future."

"Is that it?" Sandra asked. "Then let's get the hell out of here. The clock is ticking."

The trip back out of the building to the helicopter went much more quickly. As did the flight. Gunners kept a close lookout for other aircraft as they flew toward their ride out.

They landed outside another hangar. Sandra's team dismounted and formed up around her. They made it halfway to the large doors before a number of trucks burst onto the airfield and raced toward them at high speed.

# 19

Harry and his team watched the security patrols for half an hour before they slipped in. They didn't linger. Their caution proved wise when the enemy patrol they were using as cover circled back around. Someone had seen something.

The guards searched for a bit and then went on their way, likely convinced they'd been the victim of a false reading. Rex slipped away as soon as they were clear.

Harry's team made good time to the executive neighborhood where Reynolds lived. They stayed out of sight as much as possible, but they had to skulk across several roads along the way.

The house that they'd identified wasn't as extravagant as the rest in the area, but it had privacy in abundance. Set back into a forested area, it afforded the occupant a lot of isolation.

They scouted the trees, convinced they'd find both live guards and automated alarms. They found all that and more. It seemed the paranoid bastard was so worried about people slipping up on him that he'd planted antipersonnel mines.

If someone actually blew themselves up, Harry could only imagine how his mother would attempt to spin the situation to the police. Gas leak? Maybe. In any case, it would take a lot of money to hush the authorities up. He'd wager she had no idea what her security chief was doing to make himself feel safe at night.

It took them significantly longer to scout the way in than he'd planned for. The sun was up by the time they'd evaded the IR tripwires and motion sensors leading up to the grove where the house sat.

Two men patrolled the yard. He'd be taking a chance when running for the house, but Harry liked the second floor balcony as an entry point. It would hide them from casual view while they broke in and bypassed the alarm.

The man of the hour left as they were discussing how to best evade the yard patrol. They used the distraction of him walking out to an SUV to make it to the house. By the time Reynolds drove away, they were on the patio and scaling the exterior of the house.

The large balcony had a hot tub and a nice BBQ grill. It also had enough room for them to crouch down while the patrol walked below.

Jeremy worked the alarm slowly. This wasn't the time to take chances. Only once he was certain that he'd disabled the sensors did they pick the lock and open the door leading into the man's bedroom. There were no signs of a woman's presence. Or a second man, for that matter.

That made sense. If you were torturing people in your basement, you didn't want comments from the peanut gallery.

Jeremy pried the security keypad open carefully. "This is homegrown. It may take me a few minutes to hack into it."

"But you can, right?" Harry asked.

"Probably. Especially with access to the panel. Here we go. A computer port. That's helpful."

The slender man pulled a tablet out of his pack and ran a cable to the jack. "I'm running some codes to get past the login. Unless he's fiendishly clever, it shouldn't take more than sixty seconds."

It took three times that long.

"Got it. I've isolated the house from sending status changes. We can shut everything down and it'll look like it's still on to everyone else."

"Do it."

A few moments later, Jeremy unplugged his tablet. "We're good. I have it linked to my gear wirelessly. If I need to make any other changes, I can do it on the fly."

They spread out and searched the top floor. Harry spent a few minutes in the man's home office while the team cleared everything else. A set of monitors showed the yard and several spots in the forest. Reynolds had helpfully labeled the mine controls. The switch was in the off position.

Harry found a safe behind a painting, but he didn't have time to spend cracking it. He wouldn't count Jeremy out on that point, but that wasn't their mission. Unless, of course, the data they needed was inside it. Only the client could tell them if it was still in play.

He called Jeremy in to start copying files off the man's computer. Why waste the opportunity?

The security wizard ignored the ports and opened the machine. "It'll be faster if I plug right into the drive. While it's working, I'll plant a chip on the board. Even if he swaps out the drives later, I might be able to access it remotely."

"Come down when you've got it going. We can clear the first floor while you work. Then we head for the basement."

It turned out that the torture room wasn't in the basement. In the place where a normal house had a garage, Reynolds had a prison. The central portion was, as expected, a table with lots of straps and racks of tools one might see during the Middle Ages.

There were two narrow cells with excellent views of all the action. Both had occupants.

Harry didn't recognize the woman in the first cell. She wasn't in shape to tell him anything, either. Reynolds had strangled her.

Her sightless eyes stared at the ceiling from a face etched with terror and hopelessness. A zip tie bit into her neck and the torn skin around it told him that she'd been very much aware when Reynolds killed her. Based on the smell and bloating, she'd been gone for over a day.

Perhaps her body was a message to Vincent Cruz. He could hardly miss her from his cell.

The IT specialist looked to be in significantly better shape, though he wasn't unscathed. The bastard had pulled out some of the man's fingernails, broken a few fingers, and beaten him.

Cruz stared at them hopelessly. He probably thought they were there to take him out and do more nasty things to him.

"Mister Cruz," Harry said, "we're here to get you out. Where are the keys to the cell?"

The other man blinked. "What?"

"If you want to leave, now is the time to tell me how to open the door."

That got the man's attention. He stood abruptly. "Thank God. The keys are on a hook under the table."

It only took Harry a moment to find them and open the cell. "Time is limited. Did you manage to hide the data that Mister Rogers paid you to get?"

Cruz suddenly shrank back. "How do I know this isn't a trick? You just want me to tell you where it is and you'll kill me!"

That was something they'd planned for. "You have a code word from our employer. Infinity. We're for real."

The other man sagged. "Thank God," he repeated. "I didn't tell them where the drive is. I knew they'd kill me as soon as I did. It's safe."

"Is it on the BenCorp campus? We don't exactly have an all access pass."

"It's in the cafeteria computer. I hacked it and then 'fixed it' as a favor to the guy who runs the place. I didn't connect the drive, so you have to go after it. I didn't want them to be able to sniff it out over the network."

That would make things more difficult. The cafeteria wasn't in the headquarters building, but it was right next door to it. Somehow, they needed to sneak into the heart of enemy territory and retrieve it without raising the alarm.

His radio came to life. "Liberty Six, Hacker. We have a vehicle on the road. I think Reynolds is on his way back. He's in a hurry. We might have triggered something."

* * *

KATHLEEN BENNETT HAD FUMED about the situation all night. Her people had come in early and worked hard on double-checking what they knew about the space hotel project.

They didn't have any spies working on it, though she'd had a man there early on. He'd seen nothing out of the ordinary and she'd found another area of her ex-husband's business empire where he could do her more good. Or so she'd thought.

Someone had arranged for a telescope to give the orbiting project another look. She saw nothing that could hide a weapons platform. It had been another wild goose chase.

Just before dawn, she'd sent everyone home to clean up and to come back fresh after breaking their fast. They were already hard at work on what she considered plan B.

This time she wouldn't let Nathan anywhere near it. This project required a fine hand and lightning execution. Donald Reynolds would head up the operation. He wouldn't fail her.

She smiled. Her ex-husband would be screaming in frustration before the day was out. He only thought he knew what pain was. He'd learn his error the hard way.

* * *

SANDRA TOOK one look at the speeding vehicles and pushed Jess back toward the helicopter. "Move! It's an ambush!"

Someone in the back of one of the trucks opened fire on the helicopter with a large machine gun. Bullets smashed into the fuselage and the pilot slumped over. The burst also cut down the co-pilot, who'd gotten out to check something. One of the door gunners returned fire and the hostile truck rolled, throwing a man high into the air. He bounced when he hit the ground and lay still.

Jess reversed course and opened the copilot's door. "Get in!"

"You can fly?" Sandra shouted as she piled into the back with her team and the downed co-pilot.

"Well enough to get the hell out of here!"

As soon as the team was inside the aircraft, Jess opened the throttle and pulled up on the collective. The rotors bit into the air and the helicopter rose, far too slowly for her taste. As soon as she could, she pushed the cyclic forward and began building speed away from their attackers.

The sound of bullets slamming into the fuselage made her wince. She increased their speed even further and put a hangar between them and the trucks.

"Turn left," Sandra shouted. "I need to lay down some covering fire."

Jess pushed her left pedal in, skewing the helicopter somewhat to the left as it flew. As the co-pilot sat on the left side of the aircraft, she had a good view of Sandra shooting the living crap out of the trucks and the men trying to kill them.

One glance convinced her the pilot was dead. Yet another memory she'd be reliving at night.

The engine still sounded good and a check of the caution and warning lights showed no problems. The burst that had killed the pilot had taken out the radio, though. If that was all they'd lost, they were damned lucky.

The firing stopped as she crossed the airfield fence. She took her hands off the controls long enough to strap in. Sandra handed her one of the headsets from in back. The noise level immediately dropped.

"You're a woman of many talents," Sandra said over the intercom. "How did you learn to fly a helicopter?"

"Equipment needs to be moved all the time. It seemed like a handy skill to have in my toolbox. We're lucky this is an older cargo chopper. I might not have been able to figure out something more modern."

"You know Mister Scott could fly a helicopter, right? You're stuck with that call sign now, Scotty."

"That was Mister Sulu, but fine. There are worse things in life. The radio is toast. We need to warn the rest of the team away from the landing field. It'll be swarming with nasty people before they get there."

Sandra leaned in over Jess's shoulder and stared out the blood-spattered canopy. "Land on that hill over there and I'll make a call on my sat phone. We can get that poor bastard out of the other seat and into the back, too."

Jess brought the helicopter down on the hilltop, slowed the engine to idle, and looked around. There was dust behind them, but she judged they'd have some time before their pursuers could catch up. Besides, the hill wasn't on a road.

Two men opened the pilot's door and pulled the body out. She rejected the idea of changing seats. Not that it really mattered. Blood covered the entire cockpit. It looked like a scene from a Paul E. Cooley horror novel.

"Get me a rag to clean the canopy," she shouted into the back.

One of the mercenaries handed her a white cloth and a canteen. That would have to do.

It worked well enough. By the time Sandra hung up and climbed into the blood-soaked pilot's seat, Jess could see everything she needed to. "I called and warned them off. The new plan is to fly out to a container ship in the Med. He'll text me the GPS coordinates. Do we have enough fuel for that?"

"It depends on where in the Med we're talking about. Probably. I've never landed on a ship before."

Sandra grinned at her. "Considering the things you've done this week, I'll put my money on you pulling it off with panache. Let's get the hell out of here before someone else starts shooting at us."

# 20

Harry grabbed Cruz by the arm and hustled him back up the stairs. They'd have to deal with the on-site security and the men in the vehicle. With luck, they could evade them long enough to get off the grounds with the client.

"Speed it up, Jeremy. Take the drive. We're leaving now."

He made a snap decision and dug into his pack as he called Rex over the radio. "Scout, Liberty Six. Turns out, we'll be creating the distraction for you. Can you get into the main cafeteria and steal a drive from the computer? It'll be the one not connected to anything."

"Scout here. Copy. What kind of distraction will you be providing?"

"You'll know it. Liberty Six out."

Reynold's vehicle slid to a halt outside, throwing gravel everywhere. He and the driver leapt out with their guns at the ready.

Yep, they must've triggered some kind of silent alarm. Time for the diversion.

Harry reached over to the minefield controls and switched them on. "Fire in the hole." He selected them all and pressed the red button.

Reynolds had a lot more mines out there than Harry had expected. The noise almost rivaled the Mayan pyramid coming down.

It turned out there was a mine under the area where the SUV had stopped, too. It tossed the vehicle into the air when the fuel tank detonated. All the windows on that side of the house shattered and the house alarm went off. Harry felt like he was in an action movie.

As soon as things finished crashing to the ground, his people headed for the balcony. The driver opened fire and they cut him down. Reynolds wasn't anywhere in sight. Maybe he was under the burning SUV. Or maybe he was just faster than his man at finding cover.

A crash downstairs told him the guards had broken in. Time to exit stage left. He grabbed a charge and set the timer for one minute. He dropped it onto the floor inside the bedroom and made tracks.

Even with an injured client, they were on the ground in seconds. They almost made it to the trees before someone fired on them from the balcony. Harry returned the favor and the man went down. He saw someone else in the room right before the explosive charge went off and blew that corner of the house to splinters.

To say that explosions and gunfire got the BenCorp security people excited was something of an understatement. His team made it through the woods and carjacked a woman in a minivan. He left her tied up on the side of the road. He felt bad about that, but they needed her vehicle.

He stripped down to his black tee shirt. Once everyone had hunched down out of sight, he drove sedately away from the chaos. He even waved at several security cars as they flew past.

Once he reached the fence line, Harry gunned the minivan across the field and rammed the barrier. It was designed to slow people from getting in, not escaping, so they bounced over it. Security would know where they were now, but he couldn't do anything about that.

It took only a couple of minutes to get back to the warehouse. The number of sirens he heard in the distance told him that they'd caused quite the scene. His mother wouldn't like having to explain exactly what had happened back there.

Harry shooed the team toward the van that had brought them from the airport. "Back into civilian clothing. Leave anything incriminating in the minivan. Take Cruz and get going. I'll meet you at the plane when I get Rex."

They didn't want to leave him, but a cordon would go around the general area before too long. They needed to get clear. A couple of guys had a lot better chance of escaping unnoticed than a full combat team. Harry kept a pistol for defense and the smallest explosive charge he had.

The cases and equipment were gone. The unnamed men had removed anything his people hadn't used. The only sign they'd been there was the stolen minivan. It almost certainly had some of their DNA inside. The fastest and easiest solution was to burn it.

It only took a moment to put the explosive charge on the gas tank and set it for twenty minutes. He grabbed the poor woman's belongings and put them in a reusable shopping bag he found in the back. She was doing her part to save the environment. Good for her.

He put his camo with the others' discarded clothing and took a snapshot of the license plate. He'd do what he could to make up for the woman's rough treatment later. The police cars that went shooting by paid him no attention as he walked away from the warehouse.

Once he was clear, he called Rex on his cell. "Scout, Liberty Six. Status."

"Hey, man. I'm a little busy right now. Mind if I call you back in five?"

"Give me a direction to head."

"Try north."

"Copy."

He'd need another vehicle to get them clear in a hurry. Harry didn't feel like carjacking someone else, though. This was Chicago. They might shoot first.

That's when he spotted the motorcycle behind the drycleaners. A casual touch showed it hadn't been there long. Hotwiring it was a quick proposition. Another expense for his father to pay when this was all over. He put the carjacked woman's personal belongings into the saddlebags

Harry put one of the helmets on, started the bike, and took off casually. It probably wouldn't be long before the owner noticed it was gone, so Rex needed to hurry the hell up. With all the police in the area, they'd connect a stolen vehicle to the explosions fast.

A few minutes later, he parked out of sight and called Rex again. His scout answered on the first ring.

"There you are. I got you a hoagie. Where are we meeting?"

"Can you talk?"

"Not really."

"I'm on a motorcycle behind an office building." He gave Rex the address. "I can be out front when you get here if you give me an ETA."

Rex passed the address on to someone else. "We're just going out the gate. Man, there are cops and firetrucks everywhere. I hope it wasn't terrorism. I hate terrorists. I'll be there in a couple of minutes. Later."

Harry waited three minutes and drove around front. Rex was just getting out of a car. A pretty girl said something to him before driving off with a smile. He'd ditched his camo for executive wear. Where the hell had he found a suit?

His scout waved at the woman and walked over to him. He had a white bag in his hand. "The drive's in the bag with the hoagie. Man, you caused a shit storm."

"It's a gift. Give me the drive and you can have the sandwich."

"Sounds like a fair trade. I hope we come back this way someday. My ride seemed nice. Invited me out for coffee. She's single."

Harry tucked the drive into the saddlebags. "How do you do that?"

"It's my super power. Did you get Cruz out?"

"Sure did. Let's scram before the owner of the motorcycle gets everyone in an uproar. Put your helmet on so that the traffic cameras don't get our faces."

He pulled into traffic and headed away from the BenCorp headquarters. The police will probably be very interested in the torture chamber and murdered woman. His mother would be furious.

It was turning out to be a good day.

* * *

JESS flew low to stay off any curious radars and they reached the cargo ship just as the sun was beginning to set. Someone had cleared the bow, giving them enough space to land. A number of choppers from the raid circled and waited their turn. One was unloading bins as she joined the rest flying around the ship.

One of the other helicopters pulled up beside her and the pilot got her attention. He pointed at her and held up his index finger. She took that to mean she was next up for landing.

As soon as the cargo chopper took off, she cautiously approached the deck. A man waved two glow sticks at her. He had one in each hand and used them to guide her right down to the landing spot. When he crossed them in front of his legs, she heaved a sigh of relief, let the helicopter settle, and slowed the engine to idle.

A man in a flight suit and helmet helped her out and took her spot. He lifted off as soon as everyone was clear.

Sandra pulled her along as they followed a crewman to the tall control deck. One of Cradock's men was standing there waiting for them.

"The warlord took out the jet's crew and the guards we left behind," he said grimly. "I'll make him a special project in the very near future. I'm glad you managed to get clear and I'm sorry about your flight crew. It was damned lucky you could fly."

She felt a little hollow at his words. "It's been a rough few days. What's the plan now?"

"The ship docks in Italy early tomorrow morning. We'll get the fuel moved to a cargo plane and on its way by dawn. You'll meet Harry in Paris tomorrow."

"My passport won't have a valid entry stamp. Won't someone freak out?"

The security man shook his head. "I'll get you stamped when we dock. The same woman who'll get our cargo through will make sure you don't have any issues." He looked at his watch. "You should clean up and get some sleep. Things are going to be happening fast from now on."

"They've been coming fast and furious for a while," she muttered. "A shower sounds good, though."

"The captain is loaning you his quarters. If you'll follow this young man, he'll get you there."

A boy with curly black hair and bright eyes led them through a confusing maze of corridors and ladders. He bowed a little and opened the metal door for her.

Sandra went in and cleared the room. It was small, but neat. The bathroom was actually clean.

"Give me your clothes and I'll see if I can get you something that fits," Sandra said.

Jess stripped down to her underwear and discovered that her phone had a couple of missed calls and one voicemail.

Two decades ago, before cell service and wireless became ubiquitous, she wouldn't have reception on a freighter at sea. Now everything was a hotspot. Progress was wonderful, sometimes.

She played the message. It was from Rachel Powell.

"Miss Cook, I just wanted to let you know that we've identified the language. It's the lettering used in the Voynich Manuscript. No one has managed to translate it. Call me for details as soon as you get this." She left a number.

"I better call her and find out what this means." She passed her bloody clothes on to Sandra.

"Lock the hatch behind me and don't open it for anyone else. Two of our men are in the corridor. And remember, nothing classified over an unsecured line. The NSA monitors everything." The mercenary let herself out.

Jess locked the hatch and made the call.

"Doctor Powell. Jess Cook. I just got your message." She did a little math in her head and realized it must be night in Mexico. "I'm sorry for calling so late."

The other woman's voice held no hint of sleep. "I'm still up writing a report on the book for Mister Rogers. Have you ever heard of the Voynich Manuscript?"

"No. Please give me a brief rundown. And remember we're on a commercial line."

"I'll keep that in mind. The Voynich Manuscript is a hand-written codex from sometime between 1404 and 1438. They verified that time frame by carbon dating the vellum. They named the folio after Wilfrid Voynich, a Polish book dealer who bought it in 1912.

"Some of the pages are missing, but around 240 are still in the same collection. The manuscript is at Yale University."

Jess considered that. The book they'd found was from centuries earlier and it wasn't written on vellum. "You said that no one has been able to crack the meaning of the manuscript?"

"That's correct. Scholars have proposed a number of origin theories. Everything from aliens to it being a complex code. Even people at the NSA have made runs at it. The use of the letters is internally consistent, but the meaning has eluded everyone. Most of the pages have illustrations of unknown plants and medieval figures."

The engineer snorted. "Well, if the NSA can't crack it, I doubt we will either. Unless we can find a Rosetta Stone."

"To be fair, the NSA looked at it in the 1950's," Powell said. "A supercomputer might be able to crack the meaning."

"You said that there were only 240 pages left. Does that mean that there were more originally?"

"That's correct. Someone removed a number of pages and probably sold them. They're almost certainly in the hands of private collectors at this point. There's a subculture of wealthy people that want to own objects of historical and artistic significance without any intention of ever allowing them to see the light of day." Her tone indicated strong disapproval.

"Is there any chance that you can find out who the owners of these missing pages might be?"

"I'll make some calls, but I don't think I'll have any luck. These people are quite secretive."

"Do the best you can. Let me know if you get lucky."

Jess hung up and padded into the bathroom. A hot shower might make her feel clean again.

## 21

K athleen Bennett was ready to kill someone. Specifically, her ex-husband. She'd have added her security chief to the list if he hadn't died in the explosion that wrecked his house. The police and FBI were overrunning her headquarters asking the kind of questions no sane human being wanted to answer.

She might've been able to cover this up as some kind of gas explosion if Donald hadn't installed a minefield. Really? That was insane.

They'd already put out the fire and found several bodies, including one in a cell. For a few minutes, she'd deluded herself into believing the body might be that of the traitor, but her man in the police department told her it was a woman.

No matter how this played out, she'd look like an idiot or worse. Why, no Mister Federal Agent, I have no idea how my head of security smuggled all those land mines onto my facility. He was torturing and murdering people, you say? Oh, dear.

With the way this was going, they'd find a bunch of unmarked graves in the woods.

She sighed. Of course they would. Where else would that homicidal idiot hide the people he killed for sport? Could things get any worse?

As if on cue, Nathan came in and closed the door. "Well, things are certainly exciting this morning. Are you ready to let me kill Harry now?"

"We don't know it was your brother."

"Do you think it was the Tooth Fairy? It was Harry. He and father conspired to do this to you. Are you going to bend over and take it?"

The urge to reach into her desk for the pistol she kept handy was strong. "Don't you dare speak to me like that, boy. I can blame your death on Donald."

"Please. If you want payback, I'm the person to make that happen. Say the word and I'll go make them suffer."

It wasn't as though she had much choice now. With Donald gone, Nathan was her best chance of pulling off her planned revenge. God help her.

"If you fail me, I'll put a price on your head so big that you'll never get a moment's peace. This has to go exactly according to plan. The timing is critical. Is that clear enough for you?"

"I'm not a moron," he sneered. "Of course I'll succeed. Other than the girl, I've never failed you."

Kathleen brought a map up on her screen and explained what she wanted done.

* * *

JESS HAD JUST FINISHED SHOWERING when she got another call. The number wasn't familiar to her.

"Hello?"

"Jess, this is Harry. Everything came out fine. We're in the air."

A bit of tension that she hadn't been consciously aware of drained away. "Thank God. Did you rescue the man?"

"We did. My father's people have the drive. They'll assess its contents while we're in the air. How'd your thing go?" He was being circumspect because of the NSA. She really had to struggle to keep that in mind.

"It was a little more exciting than I'd imagined it would be, but we got it. I have more information about the book, too." She explained the Voynich Manuscript to him.

"That's pretty odd. The Europeans didn't know about the Mayans until almost a hundred years later."

She grabbed her tablet. "I'm sending you some images. Check out the plants in the original manuscript."

After a minute he spoke. "I've seen something like this before. On the mission before we met. There were pages like this in the office."

"Are you sure? These things look like a lot of other manuscripts of the time, except for the unknown language and unrecognizable plants."

"I'm almost certain. I didn't look closely enough to recognize the lettering, but the style of illustrations is spot on. I didn't recognize the plants, but I'm not a botanist."

"How many pages were there?" she asked.

"I had other things on my mind. A dozen? Maybe twice that."

She grinned, even though he couldn't see her. "We need to get them. Or at least pictures of them."

"No way. That bastard's security is going to be super tight."

"He doesn't have to know I'm connected with that."

"So, you just waltz in and say 'hi, I heard through the grapevine that you had these secret manuscript pages' and he lets you in for a peek? I think not. Besides, when would you do this? The schedule is tight from here on."

"We had a change in plans, too. We're on a ship about to dock in Italy. I can do this and still beat you to France."

She started pacing. "Harry, you don't understand how important this might be. Even the NSA couldn't crack the damned thing. We need those pages. It won't take your mother long to figure out the connection. Do you want to take the chance she might get these pages before we do?"

He sighed. "Sandra has to sign off on your plan. Please be careful. If it's too dangerous, walk away."

"Don't worry about a thing. I won't take any unnecessary chances."

* * *

HARRY CALLED Cradock on an encrypted line. He was already in Paris. He really needed to get one to Jess. The security man sounded just as displeased at Jess's plan as Harry was. "Dammit. Someone almost shot her at the airport. Does the woman have a death wish?"

"Shot? What happened? Tell me everything."

He listened to how the warlord had almost killed everyone on Jess's helicopter, and how she'd managed to escape. And now she wanted to go play James Bond. It made his teeth ache.

Maybe he needed to focus on the things he could control. "When does the fuel leave for Mexico?"

"In about six hours, once we dock and transship it to a cargo plane. Look, it will take a while before we have the data to plan for stealing the reactor. Get some sleep. Call me once you wake up. We should be able to make final plans by then."

"Get Jess an encrypted phone and try to get some sleep," Harry said. "Text me the number."

Harry hung up, but getting to sleep was hard. He kept imagining all the things that could go wrong with Jess's mission. And he couldn't do a thing about it.

Well, that wasn't quite true. He dialed his father's number. Maybe the old bastard could talk some sense into the crazy engineer before she got herself killed.

* * *

JESS DRESSED while Sandra stared at her as though she were crazy. "You want to do what?"

"Break back into the house you rescued the little girl from earlier this week."

"That's what I thought you said. And Harry signed off on this?"

"Reluctantly. This is important. He'll get the assault on the reactor plant set up while we make this happen."

The mercenary shook her head. "We observed the target for more than a week last time. We knew how the guards behaved and what the routine was. This time, we'd be going in blind after we stirred them up like a hornet's nest. It's crazy."

Jess didn't disagree. Yet, what choice did they have? If they passed up the opportunity, they might be up in space for months before they could try again. The forces of darkness could find out about the manuscript pages and take them.

"Don't you do this kind of thing under urgent circumstances?"

"Urgent is a child in danger of harm," Sandra said. "Getting your hands on some papers isn't in the same league."

The mercenary sighed. "You're talking about a daytime incursion. That means the help will be awake and alert. The police, too. We need to get into the office and get the papers, or at least take a close look at them. Going in shooting isn't the right answer."

"Who's the man in question?" Jess asked. "What do we know about him?"

"Alessio Romano. He's a bigshot in local politics. A judge. Word is that he's also connected to the mob."

"Is his art on the shady side?"

The mercenary shrugged. "I have no idea. That wasn't part of the mission parameters."

The phone Sandra was holding rang. She held it out to Jess. "This is your new encrypted phone. Only use it going from now on."

Jess took it and answered the call.

"Hello?"

"Jess," Clayton said. "I just got off the phone with Harry. He tells me you're on your way to see a man in Italy about some illicit art."

"That's true, though I'm kind of hoping he doesn't find out we were ever there."

"I'm somewhat familiar with the gentleman in question. He and I have had some dealings in the past. I may be able to make an introduction between the two of you, if you're willing to employ a little subterfuge."

She knew Sandra wouldn't like that, but she was willing to take a few chances. "What do you have in mind?"

"I have a security firm in Rome. Romano has hired them to upgrade his systems. I can get the man in charge to provide you a cover while you examine the building. You'd need to interface with someone knowledgeable about security, but with the right equipment, that shouldn't be a problem."

Jess smiled. "That sounds relatively straightforward. Thank you."

"Your target is a man used to dealing with the seamier side of society," he warned. "He's already been stung and he's looking to make someone pay. If he thinks you're playing him, he'll turn on you. Trust me when I say that would be a terrible outcome."

Jess didn't want that. She really didn't want it. "A security consultant can get into every room in the house. If I can transmit the images out to someone else, they can tell me what I need to know through an earbud."

"All very true, but if he gets wise, you'll be in very dire straits."

"How long would it take to get everything we need into place?"

"I can have a man in the area by the time you get there. He'll have everything you need. The company needs to confirm that Romano will see you, but I expect he's quite eager to close the holes in his security as soon as possible. Is your guard going to buy off on this plan?"

Jess looked at Sandra. "I can make that happen."

\* \* \*

CLAYTON HUNG UP. Jess's plan worried him. Project Liberty absolutely needed her to be hale and whole. Should he really enable her like this? Perhaps Harry had been right to ask him to stop her. Were these pages really as important as she thought?

He sighed. Probably. He'd make the calls. He finished just before his assistant buzzed.

"Pardon the interruption, but you have a call from the security man in Guatemala on the encrypted line. It sounded quite urgent."

"Put him through."

The light for the other line lit up and he pressed it. "Rogers."

The first sound he heard was a long burst of automatic gunfire from very close to the receiver. "Mister Rogers, we're under heavy attack! They swarmed in from nowhere and they're pushing us back. We can't hold onto the site with the underground chamber."

"Get to safety," Clayton said. "I'll call the federal police and get you support."

"I'd hurry if I were you." Another burst of gunfire sounded and then an explosion. The line went dead.

He hoped the caller hadn't gone dead, too. He looked up a number and called his man in the Guatemalan government.

Clayton hadn't expected something this bold. It had to be Nathan. He couldn't imagine how the little shit expected to steal a buried spaceship before reinforcements arrived, but the boy obviously believed he could do it. If he got away with the theft, it changed the game.

# 22

Harry woke halfway through the flight to Paris to the news that Nathan was trying to steal the spaceship. The plan was audacious. A true international incident. His brother might have to fight it out with the Guatemalan military or police.

Well, there wasn't anything he could do about it. At least his father hadn't told Jess. He'd been concerned that the events would throw her off her con. That was about the first thing he completely agreed with his father on.

They'd begun delving into the data drive and Harry now had detailed plans for the facility in Paris. He spent the next few hours going over them with his team on the plane. Cradock linked in via secure com.

The place was just as tough as Harry had expected. The sewers were indeed a trap for the unwary. The general plan they finally agreed on felt too much like the raid on his mother's headquarters for his comfort. A lot of it came down to taking bold risks.

The major difference in this case being that they'd have a lot more hardware. Including planes to get them on site very quickly. Those came courtesy of his father. He had a group of cutting edge military transports in France for an airshow.

The stealth on them was so good that they were making a few extra test runs for the French military over the next few days. The potential buyers wanted to see the planes break contact, which was perfect for Harry's strike team.

If the planes carrying his people could slip away from the test area, they could deliver Harry onto his mother's facility with devastating surprise before going back to play with the French Air Force.

One bit of good news was that they'd packed the reactor. The test wasn't going to be in Paris after all. His mother's plan was to ship it out to the US before the supposed demonstration. Apparently, the security team probing the sewers had spooked them.

At least that meant they didn't need to have Jess underfoot. They could grab the reactor while she was taking care of business in Italy. Then she could fly to Mexico on her own. They'd meet there and she could oversee the loading of the reactor into the lifter.

Finally, something was going their way.

* * *

JESS SLEPT until the ship docked. The time zone change had her body confused, but she'd been in that situation before. Sleep cured most of the trouble, given enough time.

Cradock's man hurried them past a woman who stamped their passports. Jess suspected that their entry wouldn't appear anywhere official. Which, considering the things they planned to do, was probably for the best.

The team took vans and set off before dawn. They met the man who'd coordinate with her on security matters for breakfast about an hour away from Romano's villa.

Paolo Sorrentino was an unprepossessing guy with classic Italian features. He laid some gear on the table as he sipped his cappuccino. "They tell me these are state of the art spying devices. Even a close search shouldn't turn them up. Unless of course, someone looks inside your ear." His English was excellent, with just a hint of his native Italian.

Jess picked up the device. It looked like a little torpedo with some silicone around the back. "It doesn't have anything to grab onto. How do I get it out when we're done?"

"A small hook will catch the flesh toned exterior. Without a grip, it's much harder to see. It has a small microphone that allows you to hear as well as you normally would. It's quite clever."

Jess picked up the glasses next. Classy wire frames. She'd expected ugly plastic. A quick check showed the lenses had no prescription. A good thing, since her vision was perfect. She wondered what they'd have done if she'd needed glasses of her own. Probably contacts.

There wasn't any indication of a camera, no matter where she looked.

"Okay, I give up. Where is the lens?"

"It's inside one of the nose pads."

She examined them more closely. "Now I see it. That's a good design. And there's no chance that he'll detect it sending a signal?"

Paolo grinned boyishly. "I'll load an app onto your mobile phone and it will communicate over an encrypted wireless frequency. Even though you don't know it, your phone is always pinging the towers. That will disguise the signal. The phone will record video, even if you go into an area of the building where the coverage is spotty. When you come back out, it will sync up with the base unit."

"That sounds a little worrying. What if he asks me something I don't know while we have no connection?"

"I'll be with you. The plan is for us to examine everything as a team. I'm the primary security specialist and you are my beautiful American assistant. The camera will keep your security team apprised of your personal situation at all times."

That was reassuring. Jess wouldn't have to bluff her way through a job she knew very little about. The sniper could feed her some thoughts so she didn't sound like an idiot, if need be.

Sandra pocketed the gear as the waitress came over to deliver their food. The mercenary waited until they were alone again to speak.

"The estate is big. He has a number of vulnerable approaches to the house itself. He was lax in his personal security. He didn't even turn the alarm system on. Honestly, you'd be shocked how many people shoot themselves in the foot by ignoring the most basic precautions."

Paolo dug into his food with gusto. "This is excellent. I was up early and fast food is a national tragedy."

Jess couldn't argue with that.

"When is he expecting us?"

He checked his watch. "I told him we'd be there in about ninety minutes. We should finish up and be on our way."

She glanced at Sandra. "Where will you be?"

"There's an unoccupied house nearby. We'll set up inside the woods there. All it'll take to get to you is hopping over a stone wall and running through some trees. I figure three minutes, tops. If I get worried, I'll get the team moving early."

They finished breakfast and got on the road. Just outside the town where Romano lived, she moved to Paolo's car. They'd go in separately, just in case someone was watching traffic.

The estate looked imposing. The tall wall and imposing iron gate would've kept her out. The armed men just inside were an added incentive to behave.

Paolo rolled down his window and said something in Italian to one of the men. A brief exchange resulted in the gate opening. It shut with ominous finality behind them as they drove into the lion's den.

They were committed now.

\* \* \*

HARRY'S PLANE landed on schedule and Cradock picked them up. They drove to a different part of the airfield and directly into a large hangar holding four sleek planes.

They didn't look like transports. They looked like something out of a movie, all aggressive lines and angles. That was probably to help defeat the radar. Based on the engine configuration, Harry thought they were probably capable of vertical take offs and landings.

He didn't know much about planes, but they looked badass.

"The pilots are in on the plan," Cradock said, "but not the ground crew. We'll have a meeting with everyone to plan things, but keep mum on the details even out here. You never know who's a spy."

Harry couldn't agree more. French prisons were better than many others he'd risked over the years, but he'd rather avoid the experience.

He walked under one of the wings. "Is it VTOL? How good is the stealth? How many people can each hold? And realistically, what are the chances you can really evade the French radar?"

Cradock smiled. "These are fully VTOL capable and can switch modes quickly in the air. Each one can hold two of your teams. As for the stealth, it's good.

"We have two modes. One is passive, which is what the French are buying. One is active, which we're keeping to ourselves. We'll give them a taste of what these planes can really do when these babies drop off their screens."

Harry shook his head. "I'm surprised the US is letting you sell these things to anyone other than them."

"The American government doesn't know about the active mode. With the way they've gutted the military, they can't afford them anyway. Rainforest is a true international company, incorporated through a country that doesn't care who we sell to, so long as they get their taxes. We don't need the US government's permission to do squat."

That bothered Harry, but it wasn't his fight. The American government had done this to themselves. The incredible polarization in politics meant only the most extreme politicians got into office. Nationally, the liberals had occupied the White House for the last three decades. The Senate bounced back and forth, depending on which party had more seats up for grabs, and the penny-pinching, socially stunted conservatives had a lock on the House.

That meant nothing of import happened to address the country's woes. The debt was out of control, inflation was through the roof, and any country that felt froggy could push the formerly great nation around like a schoolyard bully. Only international terrorism was able to bridge the gap, and even it never got the attention it deserved.

France was teetering on the edge of collapse. Selling them these planes wouldn't help. They needed to take their country back from the people willing to burn it down. He doubted they had the will to save themselves.

Well, that wasn't his problem. Once the country fell, these planes wouldn't be a worry anymore. The fanatics couldn't fly them.

"Have all my teams arrived?"

Cradock nodded. "They're scattered around the area, but they're here. We'll pull them in once you're ready to lay out the grand plan. We can get eight teams into the target building with four teams to cover your withdrawal. The reactor is supposedly loaded into a container.

"Word is that it's scheduled to leave early tomorrow morning. We'll probably be able to get you there right after dark tonight. That means security will be lighter than normal. They want more people on duty for the move tomorrow, so some people have the day off to rest up."

That worked. Harry gave the planes one last appreciative look. Maybe he could buy one for his company. It would sure make some jobs easier.

"Call in the teams. It's time to get this rolling."

**\* \* \***

NATHAN WATCHED the excavation with satisfaction. The earthmovers had cleared the area around the underground chamber with astonishing speed. The goal was to open the room below to the air without dropping debris on the spacecraft.

That had sounded impossible to him until an expert explained how it worked. Teams would go in through the side tunnel he'd seen the woman use. They'd fire stabilizers into the roof. A lot of them. The choppers would act in unison to lift the roof off. Then they'd lift the spaceship up on the slings the team was putting into place.

"We're ready to lift the roof, sir," the excavation boss said.

A glance at his watch confirmed that they were ahead of schedule. "Excellent. Proceed."

The local government had failed miserably at sending help to his father's guards. Most of them were dead. His men were pursuing the rest through the jungle. His mother had sown massive confusion in the Guatemalan government. No one would stop him.

Nathan held his breath as the choppers lifted the roof. The stonework was amazing. It broke into a billion pieces when they dropped it off to the side.

The spaceship looked a little worse for wear in the bright sunlight, but that hardly mattered. The limitless wealth it promised was all he cared about. That and sticking it to his father and brother.

It took them another few minutes to hitch the slings. They'd made an educated guess at the weight. Two choppers should be able to lift it.

In fact, it came up so easily that he made the decision to try one helicopter alone. That would greatly simplify the move.

It worked.

The spaceship headed out on one last journey. Several armed helicopters accompanied it on its way toward international waters and the ship that would carry it back to the US. He had fighter jets that would screen any inquisitive military presence.

He'd disguised them with Honduran markings. He could only imagine what kind of trouble that would cause. He might even be able to get some business out of the ensuing troubles.

Once it was away, he sent his people in. "Pick up every single bit of that ship. Leave nothing. Then plant the explosives. Father can waste his time digging it up to find nothing."

## 23

J ess tamped her jitters down as Paolo drove the car slowly up the drive. There were a lot of guards on the grounds. A man with some kind of rifle was just visible on the roof.

"Yeah, I sure hope Sandra doesn't have to come in after us," she said to the Italian. "I'm not sure she could manage it."

"You know I can hear you, right?" Sandra's voice said in her earbud.

Jess laughed a little. "I forgot. Are you seeing all this?"

"I sure am. Don't worry. We can get you out if push comes to shove."

The man himself met them at the front door. She could tell it was Romano because his morbidly obese form matched the description Harry had given her. He was almost a cartoon of a human being. To say that he looked ludicrous in a tailored suit was an understatement.

The initial conversation was in Italian, but Paolo switched to English after a moment. "And this is my assistant, Jessica. She's fresh from our American branch and doesn't speak Italian."

The large mobster held out a meaty hand for her. It was sickeningly damp. She resisted the urge to wipe her hand on her pants when she reclaimed it.

"Welcome to Italy, Jessica," Romano said in a deep, rumbly voice. "If the two of you come inside, I will explain the situation. One of my assistants will accompany you on a tour of the building, of course."

Obviously. He wouldn't be making any long trips along the grounds. Stairs must be a challenge.

And, as it turned out, not a worry. He had an elevator.

A man in coveralls was painting the wall beside the staircase. Whoever had done the repair work hadn't done such a terrific job. Jess could still see a few dimples. Bullet holes, she imagined. That would be an ugly reminder to the mobster of past failures.

Romano pulled a key from his vest and unlocked one of the doors near the end of the hall. It opened into an office. Her heart leapt in her chest. They might be able to get what they needed right up front. That would be a wonderful break.

Jess examined the Egyptian figurines in one of the cases as Romano sat behind his large desk. "This is a wonderful collection. Forgive me for asking, but did someone try to steal them?"

"No," Romano said with a snarl. "The bastards kidnapped my daughter and took her to America. My ex-wife, an unfit woman with the morals of an alley cat, paid someone to take her. I want this house to be a vault before I bring her back."

Paolo nodded. "Of course. We'll do everything in our power to make certain that she's safe here. Do you know how they obtained entrance to your property?"

Jess walked from case to case, slowly moving toward the one she most wanted to see.

"They came over a wall in the dead of night. They used darts to knock out my guards and myself. I shot several of them, but they overwhelmed me. The man outside is fixing the bullet holes I made. The guards who failed were severely punished."

"Bullshit," Sandra said in her ear. "Harry shot him in the ass before he even got his pistol out of the nightstand. One of the guards shot the wall when we darted him."

The pieces Jess was seeing were good. Some of the paintings looked like authentic Renaissance masters. She wondered if Romano had stolen them. Or paid someone who had. She couldn't see him climbing through a window in the dead of night.

Paolo made sympathetic noises. "Was the home alarm activated before the intrusion?"

"No. The idiots never turned it on. The intruders made their way in through the patio. The interior guards were no match for them, either. Pathetic. You must look at every door and window, scan every wall. I want no weakness left when you finish. Money is no object, but don't think to cheat me. I will know."

Jess stepped in front of the low case that held the pages. They were definitely from the Voynich Manuscript. The lettering was unmistakable.

She listened to Romano drone on with half an ear as she scanned them one by one, looking for any sign that might help them decode the book.

Her heart sang when she found something on the next to last page. It was only a few lines at the bottom, but there was the strange alien script set beside something in what looked like Italian. Or perhaps an older variant of what became Italian. She wasn't a linguistics expert.

Maddeningly, the page after it had just a few lines at the top. What she needed to see was on the back of the pages and they were under locked glass.

Somehow, she had to get this case open.

\* \* \*

IT TOOK a few hours to gather the team in another hangar. Harry led the briefing, showing them where they'd be landing, where in the building they'd be going, and running through the timeline for the assault.

The building schematics were a tremendous help. He knew which floor had the loading dock, where his mother stationed her security teams, and which paths might make for the fastest ingress.

The reactor was supposedly in a container, which meant the only means of transportation was a big rig. He had several people that could drive one, so they were ready.

Only a few roads allowed commercial traffic of that size. A cargo container was tall. If he picked the wrong street, a bridge might give them an unpleasant surprise. And, only the very largest cargo planes could even carry the damned thing. Those factors limited his options for extraction.

"Cradock, what are we doing for transport to Mexico? That'll dictate where we have to take this thing."

The large man grinned. "You'll like this. We're going to steal your mother's transport plane, too. It's on the ground at Charles De Gaul. Once you guys are committed, my team will liberate the plane. We'll fly it to the regional airport nearest the facility and be waiting for you. With all the hullabaloo, we'll be halfway across the ocean before they notice the plane is gone."

Harry liked it. "How do we keep them from using traffic cameras to determine our path? Once we're moving, we'll stick out like a sore thumb."

"I've arranged to have half a dozen legitimate cargo containers being moved around the area about the time you leave. All through local businesses that won't be traced back to us. You'll get lost in the rush."

"Good enough." Harry checked his watch. "Let's go talk to the pilots. Please get everyone that isn't cleared out of the other hangar."

"On it."

Harry and his team leaders took a van with dark windows to the first hangar when they got the all clear. Once the main doors to the hangar closed, he stepped out.

Four men in flight suits waited beside the planes. "The co-pilots are in the aircraft getting them ready," Cradock said. "Everyone has already been briefed on the plan."

One of the pilots, a tall man with a buzz cut, stuck out his hand. "Mister Rogers, I'm John McCarthy, formerly a Lieutenant Colonel in the US Marines. Call me Black Jack. I'm the flight leader. I need to say I'm damned impressed with your bravery. Damned impressed."

Harry smiled and gave him a firm handshake. "Then I've probably underestimated how scary this is going to be. Thanks for your service, sir."

"Hell, I've heard about some of the things you did in the sandbox, so thank you for *your* service. Time is short, so let me run you through the flight plan.

"We'll lift off in half an hour and run a series of engagements with the frogs. Excuse me, the French Air Force. The plan is to break contact and let them find us again half a dozen times."

The pilot patted the side of one of the aircraft. "At that point, we go active and ditch them. By the time they cry uncle, we'll have you delivered onto the roof of the target building. The bad guys won't know we're coming until the first plane—mine—drops you on the roof."

He gave Harry a smug look. "That ought to scare the living shit outta them. Everyone in that building will know we've arrived and your clock starts ticking.

"Make no mistake, we're going in hot and I expect you to unass my aircraft in an expeditious manner. Then you need to clear the LZ because the next plane is right behind me. Once we drop all of you, we circle back to pick up our hosts. Questions?"

The military speak for exiting the jet made him smile. "Are you sure you can break contact?"

He gave Harry a disbelieving look. "Seriously? They're French. That means we'll need to work extra hard to keep them from giving up before we're ready."

* * *

Jess turned back toward the men. "These are really interesting. Is there a chance I could look at one more closely?"

The fat man gave her a disapproving scowl. "You are not here to ooo and ahhh over my art collection. I've never understood why Americans are so pushy. My man will take you to examine the house and grounds. Good day."

Paolo stood and gave the man a half-bow. "Thank you for your time."

Another man opened the door and they filed out behind him. "Shall we start with the first floor?" he asked.

Jess fell back a little. "Dammit. If he'd have just been a little more accommodating, we could've been home free," she murmured.

"Don't get all tore up about it," Sandra said. "You saw enough to know there's something worthwhile. That was Italian, right?"

"It sure looked like it. If I can get that one page flipped over, we might be able to unlock enough to make some headway. The author obviously knew something of both languages."

"Don't get carried away and blow this," Sandra said. "You've already expressed an interest in the pages. You can't get back in there without him getting the wrong idea."

"Maybe I can slip away. Get in while everyone else is busy."

"Bad idea. Really bad idea. Don't even try it. Am I clear?"

Jess sighed. "Crystal clear."

They made their way through the ground floor. Jess added to the conversation when Paolo prompted her as she looked at everything. She wanted as complete a visual record as possible.

Once they'd made the rounds below, the man led them toward the patio. "Next we can look at the grounds."

Paolo frowned. "We should examine the upper floors before we make the rounds outside."

"According to the weather report, there will be rain in an hour. It would be best to look at things in the light, don't you think?"

"I have a wonderful suggestion," Romano said from the doorway leading toward the elevator. Jess hadn't seen him there. He moved quietly for such a large man.

"Why don't you take your time examining the grounds while I escort your associate on a tour above? I'll be certain to show her everything she needs to see."

"Did he really just say that?" Sandra demanded. "Hell, no. Do not go anywhere alone with this sleazeball."

Jess smiled at Romano. "That sounds like a wonderful idea."

* * *

HARRY and the men from his best two teams, now called Team One for convenience, strapped into the back of the lead plane before the ground crew opened the hangar and towed the jet out. Takeoff was smooth and easy. He wore a headset to listen as the mock war games took place. The French pilots sounded competent enough.

He mentally went back over the plan. He wanted to play out all the worst outcomes he could think of. Walking into a prepared enemy scared him the most. If his mother's people were ready for them, they might all die in that building.

About twenty minutes before the planned assault time, Black Jack called him on the private channel. "We're almost ready to break away. I got word from your large friend that the distraction group is setting off a couple of alarms in the sewage tunnels. Not enough to make them sure an attack is coming, but maybe enough to relocate some of their people to be ready for one. Your other teams are staged to provide an escape corridor for you and the package."

"Copy that, Colonel. Good luck on breaking contact."

"If you keep insulting me like that, I'm not going to buy you any drinks later."

Harry laughed.

Right on schedule, the planes dove for the deck. "Active countermeasures activated," Colonel McCarthy said. "Everyone form up on me."

The French pilots had lost the Rainforest jets before, so they didn't sound too upset. Of course, they'd always reacquired them quickly.

By the time the formation was approaching the BenCorp facility, the French controllers were getting a little frantic.

"You're sixty seconds from drop," Black Jack said. "Good luck."

"Thanks, Colonel," Harry said. "See you for that drink soon."

He hung up the headset and stood. "Thirty seconds. Stand in the door."

The red light in the rear started blinking. Harry led his people to stand under it. The plane slowed and his knees flexed to take up the pressure as the rear ramp lowered. Parking lots and buildings seemed to be sliding quickly by right below him.

The engines went full VTOL and a rooftop appeared only a few feet away. When the momentum was almost gone, Harry ran down the ramp as the jet thundered behind him. As soon as the last man cleared, the jet reoriented and lifted like a giant bird of prey, vanishing into the darkness.

He could already hear the next jet coming in. "Go!"

His people ran for the roof access as the second jet came barreling in out of the darkness to offload more of his people. It was damned impressive. He'd buy two if he could afford them.

"Alarm off, door open," Jeremy said.

Harry followed them in. Now he'd find out if their plans had a chance in hell of working. They charged down the stairs with their weapons up and hunting for targets.

## 24

Romano led Jess back to his private elevator. "Please pardon me if I sounded brusque earlier. Times such as these try a man's soul. Allow me to make up for my boorish behavior. Perhaps a glass of wine? I assure you my cellar is quite good."

"That sounds lovely. Thank you."

"Don't trust this guy," Sandra said through Jess's earbud. "He's the kind to slip something in your drink."

Jess couldn't respond, but she'd already considered that. How would Romano explain any sudden issues she developed to Paolo? There was no telling. She'd figure out how to stop him as she went.

He once more escorted her into his office. "Perhaps you should take another look around while I pour for us." His insincere and oily smile cemented the thought that he had something in mind.

Her brain raced. "I shouldn't drink while I'm working."

"What can one glass harm? I insist."

Jess went over to the case with the manuscript pages, taking her glasses off and holding them so that Sandra could see behind her.

"Yeah, he's looking at you and acting all sly. He's putting something into your glass. Don't drink it. I'm moving the team up to his property line."

She put her glasses back on and looked at the manuscript pages again. If she ever wanted to see them, she needed to figure out how to turn this situation around. And she'd like to avoid even the thought of this bastard doping and raping her.

Romano stepped up beside her and handed her a glass of red wine.

"These are beautiful, are they not? My grandfather bought them after the Second World War. Well, during it, really. No one can read them, but they look pretty."

He smiled at her. "Drink. I must know what you think of the vintage."

Jess faked taking a sip, hoping that mere contact with her lips wouldn't let the drugs into her system. "Mmm. I'm no expert, but it's good. Would you mind if I take a closer look at one of the pages?"

The fat man considered her request and then nodded. "For just a moment. These are very old, so do not touch them." He set his wine glass on a nearby case and dug out his keys.

She wiped the rim of her glass clean of lipstick and set it down beside his while he focused on the lock. She picked up his drink and took a sip, putting her mark on the glass.

The wine was actually quite good. Fruity with a hint of something earthier.

Romano raised the lid and stepped back. "You can place your glass on the other case. I don't want to risk you spilling anything on these valuable artifacts."

Jess watched with a smile as he picked her old glass up and took a sip. Karma was a bitch.

* * *

It only took a few floors for Harry to realize that they'd completely surprised his mother's forces. If they'd been lying in wait, he'd have seen them already. Even now, the rest of his teams were spreading through the building, heading for the strong points.

No alarms rang out. Had they not heard the jets? Did they mistake them for something else? He didn't know, but he wasn't going to complain.

Jeremy had bypassed the systems at the roof door. As long as they didn't use the elevators—which would've been stupid—the security teams would only see them if they were monitoring the upper floors.

Or when Team Two hit the security center.

Team Two peeled off when they got to the appropriate floor. The rest of them continued down. Automatic weapons firing in controlled bursts told him the moment his men attacked. Then the alarms went off.

They reached the ground floor in a rush. The stairwell opened into the center of the building. Rex moved out with teams three and four. They'd keep the enemy forces from getting back into the building.

Harry took his team to the interior loading dock and dove for cover when the security guards started shooting. He fired off a long burst to pin the enemy down as his men came in behind him.

The container was still where he expected it to be, thank God, already loaded and ready to move. Everyone had orders to avoid shooting the nuclear reactor, but some of the BenCorp security people decided to hide behind it. That delayed his men from securing the room.

A bullet ricocheted off the concrete beside him. He ducked lower. "Get those bastards."

One by one, the enemy fell to their fire. He tallied his men as soon as the area was secure. Two wounded, one seriously. The medic saw to them as Harry assessed the container. They'd locked it, but a bolt cutter fixed that.

The doors opened smoothly and he saw the reactor, safely disassembled and stored inside. The radioactive fuel sources were in a massive lead case. It was all here.

He checked the shipping container for bullet holes, but found none. A wave of relief washed over him. His mother's people had already hitched the big rig to the container. He climbed into the passenger seat as one of their trained drivers took the wheel.

His team opened the doors leading outside and got into a brief firefight with some security guards. These had come in SUVs. Perfect.

"Take the vehicles and make sure the gate is clear. We'll be right behind you. Rex, is everything secure?"

"Right and tight, boss. We're planting the charges now. This will more than make up for the hotel bombing. I think the whole building might come down. We'll be ready to move out in five minutes."

"Don't be late. I don't want you pinned down by any reinforcements. We're leaving now."

"Drive safe and don't rush. That's when accidents happen."

Harry laughed. "Copy that."

His exterior teams had already secured the gate. They raised the arm and waved him through. He gave them a salute. One of the SUVs rushed ahead to scout traffic while the rest settled in around the big rig.

It was early evening, so traffic wasn't as light as he wished. Still, that was a good thing. They merged with the cars leaving the industrial area without the slightest ripple.

* * *

NATHAN WATCHED the helicopter lower the spaceship into the freighter's hold with more than a hint of unease. If something went wrong, his mother would blame him. He breathed a sigh of relief when the load was down and secure.

The helicopter moved away from the ship and the crew began securing the new cargo. It would take a while to get it to the US, but this ship was one among many on the international shipping lanes. His father wouldn't find it before they had the spaceship safely to port.

He called his mother as soon as they closed the hatch and started moving.

"Mother, everything went according to plan. We have it."

"I need you to gather your people and head for France. Someone—hell, probably your damned brother—just stole my new reactor. They blew up the building. Sound familiar?"

Nathan cursed. "I thought you had it secure. Weren't you moving it early?"

"I was," she said bitterly. "Tomorrow morning, local time. He got there just before the extra security. The police are tearing up the city, but how much do you want to bet they never find it? Incompetent bastards."

"And by the time I get there, it'll be long gone. Where will he take it?"

"How the hell should I know?"

Nathan reviewed what he knew of his father's holdings. The old bastard had a lot of them in Great Britain. Of course, the reactor would be to its destination by the time he found out where that was.

"I'll direct my teams to London. If you get any more intelligence before we get there, call me."

He hung up and called for the helicopter to come back. He'd catch the first commercial flight.

He looked over the spaceship one last time before he headed up to the main deck. No matter how this played out, they'd still won. Let his father have the damned reactor. They could always build another one. This baby would give them so much more.

* * *

JESS CLOSELY EXAMINED the pages she suspected of having Italian. Her fingers itched to pick it up and look at the reverse.

"Come," Romano said. "Have some more wine."

He just wouldn't let it be, the sleazy bastard.

She took up her glass with a smile. "Don't let yours go to waste, either. We can drink up and have another glass."

The fat man smiled and took a large drink. When she did the same, he matched her until both glasses were empty. Perfect.

"That was too good to gulp," she said with a laugh that wasn't at all fake. "More, please."

"That was slick," Sandra said in her ear. "Real slick. Now play him until the drugs take effect. As fat as he is, it probably won't knock him out for long."

Romano virtually swaggered over to pour them fresh glasses. "You're very lucky, you know. Many Americans never get a chance to see how the rest of the world lives. And even when they do, they look down their noses. That's no way to take in the history and greatness of Europe."

She raised an eyebrow and sipped her fresh wine. "Really? I suppose that's true to some degree, though I'm not sure the arrogance is solely ours. So, your grandfather bought those during the Second World War? Not from the Germans, I hope."

"Of course. Who else was selling stolen art?"

Romano blinked in apparent surprise at his answer. "I mean...no, of course not. Everything was legal and above board. I don't know what came over me. My sense of humor can be somewhat odd."

Sandra laughed. "It sounds like the drug makes him more compliant. Let it take hold and we'll really get him on the record."

Jess nodded at what he'd said. "I understand. Has this villa been in your family for a long time?"

"In one form or another, my family has owned this property since the Dark Ages. It was originally a monastery. We bought it from the church and tore down the old buildings."

She asked him about the area for a few minutes as the man became drowsier. Once he seemed fully in the grasp of the drug, she decided to test him.

"What did you put into the wine?"

"A designer concoction that will make you more suggestable and interfere with your memory of the next few hours. It's completely undetectable."

Her stomach roiled at the thought of how many women he'd done this to.

"Did you use this on the American woman you married?"

"Of course. The damned condom broke and she got pregnant. I used the drug again to get her to sign a prenuptial agreement. I couldn't have her taking half my money when I dumped her."

The bastard. "So you tricked her into signing away her rights? Is that how you got control of your daughter?"

"No." His eyes were glassy now. "I never anticipated wanting the child, so I didn't specify her in the agreement. When the harpy sued me for custody, I had some of my men break into her house and take the child. She's mine. Blood of my blood. I'll kill the bitch when the time comes to take my girl back."

"Not if I have anything to say about it," Jess muttered. It was time to get him to confess to doing this before.

"Have you drugged other women?"

He laughed. "Of course. All the time. Sluts. Deep inside, they want it. Some try to get me arrested or sue me, but there's never any proof."

"Has anyone sued you falsely?"

"No. Isn't that funny? They all told the truth, but no one could prove a single thing. My friends in the judiciary dismissed the cases. I'm a judge, you know."

"And I hear you're in the mob, too. What terrible things have you done?"

He began listing a spree of horror. Killings, embezzlement, drugs, and more. He mentioned enough names to implicate plenty of other people. She made sure to ask where they'd buried the bodies and where to find any evidence of the crimes.

"You need to wrap this up," Sandra said.

Jess agreed. "Mister Romano, you tried to do something terrible to me. Give me the pages from the Voynich Manuscript to make up for it. Write out a receipt transferring their ownership to Humanity Unlimited. Make sure it's legal."

He wrote out a receipt and signed it.

"You know this is just as sketchy as that prenup he forced his ex-wife to sign," Sandra said. "It'll never hold up in court."

"Then he can sue me for them," she said firmly. "Maybe the irony will give the bastard a heart attack."

Jess folded the receipt and put it into her jacket. She gestured toward the case at the end of the room. "I'll need a briefcase to carry the manuscript pages. Please pack them carefully for me."

He took a briefcase made of fine Italian leather from a cabinet and lay it on the case beside the manuscript pages. He found some latex gloves and began tugging them on.

Jess made certain she had a good view. "Put them face down, please."

He complied and she watched the previously unseen pages as they appeared. The back of the one she suspected might have more data was better than she'd hoped. Two columns of script filled it, one in Italian and the other in the strange lettering. If anything was the Rosetta Stone, this was it.

She closed the briefcase and had Romano give her the combination.

"You've done very well. Would a second dose of the drug harm a person?"

"Probably not," he said.

"Good. Make another one."

She watched him pull a packet out from the desk, empty it into his glass, and fill it with wine.

"Drink up," she said. "Call your people. Tell them you're sending me back down and you don't need to speak with Paolo. Then go to bed. You've had a busy day and you want to get a good night's sleep. I'm not sure if it works this way, but you'll only remember you had a good time once you wake up."

Once he'd called for someone to come get her and retired to his bedroom, she spoke aloud. "Sandra, I'm on my way out. I'll find Paolo and we'll meet you at the house next door. I think we should make tracks back to Rome. We can cut out the video of the confession and send it to someone trustworthy. The police will come for him before he wakes up."

"Have I ever mentioned that you're my hero?" the mercenary asked.

"Well, you are. Now get the hell out of there before something goes wrong."

Jess grabbed the briefcase, corked the wine, and took it, too. It was the least the bastard could do.

# 25

Harry worried all the way back to Mexico. He expected to have a military jet of some kind show up to herd the stolen cargo plane to another landing spot as soon as he got close to the spaceport.

Two jets did show up, but they were obviously of Rainforest manufacture. They escorted the plane in without incident. His father stood waiting as he and his men climbed out of the plane and stretched.

"Well done, Harry. Well done. Jess's flight lands in ten minutes. She'll be just in time to get the reactor transported to pad three and begin loading. I don't know if I'll relax until it's in space."

"How long will it take to get it installed once the lifter gets it up there?"

"I believe she said twelve hours, but that seems like too short a timeframe."

That did seem optimistic. "How about the fuel?"

His father smiled. "Two loads are already in orbit. They tell me that the remainder will take two additional launches. Then we resume personnel and supply missions. We should be able to wrap those sometime tomorrow."

"So, about the time you get your primary power supply online, you'll be ready to leave? That sounds like good timing. Mother will figure everything out before too much longer. I wouldn't put it past her to try and shoot the station down."

"Wouldn't that make for some ugly headlines?" His father grimaced. "I can't believe they managed to steal the crashed spaceship. Dammit. I'm certain they moved it offshore, but I probably won't be able to figure out which ship it's on before they get it somewhere. So much technology lost."

"If you can figure it out, I'll go get it back."

His father gave him an odd look. "That might be challenging from orbit. You're going with Jess, aren't you?"

Harry felt his eyebrows rise. "What would I do up there? I'm not an astronaut."

"You don't want to walk on the surface of Mars?"

"Exactly how are you planning on doing that? I can see visiting asteroids, but without small craft, how do you visit something like Mars?"

"With the increases in efficiency, the reusable lifters will do. A number of them will stay with the ship. Fuel is available in space, too. Phobos, the larger of Mars's moons, is very much like a D-Class asteroid and probably has water inside. A lot of it.

"Eventually, we can use the high carbon content to create a beanstalk. That's a long tether that goes out beyond geosynchronous orbit and uses elevators to move people and cargo from the surface to a station in orbit."

"Are you serious?" Harry asked. "You'll build a space elevator?"

His father nodded. "Yes. The gravity is much weaker on Mars. That means the carbon nanotube cables would be much shorter and slimmer. A number of scientists and science fiction authors have explored the subject. I intend to explore the reality."

He shook his head. That sounded almost as impressive as exploring the solar system.

"Back to the subject," his father said. "You could be one of the first humans to walk the surface of another planet. As one of the owners, perhaps even right behind Jess."

"You're not going?"

The older man shook his head regretfully. "Alas, no. I'm far too old for that kind of nonsense. Besides, I have a covert war to fight here on Earth. Once the ship leaves orbit, everyone is going to go mad. Your mother in particular, but also the various governments that see they've missed the boat. I foresee a number of attempts to nationalize the company. My work will be to keep that from happening."

The noise of another plane landing announced Jess's arrival. Harry considered the offer. Did he want to go? His work on Earth was satisfying, but this was a once in a lifetime opportunity. What could he contribute once they were in space?

Admittedly, going with Jess had its appeal. He'd grown quite fond of her in the last few days.

The airplane taxied up to park beside the cargo plane. A motorized stair positioned itself and the passengers started making their way down. Jess was in the lead with Sandra right behind her.

The blonde engineer came up to him with a huge grin on her face and grabbed him in a tight hug. "We did it! We got the reactor and the papers! That'll show your mother!"

His indecision vanished as he held her in his arms. He knew his body was making a hasty call, but he was willing to see what happened. He felt a little more alone when she pulled back.

"I'm sorry to burst your bubble, but we didn't get our way in everything. Nathan stole the buried spaceship."

Her face fell a little. "Dammit. Well, maybe we can find another one. One in better condition."

She turned to his father. "Did the fuel make it up?"

"Half of it has. The other half is loading now. It will launch just before the reactor does."

"Excellent! I need to start moving the reactor. Excuse me."

The two men watched her run to where they were unloading the cargo container. His father spoke after a moment. "How can any project with her at the helm fail? She's like a tornado."

Harry hadn't agreed with his father so completely in years.

NATHAN'S PHONE WOKE HIM. Even at cruising altitude, there was no escaping his mother. All passenger aircraft had satellite links these days. The other first class passengers glared at him, but he ignored them and answered the call.

"Hello, Mother. Have you located your property?"

"The bastard stole my plane. With all the confusion, no one noticed the pilots had disappeared. The French police found them locked up in a hangar at a regional airport."

That made things more complex. With an aircraft, the reactor could be anywhere in the world.

"Do you have a transponder on the plane?"

"They disabled it, but that doesn't matter. My spy at the Yucatan Spaceport said they landed there just a few minutes ago. Turn around and get back there as soon as you can."

He rubbed his face and checked their location. The plane was almost ready to land at Heathrow. "You know all my assets are landing in London, right? It will take at least a couple of hours to get on our way back. Figure half a day to get to Mexico and begin planning a mission. Why the hell did they take it there? To slip it across the US border?"

"I have no idea. My man is keeping an eye on the situation. Stop complaining and get your ass in gear. I want that reactor back in my hands before they get it somewhere we can't recover it." She hung up before he could respond.

Working for his mother was becoming a chore. Nathan turned his phone off when the flight attendant told the first class passengers to do so. He'd call his men as soon as he landed. There was just enough time to get a decent meal while they refueled. He'd order something for his men and they'd eat on the flight back to Mexico.

* * *

JESS FRETTED while loading the reactor on the lifter. There was no room for error. One mistake and the whole project could go up in flames.

She'd planned on an hour to load, but the painstaking process took almost 90 minutes. With that high stress task done, Jess retreated to the control center for pad three.

Harry was already there waiting. He handed her a bag.

"What's this?" she asked. It smelled good.

"A meatball sub."

"It can wait until they fire this thing into orbit."

"And then you'll say you can wait until it docks. Or some other milestone. Eat the damned sandwich. I have a glass of tea, too."

It was easier to eat than argue. She sat at one of the empty consoles and looked at the main screen. The countdown clock showed only a few minutes until launch. Her first bite brought her hunger to life. The sub was delicious.

"I hear you got the pages," Harry said as he took a seat. "Congratulations. Sandra said you kicked some ass, too."

"The police arrested Romano a few hours after I left," she said smugly. "And I forwarded the edited video to his ex-wife through Sandra. She's going to get a chunk of his fortune for her daughter, I think. Once the prenup is voided, she'll be in a good position to take over the bastard's assets."

Harry grinned. "Remind me never to get on your bad side. Did the papers have everything you needed?"

"I'll know once Doctor Powell takes a look, but I think they might. It looked like it had a long segment of medieval Italian and the unknown language. That might be enough to figure most of it out."

"My father asked if I was going on this mission," he said. "What do you think?"

She looked at him in surprise. "Well, of course you are. You think this is all for physicists and pilots? You'd be exploring where no man—or woman—has ever gone before."

"He said we might be going down to Mars, and that as an owner of Humanity Unlimited, I could be one of the first few people to step onto an alien world. Behind you, of course. As the senior owner present, you should go first. I hope you come up with something suitably historic to say by then."

Jess froze with her sandwich halfway to her mouth. "Oh, shit!"

"I'd seriously recommend something classier."

She swatted him. "You know what I mean! Me? The first human on Mars? Are you serious?"

"Why not? Though, to be fair, you might not be. Aliens, you know. They might have been there before us."

That was true. "Yes, but I'd be the first modern human. Wow. No pressure."

The flight director called out. "Jess, we're about to launch."

She rose to her feet and stepped over to his console. The timer was down to fifteen seconds. She watched it slowly drop to zero. The engines ignited right on schedule and the lifter rose from the pad.

In less than a minute, it was lost to sight. Ten minutes later, it was safely in orbit. It would dock in four hours.

Then the real fun started.

* * *

CLAYTON LOOKED up when his assistant knocked on his door. "Sir, the courier is here and you have a call."

"Who is it?"

"Your ex-wife."

That surprised him. He'd lost count of the number of knives they'd planted in one another over the years, yet she'd never called him about any of the incidents. Not even to gloat when she'd won.

"Keep her on hold. If she wants to talk to me, she can wait for me to finish my business. Send the courier in."

His assistant ushered in a young woman in a casual suit with a flat package. He closed the door behind her.

"Set it on the desk and I'll sign for it," Clayton said.

The papers were straightforward and he had the woman on her way in only a few minutes. Alone with the package, he spent a few minutes carefully opening it. They'd protected the contents very well, just as he'd asked. The old pages of the Voynich Manuscript had cost him a significant amount of money. Yale hadn't wanted to give them up, but they could use the funds he'd offered for so many other projects. And the endowment hadn't hurt, either.

Clayton didn't know if the pages themselves would provide any extra clues, but he doubted that anyone had analyzed them rigorously since they'd been stored away. They might contain any number of undiscovered secrets.

Doctor Powell could examine them with the newly acquired pages. Well, she could once she and her associate had set up shop in orbit. They were going along, of course. The odds were very good the explorers would find new artifacts in space and Clayton wanted them preserved correctly.

Then he answered his ex-wife's call. "Sorry to keep you waiting, Kathleen. Business, you know."

"The wait only makes me more determined to hurt you," she said. "What the hell are you doing, Clayton? You stole a nuclear reactor from me and shot it into orbit."

"And you stole an ancient spacecraft from me. You also killed dozens of people and blew up my hotel."

"Which you got even for when you destroyed my research facility. Drop the faux outrage."

He shook his head. She'd never understand the difference between them. Or realize that she was a monster. "What do you want to talk about, Kathleen?"

"To tell you the kid gloves are off. You and Harry aren't on the safe list anymore. Keep looking over your shoulder, Dear. One day, Nathan will be there and you'll die."

"You can't believe how little that actually matters to me. Send whomever you like. I'll return them to you in a body bag."

He hung up the phone and pressed the buzzer. His assistant answered at once. "Sir?"

"I want security around the spaceport tripled. No one gets onto the launch pads or into this hotel without being cleared."

He stared out the window. Phase one was almost complete. If he could just hold things together for a while longer, he'd take all the marbles.

# 26

Harry made time to talk with Rex, Sandra, and Jeremy. The rest of his people were coordinating with the Rainforest security people to keep things sane while the last of the launches were taking place.

The four of them wedged themselves into a booth at the hotel restaurant. It was deserted. He got right to the point. "I wanted to let you know that I'm going up to the station."

All of them stared at him. Rex finally spoke. "Look, I know I told you to stay close to your lady friend, but that might be a little too much commitment. Stalkerish, even."

Sandra smacked Rex on the back of the head. "Sexist jerk. That sounds exciting, Harry. Maybe you'll miss all the fallout of the theft, if you'll forgive the pun."

"I might be able to miss all that and more," he said. "Before I talk about it, I wanted to make you three an offer. You're the best people I have and I want to keep you with me. I'd pay very good money if you'd join me."

Jeremy grinned. "In space? Hell, yeah!"

Harry smiled and shook his head. "Not so fast. There's a lot more to this situation than you know. Let me lay it all out for you."

He spent the next ten minutes explaining the whole space station being a spaceship surprise and the alien tech. That kept them quiet for a while.

Sandra was the first to speak. "So, you want us to leave the Earth and fly to Mars. Why?"

"Because I want people I can trust at my back."

Rex nodded slowly. "Sure. Hey, I wasn't doing anything for the next few months anyway."

Sandra and Jeremy also agreed.

With their buy in, he relaxed. "Great. There's room on the lifter for all of us. With luck, the last of the supplies will be on the ship tomorrow."

Harry looked at his watch. "You have enough time to pack a bag. They'll provide everything ordinary, so limit yourselves to personal items and luxuries. Meet me in the lobby in two hours."

\* \* \*

Jess already had her personal belongings on the ship, so she stuffed her bag with coffee, tea, and chocolate. They were going into deep space. There was no such thing as too much caffeine or chocolate.

Even though she shouldn't take it into space, she put her pistols, holsters, and spare magazines in the bag, too. A few discreet inquiries with her guards got her a few boxes of ammunition. She'd turn them over to the ship's captain. Maybe. She might just keep them close until they were safely away from Earth.

Once she'd stuffed her bag to the limit, she went down to the lobby. The bag was heavy enough to make her feel like a pack mule.

The other elevator opened and Harry walked out with Sandra, Rex, and the security guy at his back. Jeremy, that was his name.

She waved. "Hey. You guys excited about going into space?"

Harry shrugged. "Excited might not be the word I'd choose, but I'm ready to go. What happens next?"

"A van will pick us up in a few minutes and drive us to pad one. We'll get into suits and board the lifter. Once we're all aboard, they'll launch when the station is at the right point in orbit. About an hour from now."

Sandra hefted her bag. "Where do we check in our baggage?"

"They'll put it in the back of the passenger cabin when we board the lifter."

The elevator opened again, and Clayton Rogers strolled out. "Ah, good. I was afraid I might miss you."

He extended his hand to Jess. "My deepest congratulations on the magnificent engineering marvel you've helped design and build. This achievement will see humanity finally leave this planet for good. I couldn't be prouder to be a part of such a grand venture. You'll keep me up to date on everything you find?"

She shook his hand firmly. "Of course I will. This is a wonderful adventure. Thank you for allowing me to be part of it."

The older man turned his attention to his son. "I know you don't trust or approve of me, but that doesn't matter. You're helping to do something important. Keep her safe and enjoy the ride."

Harry took his father's hand. "Don't make me regret this."

The van pulled up out front. "Our ride is here," Jess said. "Let's mount up."

The trip out to the pad took longer than she'd expected. Security stopped them twice, comparing the passenger's faces to something on their security tablets. They searched the bags and scanned everyone with detection wands.

She expected trouble about her weaponry, but the man in charge of the checkpoint made a short call and put everything back. Clayton had cleared them to take weapons up with them.

The launch pad towered over the area where the van stopped. A protected door led them into the concrete base. The changing room wasn't large, but a partition separated it in two for modesty.

Jess stripped down to her underwear and put on a ship's jumpsuit in light blue. Once Sandra was ready, she picked up her freshly bagged clothes and led the mercenary through the door into the suit room. The three men were already on the other side.

Technicians fitted them into suits in short order. Gone were the days of bulky, hard to wear vacuum gear. These were relatively light and flexible. Not as much as the rotted suits in the crashed ship had been, but much easier to wear than twenty years ago. The helmets were clear composite. They'd be able to communicate through built-in radios.

They went up the elevator one at a time. A technician on the upper level escorted her into the lifter, helped her secure her gear, and strapped her in. Even though she'd been on a number of flights, she still got the safety lecture. She listened intently and reviewed it in her mind once the man left for the next passenger.

The two pilots were going through their checklists. The passenger cabin had three seats side-by-side and four rows. She didn't know the other passengers, but waved anyway.

They strapped Harry in beside her and she had him switch to a private channel once he was settled in. "I'm so excited. This is really it."

"At least you have some idea of what we're getting into. Tell me about the ship. How many people does she carry?"

"More than you might think possible. The torus has three levels with the floors arranged so that our feet point outward. They rotate twice a minute giving the outermost level 95% of Earth's gravity. The innermost level is about 85%."

He looked impressed. "How many people are aboard?"

She smiled. "Get ready to have your mind blown. The torus supports about 2,500 people with plenty of space left for manufacturing, research, and cargo. It's a mobile colony. We've been sneaking them up over the last six months as the ship came online."

Harry looked a little stunned. "Considering how much the first international space station cost to house just six crew members, my father invested a lot more into this project than I thought possible. Even considering how he's lowered the launch costs. I was thinking fifty or a hundred people, max."

"We need a lot of people. We're planning on dropping off three mining outposts. They'll have a lot of work to do. They'll be building stations similar to the ship for long-term colonies, at some point.

"We have habitat plans that would support more than half a million people in one massive space station. They'll be building one like that in Mars orbit once we get to mining Demos and Phobos."

He shook his head. "That's staggering."

"Your father thought big. He wants to get mankind off Earth in a permanent way. Imagine colonies around Venus and Mars. The asteroid belt. Jupiter and beyond. Ultimately, millions of people. Even billions at some far off future date. The planet that gave mankind birth would no longer limit us."

The pilot turned in his seat and spoke over their radios. "Welcome aboard. I'm Lenny Kawasaki and I'll be your pilot today. We hit the burners in about ten minutes. Once we reach orbit, we'll have another three and a half hours to get to our destination. Thanks for flying with us and we hope you'll choose Humanity Unlimited for all your orbital launch needs."

Harry seemed disinclined to talk, so Jess settled back and meditated. The engine ignition caught her a little off guard, shaking her and then pressing her back into her acceleration couch firmly.

The boost to orbit took just over ten minutes. They didn't have windows, but the small screen above the pilot' cubby showed the view. It was breathtaking.

Once the engines shut off, they were in microgravity. Basically, they floated. The pilot allowed them to unbuckle once the lifter was on course. Jess decided to stay where she was.

Watching the mercenaries figure out how to move around was fun, though. They were surprisingly adept at it, though they had a tendency to overshoot their marks.

The fun and games kept them from being bored while Jess reviewed the data dump from the ship. They'd unloaded the reactor and had it roughly in place. She'd see to the final connections once she was on board, but she was satisfied with the work that her people had done so far.

* * *

HARRY PLAYED AROUND for a while and then buckled back in to watch Sandra, Rex, and Jeremy. The sniper was trying to figure out how to compensate for zero-G when she tossed a ping-pong ball toward a small basket someone had taped to the far wall.

Apparently, this was a fun game for everyone. They'd try to get the motions just right and mostly fail miserably.

"This is more complex than it looks," Sandra said after a while. "I'll figure it out, though. I wonder how a shooter does her business without gravity. The recoil would shove her hard enough to screw up her aim. And the slug might penetrate the hull."

"They might not have weapons in space."

She stared at him for a moment and laughed. "Stop trolling me. Of course they have weapons in space."

Rex held onto the back of one of the chairs. "Maybe it uses compressed air and frangible rounds."

That made some sense, Harry decided. Over-penetration would be a bad thing in space. "Most of the ship has gravity, just not as much as you'd expect. It would mean knowing how to shoot in every level and being able to compensate correctly the first time. That could be fun."

"But the central area doesn't have gravity, right?" Sandra asked. "I bet I could manage something, but it'll take time to develop the right skills and tactics to secure the whole ship. I know what I'll be doing most of the trip out. Chasing Rex around."

"Just what I'd been hoping you'd say."

"You are such a pervert."

The big scout laughed. "Hardly that. It's all natural."

"I want to get a good look at their systems," Jeremy said. "They must be seriously advanced."

Jess tapped Harry on the shoulder. "We're almost there. Check the screen."

Harry watched the small dot grow into a ship on the screen. The lack of reference points made it hard to tell the size until they got close. Liberty Station was huge.

The shaft the torus rotated around was shorter than he'd expected and he couldn't see any sign of the engines Jess had spoken of. Four massive spokes connected the rotating torus to the spine, helping it rotate majestically. The torus was thicker than he'd imagined, too, but there were thousands of people in there.

Three long arms projected from the ship above the torus. He suspected there was a fourth that he couldn't see because of the ship itself. One looked like a dock. He could see two lifters attached to it. That gave him a new sense of scale. The station was even bigger than he'd thought.

One of the remaining arms held a solar array. The other held three large disks that looked ready to drop. Maybe the mining equipment Jess had mentioned.

As they came around the station, he saw a similar set of discs on the far side of the ship on the last arm. He'd have to ask about them when they had time.

A smaller disk, about a third the size of the torus, but just as thick, sat on the top of the station. It was rotating in the opposite direction from the torus. The ship looked amazing.

"We dock at the end of the arm to the left," Jess said. "We'll get off in zero gravity and unload the cargo they brought up. You guys can settle in and take a tour of the ship while I get the reactor installed. By this time tomorrow, we'll have left Earth—and our troubles—behind."

## 27

J ess fidgeted during the approach. In space, ships and people moved slowly and carefully. The lifter edged close to the docking arm and allowed the clamps to lock it down.

The pilot instructed everyone to stay in their seats until someone came to get them, unless they were zero-G certified. Which she was.

She unbuckled, spun over her seat, and launched herself to the handhold beside the personnel lock. She opened a cubby, retrieved a line, and went back for Harry.

"You can get out of the suit, now. They'll pack it away for you."

Jess helped him get his suit off and then stripped off her own. She folded them and strapped them into their seats.

She held up the line. "Let me hook us up. Until they're satisfied that you can maneuver on your own, you'll need to be paired up with someone who can keep you from hurting yourself or others in microgravity."

"Does that take long?"

"That depends on the person. I think you'll take to it quickly. Sandra, too. Rex, well, maybe by the time we get to Mars."

"Hey," he said mildly.

She laughed. "I'm sure you'll do fine. Okay, use your hands to gently push on the chair and send yourself toward the handholds. I'll be right there with you."

Harry shoved off with too much force, but not as badly as some she'd seen. He also tumbled in the air because he was off balance. She let him hit because it wouldn't hurt him and it would teach him a lesson.

He looked chagrined. "That didn't go so well."

"You'll pick it up. You ever go scuba diving?"

"Sure. Is this like that?"

"Only in that you had no idea what you were doing before it all clicked into place in your head. This will be the same. Everyone gets the hang of it eventually."

She led him through the airlock. A pair of attendants was just arriving to bring the new crew on board. "I'm certified," Jess said. "I've got this one."

The ship's air smelled different from the lifter. A shade more metallic, but not as stuffy. It definitely wasn't like natural air, but it was good enough.

Planting her feet on the hull, she grabbed his belt. "Hold still. We could use handholds, but I'm in a hurry."

One light push sent them floating the direction she wanted. She was pleased to see that she'd accounted for his mass fairly well. They'd only miss her point of aim by a few feet.

They drifted with deceptive slowness and she stopped them at the hub. She pulled them around the corner into the spine. The spokes to the torus were only a short distance away.

Unlike the rest of the spine, the torus's hub rotated. So, each spoke made a trip around the spine twice each minute. That took some getting used to.

It had also taken a tremendous amount of engineering to account for the edges. The spine was inside the moving hub so that conduits, pipes, and supports could run along the entire length of the ship. The junction with the spokes could even seal if there was an explosive decompression.

Jess got Harry to the hub. "See how the ladders have arrows?" she asked. "That's direction of travel. It's awkward to run into someone going the other direction. If you do, the person in the wrong has to back up.

"There are also elevators. We built the doors into the spokes since the cars can't come all the way into the hub. We cinch cargoes into the hub and match speeds. It's a bit complicated, but it greatly simplifies boosting the ship."

"Seems straightforward enough. We're in zero-G. That changes as we go down, right?"

"Right, though we don't use up and down. Too confusing. Going toward the torus is outward and going toward the spine is inward. In the torus, the direction of rotation is spinward. The other is antispinward."

He considered that. "How do you know which is which?"

Jess smiled. "You can feel the rotation. I'll show you. Come on."

She moved ahead of him. "Always keep one hand on a handhold until you're certified. Then you can do this." She lightly shoved off and coasted above the handholds. After a dozen feet, she stopped herself. It would ruin her image of competence if the line yanked her up short.

When the centrifugal force grew strong enough, they switched directions and it felt as though they were climbing down a ladder. The pull grew stronger with every rung until they came out in the innermost torus level.

Jess unhitched the line and put it into a cubby with others just like it. "Let's get you settled in and I'll be off."

She led him down the corridor. "See how it curves up in each direction? It always makes me think of hamsters in their exercise wheels. And plenty of people get their exercise in just that way. Walk long enough and you'll get back to where you started."

"You said we could tell which direction we're spinning. How?"

She stopped. "Close your eyes. Turn in the direction that feels like you're moving toward."

He paused and turned to spinward. "That's weird."

"Your inner ear knows when you're moving, even if your eyes tell you you're not. Also, check this out. Do you have a coin in your pocket?" It usually took a while before people stopped carrying money around with them.

"Probably." He found one and held it out to her.

"Drop it."

He let it go and it fell to the deck, but not in a straight line. The coin fell in a curve, angling toward antispinward.

"Whoa!" he said, grabbing the coin and doing it again. "What the hell?"

"That's the Coriolis Effect. We're rotating, but the coin is falling directly away from the spine. As we move, that direction changes from our perspective. So, the falling object curves. If you toss a ball, you'll have to deal with the same physics. It'll seriously screw up your basketball game."

"And shooting. Sandra will be seriously dismayed."

Jess laughed. "We don't have any shooting ranges, so that won't be a problem. You'll get used to it after a while. Come on."

She led him to a cross corridor and down to her room. "I'm here. I reserved the room across for you. We assigned the others rooms on this corridor. Your personal gear will arrive once they start unloading the lifter."

"People get single occupancy rooms in space?"

"They do when we have enough to go around. The rooms are small compared to those on Earth, but they're large enough. I really need to go look at the reactor, so you'll have to hang here for a bit. Someone will be along to give you a real tour shortly."

She grabbed him by the shoulder. "Welcome to space, Harry."

\* \* \*

HARRY GAVE his new home a short walk-through while he waited for his guide. He'd expected the room to be something like a cruise ship cabin, but it was more like a small apartment. He had a living room, a kitchenette, a bedroom, bathroom, and a spare room that he could use for anything he wanted, he supposed.

The bed was a queen and already made. Built in dressers and closets had basic supplies like new underwear and ship's suits like the one he wore. The ones in his closet already had his last name on the breast. A quick check showed that the bathroom had basic supplies, as well.

The kitchenette had a microwave to heat things up, and a small oven to bake. The two-element stovetop would suffice for his cooking skills. A small fridge stood ready, but was empty.

A buzz at the door announced he had a visitor. A short Asian man with silver oak leaves on the shoulders of his jumpsuit smiled at him and extended a hand. "Mister Rogers, welcome aboard. I'm Captain Lee, the commanding officer of Liberty Station."

Harry shook the man's hand. "Captain, it's a pleasure to meet you, but I'm sure you're a very busy man. You don't need to show me around."

"It's no problem at all. I needed a break, so I thought I'd give you a tour of the ship's common areas and then have lunch. I realize it's after dinnertime down at the spaceport, but we run on GMT up here. Have you looked around your quarters? I hope they're acceptable."

"They're bigger than I expected, actually. So is this whole ship. She's amazing."

The officer grinned. "Yes, she is. Come on and we'll stroll down to the public section of the torus. Your bag should be on your bed when you get back from lunch."

"Is there a lock for the door?"

"No. Where would someone take a stolen object? We don't use money directly on the ship. Everyone gets their pay electronically and purchases come out of those accounts at the public stores. Meals are part of the pay, so no charge there."

They walked back to the main corridor and then headed antispinward. Harry nodded and smiled politely at the people they passed. "What about secure areas of the ship like the bridge and engineering?"

"Those are locked. Only authorized personnel can access them. The control consoles are locked, as well."

They passed out of the housing section and into what looked like a park. Harry stopped and stared in amazement. There was grass on the ground and small trees under a large, opaque dome. The lights seemed to be about the same color as the sun.

"This is one of our habitat zones," Lee said, smiling at Harry's bemused expression. "We have other areas for growing food hydroponically, but places like this let the crew have a taste of home."

"I'm surprised you don't have a view of space here. Radiation?"

The officer shook his head. "Not exactly. We have a powerful magnetic field that will protect the ship once we leave Earth. Impact shielding and water surround each hull. Micrometeorites are a concern, as well as cosmic radiation that might be too energetic for the magnetic field to stop. There *are* a few viewing areas, but we thought the habitat zone wasn't the right place for them. We'll look at one before we stop off in the cafeteria."

Harry mulled that over. "I saw my cabin had a kitchenette. If there's a cafeteria, what use is it?"

"Want to watch something on the screen while you snack on some chips and dip? Maybe make a grilled cheese sandwich or an intimate dinner? That's why we put one in every set of quarters. Feel free to use it or not, as you like."

He saw movement in one of the trees. Something was up there. An orange cat walked out on a limb and stared haughtily down at them. It crouched and leapt to another branch, seemingly accounting for the Coriolis Effect with ease.

"You have cats," he said, surprised. "Do you have pests?"

"Not that I'm aware of. The screening process was good enough to make sure we didn't get rodents or insects. Vacuum does wonders for that. No, we have some cats and dogs as common pets. They're all domesticated and friendly.

"We have several crewmen dedicated to seeing to their health and wellbeing. Given how quickly they breed, we should be able to start allowing private pets in a few years."

The area next to the park was similar to a mall, with all kinds of stores. Many of the people were dressed casually. Harry was glad he'd brought some of his regular clothes.

Lee gestured around them. "You can buy any number of personal items in these stores. They're charged to your account."

"How do they know who I am?"

"That's a good question. We'll get you set up with a chip in your palm. The ship will know who you are and be able to track you anywhere inside the hull. That's partly for safety. We don't want someone wandering into a dangerous section of the ship."

"It's also a security feature," Harry said approvingly. "You know if someone enters an area they aren't cleared for."

"True enough," the captain agreed. "That isn't the reason for them, though. We've vetted every member of this crew very thoroughly. The cafeteria is just ahead, but let's go see the observation level first."

That required a detour to the edge of the habitat area. A short set of stairs led them up to an airlock. The doors stood open and he could see a wide room with a clear ceiling. The central spine of the ship was directly overhead and shone brightly in the sun. The Earth occupied one side of the view, seeming to spin quickly.

"It's beautiful," Harry said. "I think I'd get a little dizzy if I had to watch it all the time."

Lee laughed. "Most people feel that way at first, but the mind adjusts just as well as the body. The micrometeorite protection for this area is under the deck. If you're ever here and this section loses pressure, there are hoods and oxygen canisters in the lockers against the wall. Keep calm, put one on, and go to the lock. It has two doors, so you can get back into the habitable area."

Harry pointed at the section of the spine facing toward the Earth. "Those are the engines? They don't look the part."

"Appearances can be deceiving. The hull there is on hinged arms. When the time comes to boost, it opens like a flower. And, once we reach a new orbit, the hull closes and we can use the equipment mounted there. We get the best of both worlds."

Harry watched the universe turn for a few minutes in silence. This made him feel almost insignificant. The entire Earth could vanish and the rest of the galaxy wouldn't notice.

"What's the plan going forward?" he eventually asked.

"We're still bringing the last of the crew and supplies aboard. We have another dozen lifters coming. Once the new reactor is online and our current one is playing backup, we'll disassemble the solar array and put it into storage. That will give us six docking points for the lifters.

"Once the last of them has unloaded, we'll rotate the ship so the engines are in line with our orbit around the Earth and start boosting. We'll break orbit on a course for the comet Miss Cook found the coordinates for."

"How long will it take us to get there?"

"It's not all that far away, so about five days. We'll boost to a speed somewhat faster than it and coast into the same orbit. Then we'll decelerate to match speed."

Harry took one last look at the Earth. "I can only imagine how that's going to freak them out down there."

"No doubt," Lee agreed. "I'm afraid it's time to go get some food. I have to get back to the emergency bridge. We're using it to monitor the reactor installation. We'll have plenty of time to get to know one another as we head to Mars."

Harry followed the captain out, but he couldn't tear his eyes away from the glory of the view until it was out of sight. This would be an amazing trip.

## 28

"**D**on't move it so quickly!" Jess said.

Chief Engineer Ray Proudfoot gave her a look. "Jess, take a breath. I promise I won't slam the radioactive material into the reactor."

"Sorry. It's been that kind of week. Just go extra slowly."

She watched him resume moving the manipulator arm that held the fuel. He inserted it into the reactor and locked it in place. She double checked the work and nodded. "Good. Really good. Thanks."

A nuclear reactor wasn't like a light switch. She couldn't just press a button and have power. She had to bring it online in stages. It would take about six hours to get the reactor to full output, but they didn't need that kind of power on a spaceship. They'd wanted the unit for its portability and longevity. For their purposes, one-quarter output was more than good enough. It would take them two hours to get it up to that.

Step by step, she and her team walked through the process. In an hour, the reactor had taken over supplying power to the ship from the weaker unit that the UN had approved. That anemic reactor would make a good backup, but it couldn't do more than keep the lights on. They'd need twice the power to generate the protective magnetic field and fire the engines.

"Power output at 25%," the chief engineer said at last. "Lock it down. Great job, everyone."

Jess relaxed a little. The hardest part was over. At least until they fired the main engines.

She headed for the hatch. "I'm going to the emergency bridge. Let me know if you see any unusual readings."

"Relax," he said. "I have everything under control. Go get something to eat and maybe have a glass of wine. You're wound up pretty tight."

"I will. I even brought a fresh bottle of wine. I hope it made the trip okay."

She left the power center and made her way forward in the spine to the emergency bridge. Her chip allowed her access to every portion of the ship, so all she had to do was wave her palm in front of the reader and the hatch slid open.

The emergency bridge wasn't very big, but it was close to the reactor room. The large screen up front took up the most space. It showed the Earth spinning below the ship. Four angled control panels allowed the officers to monitor various parts of Liberty Station. Several observation chairs could fold down from the rear bulkhead.

They were almost ready to shift operations to the control deck. That would be a big improvement since it had gravity. This one would now be reserved for unforeseen crises.

Lee glanced up as she came in. "I see the new reactor is providing power. Well done, Jess. All systems are in the green and we'll be ready to break orbit tomorrow morning. There are ten lifters still in the queue. The next two will lift in half an hour. The launch windows are 90 minutes apart. Once they dock, we'll unload them.

"We'll get a good night's sleep while that happens and be on our way shortly after breakfast." He looked pleased. "It's hard to believe we made it."

She took a slow breath and shook her head. "I'm not counting on that until we're away. If things look good, I'm getting something to eat and have a glass of wine."

"Have two. Goodnight, Jess."

"Goodnight, Captain."

It only took a few minutes to get to her room. She hesitated and then buzzed on Harry's door.

She smiled when he opened it. "Good. You haven't gone to sleep. I wanted to see if you were up for dinner."

"Sure. We'll have to go to the cafeteria, though. I don't have anything to fix."

"We can go to my place. I have some steak. And wine. I brought a fresh bottle. Did you get your gear?"

"Yup." He stepped into the hall. "I've put everything away and I've been scanning the entertainment channels. You've got the full spectrum up here. I'm especially impressed with the sports lineup."

Jess opened her door and led him inside. "We get the feed straight from the commercial satellites. Some of the channels will continue once we get going. The transmitter that we'll be communicating with has a lot of bandwidth. The library is fairly extensive when it comes to movies, too. One of the benefits of Rainforest being the leading provider of streaming entertainment."

She found her freshly acquired bottle of wine and opened it to breathe. "We got the power online. We're almost ready to go. How are Sandra and the rest getting along?"

He followed her to the kitchenette. "Pretty good. They're off exploring."

"Why didn't you join them?"

"I'll do that tomorrow. I wanted to review what my people back on Earth have found out. There's still no sign of Nathan, but my mother swore revenge. We need to be on our toes."

Jess put two steaks into the oven. "They can't even get to us up here. I hope. I can't wait to watch the news channels when they notice we're leaving. It will be awesome!"

Harry didn't seem convinced. "I'm not resting easily until this is over. Can I toss the salad?"

It would be a tight fit in the kitchenette, but she didn't mind. "Be my guest."

\* \* \*

NATHAN MET the paid weasel outside the spaceport. Security was tight, so it was easier for the man to come to him. They'd broken into a small warehouse. It looked disused, so he'd taken the chance. It was large enough for his team to assemble.

The cadaverous man looked nervous as he walked in under guard. "Mister Bennett, I can't be gone long."

"You can be gone as long as I say. My mother tells me they took our reactor to the space station. I want you to tell me how I can get it back."

"Impossible. If it's up there, it can't be retrieved."

He punched the man in the gut, smiling as he folded and retched.

"You don't tell me what's possible. You take my instructions and make them happen. How can we commandeer one of the lifters and get to the space station? Once we get up there, no bunch of scientists is going to stop me from doing what I want."

"You don't understand. That's impos—"

Nathan slapped him. Hard. "I'm getting tired of your excuses. I understand the spaceport is at a heightened state of security. Figure out how to get my men past it to one of the pads. Tonight."

The man rubbed his face. He was sweating heavily. "Security is exceptionally tight, Mister Bennett. It will take me several hours to see what options we have. Perhaps if you waited a while for things to calm down, it would prove simpler to get you up there. It's not like a space station is going anywhere."

"Not that I need to explain myself to you, but I might be able to steal it back if they haven't installed it. You have four hours to get back to me. Go!"

It took almost the full four hours for the man to return. He shook like a leaf, so Nathan was prepared just to shoot him, but the man had a plan.

"They're still loading personnel and supplies. There are four launches left on tonight's schedule. Two lift within the next hour, so I can't get you into the secure area before they go up. One of the last two is a personnel launch. It will need to be that one.

"Security examines each vehicle going to the pad area closely, but I've discovered an old service tunnel that isn't used anymore. It goes past both perimeters."

The man took a deep breath. "You can't just walk in and hijack the lifter. The pilot can tell the control center something is wrong in so many ways that you'd never notice. The weapons need to go into bags. They're stored in the cabin. Once the lifter docks on the station, you can take action. Not before. You have to pretend to be the real crew until then."

Nathan could work with that. "How will you get us into the spaceport?"

"Through the employee entrance. I brought paperwork for you. There's a bus outside. You're new hires, already vetted by me. Once I get you in, you have to pay me off. They'll know I helped you in."

"Of course. You'll get everything you're owed and more. Get my team where it needs to go and I'll make the call."

The bus ride was stressful, but the paperwork got a dozen of his men past the guards. The spy drove them to a rundown area of the spaceport and stopped beside a decrepit warehouse. They made their way inside.

The man gestured toward concrete steps leading down into the darkness. "The stairs go to an old access tunnel. It exits in a building much like this one." He handed Nathan a hand drawn map. "Go west several blocks from the exit and you'll find the main thoroughfare. A bus with people is going past there in half an hour on the way to pad one. The pad crew won't check ID."

"Is that all I need to know?" Nathan asked.

"Yes."

Nathan smiled. "Excellent." He drew his knife and stabbed the idiot in the throat. He wiped the blade on the man's jacket and sheathed it as the fool writhed on the floor, drowning in his own blood. "Say hello to all the other suckers when you get to hell."

His team fell in behind him as they made their way into the tunnel. It was nasty, but not as bad as the jungle had been. Rats and roaches he could handle.

With the security lockdown, there weren't any people wandering around the area where the tunnel led. His people were able to find the target road without any problem. They set up an ambush and waited. If this really was the last flight of the night, he couldn't afford to miss it.

He heard the bus coming about the time he expected and stepped out into the road. He held up his hand with authority as it turned the corner.

It slowed to a stop and the driver stared at him in confusion. "We already passed the screening zone. What now?"

Nathan aimed his pistol at the man and grinned. "Now you raise your hands. If you reach for that radio, I'll shoot you dead."

That got everyone in a terrified, but cooperative mood. His men rushed the bus and started pulling people off. The driver and twelve passengers. They herded them back to the warehouse and returned alone. His father's people wouldn't find the bodies until long after this was over.

They drove to the pad and parked. Nathan pointed to one of his men. "Drive the bus to a different area and go back out the way we came. Tell the rest of the men to head back to the US. You're done here."

The preparation crew didn't realize anything was wrong and got them all fitted into spacesuits. They helpfully loaded the bags laden with weapons and explosives into the lifter and strapped his men down.

One of the pilots—a woman—turned toward them. "Welcome aboard. We're the last personnel flight to Liberty Station. They must've saved the best for last. We'll launch in ten minutes and dock in four hours. Sit back and relax."

Nathan did exactly that after launch. He fell asleep. All this flying around was catching up with him.

He woke when the lifter was settling into its dock with a thump. The pilot again turned and held up a hand. "No moving around until you have an escort, unless you're zero-G certified. Welcome to Liberty Station."

The weapons were just a few feet away, so Nathan unbuckled and pushed himself toward them. He missed by a wider margin than he'd imagined possible and hit hard.

"Sir? Are you okay?" the pilot asked. "You need to stay still."

Nathan opened the door and grabbed one of the bags. It didn't matter which. They all had weapons. He pulled a pistol from inside and surprised the pilot with it just as she got to him.

"Don't move," he said. "You at the controls. Touch anything and she dies now and you'll be right behind her."

It only took them a moment to subdue the pilots, remove their helmets, and tie them to chairs in the passenger compartment. Their escorts opened the airlock just as they finished. They took one look inside and fled. Several of his men fired at them and missed. No matter.

"Two of you stay here and keep our ride secure. The rest of you, bring our gear. It's time for some payback."

## 29

"Harry! Wake up!"

He woke abruptly and blinked at Jess. She was standing over his bed. "What?"

"We're under attack!"

That got him moving. He threw the covers back and grabbed a fresh set of coveralls from his closet. He briefly thanked God that he didn't sleep in the raw. "Tell me."

"Someone hijacked a lifter," Jess said, her hands gripped into a ball in front of her. "It has to be your brother. He's here."

He put his shoes on and grabbed a pistol belt out of the lowest drawer. "What's he doing?"

"We don't know. The captain called me. One of the pilots was talking with them and they heard enough to realize what was going on before he cut off. They shot at men inside the ship."

Harry slid a pistol into the holster and grabbed his extra magazines. "Do we know where they are?" He grabbed a backup pistol and clipped the holster at his spine.

"In the spine. Maybe he's after the reactor."

"Can they take it?" He headed for the door. Time to wake his team.

Jess followed along behind him. "No. It would take days to cool off enough to remove. But he likes blowing things up. He could destroy the ship if wanted to. One bomb would turn it into a radioactive wreck."

Sandra was just down the corridor, so he pounded on her door. He explained the situation in a few words as soon as she opened it.

The sniper cursed and headed for her bedroom. She'd gather the rest of the team.

He focused on Jess. "What about security? Surely this ship has people trained to defend it."

She wrung her hands. "I don't think they ever expected someone to get an armed group on the ship. The command team is on the emergency bridge. Nathan has to go right past it to get to the reactor room."

"I need to talk to them right now."

Jess took him into her quarters and picked up a regular looking phone from a holder beside the couch. She dialed a number and handed it to him.

He heard it ring once before it picked up. "We're a little busy, Jess." It was Captain Lee.

"This is Harry Rogers, Captain. I need your security team to gather at Jess's room with everything they have."

"That won't be much. Tasers only. We never expected an armed incursion like this. Since the pilot reported a full load of passengers, there must be a dozen of them. I don't know how many they left in the lifter, but we can't fight something like that easily."

"Where are they?" Harry asked as his people arrived at the door, heavily armed.

"They're in the main corridor heading toward the emergency bridge, reactor room, and engineering. I've ordered the other areas to evacuate and lock down, but these men can probably force the doors. I told the incoming cargo lifter to stay clear and I'm rousing the other pilots now."

Harry decided not to wait for the security forces. Tasers wouldn't be of much use. "Send the pilots along with the security people. I assume you have a real weapon on the bridge. Try to hold them off for as long as you can. We're coming."

He looked at Jess after he hung up. "Take the remaining lifters, if you can. Get them away from the ship. Nathan isn't suicidal. If he has no ride home, he won't blow up the ship."

Once she nodded, he headed for the corridor. Sandra, Rex, and Jeremy were waiting. "Let's go end this once and for all."

* * *

NATHAN HELD BACK when they blew the locked hatch to the emergency bridge. A good thing, since someone inside opened fire and hit the first two men through the door. The next two spun out of control as soon as they opened fire. They must've hit the bastard, though. The firing stopped.

He looked in and saw more destruction and blood than he'd hoped for. He needed people with authority and he needed them alive. This had seemed like the perfect place to look, since they'd marked it so prominently and it was on the way to the engineering spaces.

Three of the men in the room were floating uncontrolled and bloody. Some of the control panels were smoking and the main screen was dark with a number of holes in it.

The captain of the station was easily identifiable with his silver oak leaves, but he wouldn't be useful. Dead men rarely were.

One of the others was similarly dead, one badly wounded. A fourth man had his hands up.

Nathan shot the wounded man. A mistake, as he spun out of control until someone grabbed him.

Once he'd righted himself, he glared at the remaining crewman. "You've made things harder than they needed to be. Where's the reactor you stole?"

"In the reactor room," the man said, obviously terrified. His name tag gave Nathan a name.

"Williams, you'll want to be more specific than that if you want to live. Where's the room?"

"Aft of here on the main corridor."

"Good. Bring him," he said to one of his men.

The captain's aim had been good. The two men he shot were dead. Nathan's incursion party was down to eight.

Two of his men struggled to move the prisoner slowly through the zero gravity. All of them struggled, truthfully.

The reactor room was clearly marked. Nathan pointed his pistol at the man's head. "Open it."

Williams held his palm over the plate beside the door and the hatch slid open. Expecting more gunfire, Nathan sent his men in first.

The room was unoccupied. "Where is the crew that belongs here?" Nathan demanded.

"The captain ordered them to run."

Nathan grunted. Effective and inconvenient. He didn't know anything about nuclear reactors, but this one looked like it was operating. That couldn't be good for his plan to steal it back.

"What is the status of the reactor?"

"They brought it online last night," the prisoner said.

No, stealing it back wasn't an option. There were probably more of them than he had bullets, too. Eventually, they'd overpower him and his men. Mother wasn't going to be happy.

He shot Williams in the head, making sure to grab something as a brace first. The blood spatter in zero-G was impressive.

"Plant the explosives."

* * *

JESS RALLIED the security people and led them into one of the spokes. It let out into the main corridor of the spine, which was a dangerous place, but there were access panels leading to some of the maintenance crawlspaces. They were tight, but safe, methods of getting close to the docking arms.

She'd sent pilots to get the craft on the opposite arm free. Several others remained with her party to get the rest, if they could. A dozen meters of vacuum was as good as being on the other side of the planet.

Jess had brought her pistol and was steeling herself to the probability she'd need to use it. Those bastards had hostages. Of course, if she did, the lifter would almost certainly lose pressure. They'd need to act fast.

Once they were close to the compromised docking bay, she peered out from an access panel. The airlock to the hijacked lifter was open and no one was in sight. There were several crates secured to the deck. They'd provide a little cover once the security team exited the crawlspace.

She turned to the man behind her. "Spread out once I go in. I won't lie. Some of us will probably get shot, but we can't let them have a way off this ship or everyone dies."

He nodded grimly. "We're behind you."

Jess looked at the pilots. "You get the other lifters clear." She floated to the crates. She'd only just arrived when a man came out from the lifter's airlock. The security man pulled the access panel closed behind her while the intruder was looking up the arm.

The mercenary scanned the compartment and floated there, blocking her way into the lifter. If he stayed, there was no possibility of getting in quietly. She'd have to shoot him and that would warn any of his compatriots still inside.

She quietly took one of the bullets from her spare magazine, estimated the angle she'd have to toss it to hit near the arm, and gave it a light push.

The bullet floated slowly enough that it didn't grab the eye. It bounced off the bulkhead beside the arm. The sound of metal on metal got the guy's attention. He made a clumsy jump to one of the crates close to the airlock and peered around it.

Jess pushed off and sailed across the docking bay toward the airlock. She hoped she didn't have to shoot him, because that would send her tumbling in some unexpected direction.

She touched down beside the lock as softly as she could and slipped inside. He wouldn't be able to see her if he looked back now. This was the time to act.

"Everything okay, Zack?"

Jess made a guess of which direction that voice came from and slapped the airlock controls. The hatch behind her slid shut and locked. That gave the guy some warning, but he wasn't expecting her to come out shooting.

Because it was insane. Her first shot missed him as he opened fire on her. The loud whistling sound told her that she'd probably shot one of the viewports up front. If it failed catastrophically, she'd die quickly and horribly.

His bullets tore into the side of the lifter. Some of the ricochets must've went back into the cabin, because someone screamed.

Jess jumped for the first seat and shot the mercenary center mass. He grunted and fired until his weapon ran out. Jess bounced off the bulkhead, grabbed a pipe, and shot the man until he stopped moving.

The sound of leaking air came from all around her. Someone was pounding on the airlock. Probably the other mercenary.

One of the pilots slumped in the acceleration couch they'd tied him to while the other struggled to free herself. "He's hit. We need to get out of here and give him first aid."

She untied the woman. "I'll look at him. Disengage the docking clamps and get us away from the ship."

"We're leaking air and one of the ports is cracked. You don't have a suit. If it blows, you're dead."

"I'll make do. Hurry."

Jess examined the pilot's wounds while the woman put her helmet on and climbed into the cockpit. The man was in bad shape. Really bad. She had to get him out of his suit to treat him, and that meant the dropping atmospheric pressure would kill him. A no-win scenario.

"We're free," the pilot said. "The cargo lifter is holding position just ahead of us. We're at 60% pressure and falling fast. You don't have more than a couple of minutes."

Jess wracked her brain for a plan.

* * *

HARRY FOUND someone to lead them to the reactor room. Once he knew they could find it on their own, he sent the guide away. Speakers had begun a kind of hooting alarm. A recorded voice advised people to seek shelter in their quarters and prepare for possible decompression. He hoped that wasn't a reality.

Sandra got as close to the central corridor as she could and used a compact mirror to peer around the corner. "Four armed men in the hall, two looking in each direction. They're wearing pressure suits with the helmets hinged back. None of them is your brother. He must be inside the reactor room."

"I like those odds," Rex said. "We can pin the bastard down. Then we take him out."

"Without damaging the reactor?" Harry wasn't sure how that would work out. Still, he didn't have a better plan. "You sure you can shoot straight without gravity?"

The sniper grinned at him. "Oh, yeah. That just means no drop. The trick will be dealing with the recoil. It also means the bastards will miss those critical first few shots."

Harry sighed. Time to act. "How do you want to do this?"

She readied her combat rifle. "You three hold onto me and the ladder. I'll pop up like a jack in the box and let them have a piece of my mind."

It took a moment to figure out how to do that. "Go," he said.

The sniper raised herself and fired. Her whole body jerked back. The three of them kept her from flying loose. She fired again just as the enemy shot back with a fully automatic burst.

Sandra didn't flinch even though Harry heard bullets bouncing off the bulkheads. She fired twice more. "They're coming this way! Back up!"

They released her and retreated up the spoke until they found cover. Harry grabbed a pipe, aimed his pistol, and shot at the men pouring fire at them. It took a minute, but their limited experience in low gravity carried the day.

They cautiously went back toward to spine and looked out. He counted six bodies floating there. A noise from one of the other spokes drew his attention.

Two men were rushing down it. One of them looked like Nathan.

He sent the others to check the bodies. He didn't want someone to ambush them by playing possum. The enemy was dead or dying.

"The reactor room is clear," Rex said. "Of people, anyway. I think they planted a booby trap."

"Jeremy, see what you can do."

"Let me tie off Rex's leg first," the security specialist said.

A glance back showed that the scout had taken a round.

"I've cut myself worse shaving," Rex said. "Get in there. I'll handle this."

Harry had no choice but to trust them to do their jobs. "Sandra, take that spoke and cut them off. We'll box them in between us."

Sandra dove down her spoke and he headed for the one his brother had taken. A scream sounded from inside it. One that cut short abruptly.

He peered around the corner and saw one of the men was almost to the other end of the spoke, climbing down the ladder as fast as he could. A form was sprawled in the corridor below him.

The torus looked as though it was over his head, but he knew from experience that the perspective was false. If someone pushed themselves too hastily, they'd find themselves falling. One of the men had obviously missed that until it was too late.

He wished he could believe it was his brother, but that would be too lucky.

Harry took aim and fired at the fleeing man with slow deliberation. The Coriolis Effect screwed him up and none of his shots found their mark. He hoped none of the bullets went all the way through the outer decks. If they had, someone would need to find them and patch the leaks.

His brother fired a salute back at him, grabbed the body, and dragged it out of sight.

Dammit.

## 30

Nathan stripped his man of ammo and explosives. If he couldn't get back to the lifter, they wouldn't make much of a difference, but he'd gotten out of worse predicaments in his life. He'd started toward the lifter, but spotted several men with weapons waiting for him and reversed course. There was no way they'd make it to the lifter under fire with their lack of zero-G experience.

There weren't any convenient hostages where he was now, so he ran. The corridors all looked alike. They had to have escape pods of some kind in case of a serious emergency. Like, for example, a reactor explosion.

He was out of sight from the ladder when he heard someone jump down. Probably his asshole brother. He needed to lose him fast.

The corridor opened up into a wide area with trees and grass. If he hadn't been running for his life, he'd have gaped. Instead, he bolted across it and spotted a sign over a nearby side corridor that read "viewing room." He didn't know if that also held a way out, but he'd try it.

Nathan bolted down the featureless corridor and up the stairs. He stared at the space station rotating over his head for a moment. It was a lot bigger than he'd expected.

There wasn't any time for this. He started looking for escape pods. There were many access panels, but none of them was large enough for a person.

"Throw down the weapons."

He looked back the way he'd come and there his brother stood, hiding behind the hatch with his pistol aimed and ready.

Nathan sighed and dropped the rifle. "Well, it seems as though you have me."

"Kick it over. Hands on your head and keep them there."

A light kick sent the rifle about halfway to the hatch. His brother gave him the stink eye, but came in slowly. He was ready to shoot, but Nathan bet the weird rotation would make him miss. All he needed was one chance.

When Harry was almost to the rifle, Nathan threw himself aside. His brother fired and missed, giving Nathan enough time to get a grip on a grenade he'd had behind him and pull the ring.

"I'd stop right there unless you want to go up in a bright flash. Put the pistol down. Who's holding all the cards now, big brother?" Nathan gloated.

* * *

Jess tried to staunch the flow of blood, but the pilot stopped breathing. She closed her eyes for a moment and then headed for the cockpit. "He's gone. Can the other lifter dock with this one?"

The woman sighed. "Dammit. You don't have time for them to decide to trust us. There's an emergency suit in the airlock, and enough air to put it on."

Jess climbed into the lock and shut the hatch. It didn't have an exterior viewport, but she could see into the ship. She knew when the shadows became as sharp as knives that the interior was in vacuum.

She opened the valve marked emergency air and a reassuring hiss began. It didn't last long, but she wasn't as dizzy. The locker right next to the nozzle had suits that were exactly like the one she'd worn on the trip up.

It took her a few minutes to get one on and make sure the air was feeding correctly. She reversed the airflow and brought the airlock down to vacuum. Only then did she open the interior door.

The pilot looked over at her as she sat down. "The other pilots don't know if they can trust us, so we're all waiting for word from the station. The reserve watch officers are in the main control center. Apparently, there's still at least one hostile aboard and they rigged the reactor with explosives."

"This week just keeps getting better," Jess said bitterly. "Can you turn us toward the station?"

She prayed as the lifter reoriented itself and they began waiting.

* * *

Harry considered his options. If he let Nathan out of this room, more people would die. Was he willing to let that happen?

No.

"If you let that go, you'll kill yourself," he said. "Your ego won't let you commit suicide."

"Then I'll have to trust fate." His brother tossed the grenade at Harry and dove away.

Harry threw himself forward and swatted the grenade back at Nathan. He rolled as he hit the deck and was looking away when it went off.

The blast smashed him into the wall and knocked many of the storage areas open. He grabbed for one as the clear ceiling gave way. The air chuffed out into space, dragging him with it, and he missed his grip.

Several hoods flew past him and he managed to snag one. He quashed the panic threatening to overtake him and read the instructions. Seconds later, he had it on and he was breathing canned, nasty, wonderful air.

Nathan was tumbling near him, struggling to get his helmet on. It looked as though they'd both be flying off into the darkness of space.

Well, screw that. Harry drew his backup pistol, lined up on his brother's head, and pulled the trigger.

Which sent him spinning wildly. He had no idea if he'd hit the asshole.

He watched helplessly as he tumbled past the spine and flew out into space.

* * *

Jess saw the flash from the torus and gasped. "Something exploded! It wasn't the reactor."

The pilot leaned forward. "That looks like one of the observation bubbles. People watch the ship from the inner ones and space from the outer ones. I wonder why it blew."

Something flashed near the spine. Jess frowned. "That looked like a gun. Can we move closer?"

"So someone can shoot at us?"

"I doubt they'll be in any condition to use a weapon by the time we get there, but if that was a friend, we need to see if we can rescue them."

The pilot brought the lifter to life and moved in. "Based on the angle, they probably missed the spine. We'll circle around to the other side and see if we can spot them."

Jess scanned the darkness and spotted a series of shots. "There! Someone is shooting. Maybe they're trying to get back to the ship."

"We'll go slowly so they don't try to shoot us," the pilot said as she refined their course.

The lifter had radar, but that wasn't any use in finding a person in space. The pilot did three passes and spotted something on the last one. "There. That's a person."

Jess saw the tumbling body. She couldn't tell if it was male or female at this distance.

The pilot nudged the lifter around in front of the body. "Go open the outer airlock door. Use one of the lines to secure yourself. You don't want to get separated from the lifter."

"Got it." Jess grabbed one of the lines, made her way into the airlock, and secured herself. Then she opened the outer airlock door.

A man was spinning wildly about ten meters away. He was coming toward the airlock slowly.

"He's almost here," she said to the pilot.

"I'll catch him in the airlock. Don't let him hit your helmet. Hold him while you close the outer hatch. Pressurize and see if you can revive him."

"He's wearing some kind of hood. He might still be alive."

Jess grabbed the man's arm and stopped his rotation. It was a good thing she'd secured herself. She pulled him in, closed the exterior hatch, and started the air flowing.

Only then did she get him turned around. "Harry!"

He looked a little rough, but he was awake and smiling. The air pressure rose high enough that she could hear him. "I'm a big fan of your timing."

"Are you okay?" She scanned what she could see of him. His left leg had a large splotch of blood, but otherwise he seemed uninjured.

"I think I caught a piece of shrapnel, but I'll live. That beats what's happening to Nathan as we speak."

The pilot called over the radio. "How is he?"

"Hurt, but alive. We need to get him back on the ship."

"The docking bay is clear. I'm taking us in now. Stay there."

Jess returned her attention to Harry. "Your brother was with you?"

Harry nodded. "He blew out the observation bubble. We both went flying. I took a shot at him, but that worked out spectacularly badly. He was wearing a suit."

"Hopefully, he's flying off into space and dies a horrible death," she snarled. "We're heading back to the ship. I heard something about explosives."

"Nathan rigged the reactor. Jeremy and Rex are trying to disarm the charges. I need to get back there as soon as I can."

She couldn't see outside, but she felt the lifter dock.

"You can exit the airlock," the pilot said.

Jess opened the outer hatch and sagged in relief when the members of the security team were waiting for them. They'd captured the mercenary and tied him to a crate, where he glared at everyone.

Harry ripped off his hood. "Get me to the reactor room. And have someone tie that guy up and bring him along. We can guard him better there."

She grabbed Harry and shoved off down the arm. Perhaps a little faster than was wise, but she managed to keep them from bouncing off anything.

They made the corner and sailed past the bridge. The mercenaries had blown the hatch open and she had a glimpse of blood inside. The thought of Captain Lee and the others being dead infuriated her. First Abel Valdez and now Lee. Two close friends. Would she ever stop losing people to these bastards?

There were several people gathered outside the reactor room. She used them to stop their forward momentum. "Sorry!"

Harry grabbed the handhold and rushed into the room. She followed, hoping desperately that he could save them all.

THE FIRST THING Harry saw when he came in was Jeremy working on a bomb. "Tell me you have this," he said as he came to rest beside the man.

"It's a tough one, boss," his security man said. "It's got all kinds of redundancy and anti-tampering features. The timer gives us less than five minutes and this is only one of six."

That didn't sound good. "We need to evacuate the ship."

Jess shook her head. "Even with the escape pods, I don't know that we'll get everyone off."

"If the damned things didn't have motion sensors, we could get rid of them," Rex said.

"How does a motion sensor work in zero-G?" Jess asked. "It should've caused the bomb to detonate right away."

Jeremy stared at her for a moment and dug back into the bomb. "It has to be a dummy. We can move them."

Harry grabbed Jess's shoulder. "Where's the nearest escape pod?"

"Grab the bombs and follow me."

Sandra came in then. "All of the intruders are accounted for, except Nathan. One is alive and the rest dead. Where did your brother go?"

"Into space," Harry said. "Take charge of the prisoner."

He and the others took the six bombs and followed Jess to an elevator. It took them to the exterior level of the torus. A long row of escape pod hatches was marked in red on the floor.

She flipped open a recessed control and opened the hatch. It slid sideways into the deck revealing another hatch. This one also opened at her touch.

The escape pod looked like it could hold a couple of dozen people.

Harry climbed in and secured the bombs to the walls. They had less than a minute to go.

He scrambled out. "Launch it."

Jess reached out, grabbed the prisoner, and yanked him over the opening. He fell in with a wail before Harry could react.

The blonde engineer hit the controls and both hatches slid shut. A thump vibrated the deck as the pod ejected.

"Why did you do that?" he asked softly.

Jess defiantly stuck her chin out. "That bastard helped kill my friends and tried to commit mass murder. He had it coming."

Harry couldn't disagree with her logic. "The people in Geneva probably wouldn't approve."

"Then let's not tell them."

The deck shuddered, almost knocking them off their feet. Harry hadn't expected to feel the explosion in the vacuum of space. The pod must've detonated fairly close to the station or the blast was larger than he'd imagined.

He helped steady Jess. "We need to get a status on the ship. And to call my father and see what we do now. We've lost the command crew."

She nodded. "Let's get to the bridge."

It was located at the front of the ship. The room had six spacious consoles and a large screen. Two men and two women manned the controls. The gravity here was less than in the torus, only about Mars normal.

One of the women stood. "Mister Rogers. Miss Cook. I'm Lindsay Waller. Liberty Station's reserve pilot."

Harry gestured toward the screen. "Did the bombs go off? What's the condition of the ship?"

"The bombs exploded short of the atmosphere," the pilot said. "The ship is in good shape. The emergency bridge is wrecked, but other than the blown out observation port, a lot of leaks to plug, the damaged lifter, and the two ejected escape pods, everything is fine."

Harry looked at Jess. "Two pods. We only used one." He returned his gaze to the pilot. "Who ejected on the second?"

She shrugged. "We've accounted for everyone. Maybe it was a malfunction?"

He cursed under his breath. "It never worked out that way in the movies and it probably isn't true now. Dammit. My brother somehow survived me blowing him into space. He escaped."

# 31

Nathan stared out over the waves from the hatch of the escape pod and enjoyed the strong salty smell of the ocean. His idiot brother had almost killed him, but he'd overcome everything. Luck was his bitch. The bombs he'd planted should've already destroyed the station. Victory was his.

He hoped he wasn't too far from civilization. In any case, his sat phone should be able to get him a lift.

His mother answered after a few rings. "Nathan?"

"Alive and well, Mother. We couldn't retrieve the reactor, but I planted explosives on the space station. You should've seen it blow up by now."

"Something exploded in orbit, but the station is still there. Maybe you only damaged it. That could be good enough, I suppose. Where are you?"

"In the middle of some ocean. I can give you GPS coordinates. I need a pick up." He recited his location.

"I'll send someone," she said. "This war with your father is only starting. I want you back here as soon as possible."

She hung up without another word. Nathan climbed back into the escape pod. There had to be something to eat in here somewhere.

★ ★ ★

CLAYTON LISTENED to his son explain the events from orbit with a mixed sense of anger and relief. It could've been so much worse.

"I obviously failed in providing enough security," he said at last. "I needed a heavily armed cadre of troops there to protect the station."

His son shrugged. "It was hard to imagine this happening. What about the people who were supposed to be on that lifter?"

"Dead. We found them in an old warehouse. It had a tunnel right under the security cordon. I have people searching every building for more. We also found one of my executives with his throat cut. Probably the leak."

"That sucks," Harry said. "The engineer said the ship is fit to boost. We still have the reserve pilot. The captain and primary pilot died on the bridge."

Clayton shook his head. "That won't do. I'll find someone else who can learn to pilot the ship. Call your people. We have two lifters held in reserve. That's two dozen more security people. Have them pack whatever weapons you think you'll need. Hell, pack things you don't think you'll need. You should be prepared if anything like this happens again."

Jess leaned over Harry's shoulder. "We should've put weapons on the hull. It'll take us a few days to replace the panels in the observation room, but we can do that while in flight. I'd really like to break orbit as soon as possible."

Clayton couldn't agree more. "I have the lifters under heavy guard. No one will be using them without authorization. The only other ways into orbit are the spaceports in China and India. I'll warn both of them."

He checked his screen. "Let me make a few calls. We'll launch as soon as we can. Get things ready on your end." He terminated the connection.

That had been entirely too close for his comfort. He needed to get the ship on its way before something else went wrong. He picked up his phone and called his assistant.

* * *

TEN NERVE-WRACKING HOURS LATER, the last two lifters docked with the station. Harry had spoken with his people on the ships, so he was certain there wouldn't be any trouble. He still had all four trained fighters on hand to welcome them. Armed to the teeth.

He relaxed when his people came out the hatches. The addition of two dozen of his men and women took the edge off his anxiety. They'd keep one of these lifters to replace the damaged one. They'd already jettisoned it. The pilots that had just brought them up would go back down in the remaining one.

Harry knew one of the new pilot trainees. Lieutenant Colonel "Black Jack" McCarthy. The tall man floated out of the lifter with a huge grin. "Momma always wanted her boy to be an astronaut."

He pulled the pilot over to a crate and shook his hand. "We're glad to have you with us, Colonel. The crew will get your stuff into your new quarters while we break orbit. I don't want to give my mother or brother another chance to screw us up."

By the time they made it to the bridge, the departing lifter was undocking. The one that had been holding position was ready to reattach to the ship.

He introduced McCarthy to Waller. The two pilots immediately started talking shop.

While that was going on, Harry commandeered a station and called his father. It was night, but he knew he was waiting for them to get on their way.

Harry was surprised when he only got audio. "Is your screen broken?" he asked.

"I'm on my jet, but not in my office. Mexico might get a little warm for me once everyone discovers I've been building a spaceship. I have a little island nation that's considering electing me president for life. In exchange for a very substantial payment and jobs at the new spaceport I plan on building there, of course. It's recognized as a nation by the UN, so that might give me some cover."

"Are you expecting a lot of trouble?"

His father laughed. "Oh, hell yes. The UN will hold endless hearings. Every gasbag on the planet will call for my head on a platter and demand that I bring the ship back at once. The US government is going to have a conniption. Things will be very exciting. I'm sure that they'll attempt to nationalize all my holdings. That won't stop me, but the fight will be long and glorious."

"Good luck, then. Captain Waller tells me that we're about ready to break orbit."

"She's only the command pilot, and while competent at that task, has no leadership experience. I think you would be best suited to that role."

Harry stared at the display in confusion. "Me? I don't know the first thing about running this ship."

"And you don't need to. You know how to lead. The subject matter experts can handle the details for you. Learn as you go, just like Colonel McCarthy. Right now, everyone needs a confident, steady hand at the helm. That's you.

"Miss Cook will be your second. She knows every aspect of Liberty Station. She can teach you about it while you show her how to be a leader."

He looked over at Jess. She was staring at some readouts on one of the other consoles. "I think she's already learning that. Fine. We'll break orbit in fifteen minutes or so."

"Allow me to wish you the very best of luck. Humanity is counting on you. I'll keep you up to speed on events here as they unfold."

Harry ended the call and walked over to Jess.

She looked up. "We're ready. Both lifters are docked and the engines are uncovered and ready to fire."

"My father thinks I should assume command of the ship. What do you think?"

Jess beamed. "That's the best news I've heard all day."

"Then let me bring you down. He said you should be my second in command."

"Me? Is he smoking crack?"

Harry laughed. "Doubtful. He just thinks that you'd make a good counterbalance. You know the ship better than anyone else and I've seen how decisive you can be."

"That wasn't me being decisive. That was me being impulsive. I'm not leadership material."

"And I'm not trained to run a spaceship. We'll both have to learn as we go. Are you ready?"

Jess took a deep breath. "Ready, Captain."

"Just Harry, please."

He returned to his console. "How can I speak to everyone on the ship?" he asked Waller.

She reached past him and tapped the controls. "Hit the green button to activate the speakers. Hit it again to close them."

He smiled at her. "Thanks. As I just told Miss Cook, my father has appointed me as the captain of Liberty Station. I'm sorry if that steps on your toes."

The woman held her hands up. "I'm a pilot, third in line for flying the ship. I have enough on my plate becoming the command pilot. You can gladly have the sleepless nights."

"Tell me that in a month."

He touched the button. A chime sounded from the speakers overhead. "Attention, everyone. This is Harry Rogers. You don't know me, but after the terrible events that took Captain Lee from us, I'm assuming command. Miss Jessica Cook will be my second."

Harry paused a moment to allow that to sink in. "We're going out to explore the solar system. There are many things that you don't know yet, but I'll be talking with all the section leaders as soon as possible. You deserve to know what we're looking for and what we hope to find.

"For the moment, just accept that this is the most exciting and important voyage of exploration humanity has ever undertaken, bar none. If we find what we hope, you'll be helping to free mankind to explore the universe.

"Think about that as we get under way. We're breaking orbit in ten minutes. Do whatever you need to do to get ready. Inform your supervisors if there's a problem. Rogers out."

He touched the button again to shut off the speakers. "Ten minutes, pilot."

She looked at her console. "Orbital mechanics being what they are, I can work with that. We'll start out slow and build thrust as we come into the best course. Just as a heads up, if you'd waited twenty minutes to say that, we'd have been on the wrong side of the planet and would've needed to wait."

Harry felt a little chagrined. "I've obviously watched too much television. Let me rephrase. When would be the optimal time to break orbit?"

She turned in her seat. "Just over fifteen minutes."

"Go with that."

"Aye, sir. Rotating the ship to bring the engines into the correct position for burn."

*　*　*

JESS WATCHED the countdown clock until it hit zero. She'd been in communication with Ray Proudfoot for the last five minutes and everything was ready. Right on the mark, the engines began firing.

The fuel pellets dropped one at a time into the fusion chamber and intense magnetic fields crushed them until they ignited. The thrust from each burst wasn't massive, but one after the other they got the ship moving. The ship slowly began rising into a higher orbit. The consoles and seats rotated until they found a balance between the thrust and the centrifugal force.

They'd continue to burn for several passes around the Earth before they escaped its gravity. The fusion burn would be visible below. She wondered how long it would be before anyone noticed they were leaving.

*　*　*

THE RINGING PHONE woke Kathleen Bennett from a sound sleep. No one called her at night unless something was terribly wrong.

"Bennett," she said groggily.

"I'm sorry for waking you so late, ma'am," her assistant said. "Something serious has come up regarding the space station. It's leaving."

"What? Is it falling out of orbit?"

"No, ma'am. It has some kind of thruster that we couldn't see. It's firing now. The astronomer you paid to keep an eye on it feels certain that it's leaving Earth orbit. It's not a space station. It's a spaceship."

She sat bolt upright. "Is my son back?"

"Yes, ma'am. He arrived an hour ago and went to bed."

"Wake him. I want a full team in my office in twenty minutes."

Kathleen hung up and began dressing hurriedly. She didn't know how they'd missed this, but she knew what it meant. Her ex-husband was going to wherever that crashed ship had come from. She was certain of it.

She wouldn't let him steal a march on her. Somehow, she needed to get in front of this.

\* \* \*

JOSH QUEEN, the secretary of state for the United States of America, woke at the first ring of his phone.

"Yes?"

"I'm sorry to disturb you, sir. Something has happened." The man outlined the events in orbit.

Queen sat up and slowly nodded. "The president will need to know about this first thing. Contact the owners of this station and demand to know what they think they're doing. I want details on my desk in an hour.

"And Paul, don't let them push you around. This is a direct threat to the United States of America. I don't care who they think they are, no one secretly builds something like this in orbit around our planet. They might have nuclear weapons. They'll answer to us directly or suffer the consequences."

He rose, looked at the clock, and started getting dressed. Today would be long and difficult. At best, someone had built an unauthorized spaceship, duping the American government. At worst, they were threatening the stability of the greatest nation on earth.

He couldn't allow that to stand.

# MAILING LIST

Want more? Grab *Freedom Express* today or buy any of Terry's other books below.

Want Terry to email you when he publishes a new book in any format or when one goes on sale? Go to TerryMixon.com/Mailing-List and sign up. Those are the only times he'll contact you. No spam.

Did you enjoy the book? Please leave a review on Amazon or Goodreads. It only takes a minute to dash off a few sentences and that kind of thing helps more than you can imagine.

You can always find the most up to date listing of Terry's titles on his Amazon Author Page.

## The Empire of Bones Saga
*Empire of Bones*
*Veil of Shadows*
*Command Decisions*
*Ghosts of Empire*
*Paying the Price*
*Reconnaissance in Force*
*Behind Enemy Lines*
*The Terran Gambit*

*The Empire of Bones Saga Volume 1*

## The Humanity Unlimited Saga
*Liberty Station*
*Freedom Express*
*Tree of Liberty*

## The Fractured Republic Saga
*Storm Divers*

**The Scorched Earth Saga**
*Scorched Earth*

**The Vigilante Duology with Glynn Stewart**
*Heart of Vengeance*
*Oath of Vengeance*

# ABOUT TERRY

#1 Bestselling Military Science Fiction author Terry Mixon served as a non-commissioned officer in the United States Army 101st Airborne Division. He later worked alongside the flight controllers in the Mission Control Center at the NASA Johnson Space Center supporting the Space Shuttle, the International Space Station, and other human spaceflight projects.

He now writes full time while living in Texas with his lovely wife and a pounce of cats.

www.TerryMixon.com
Terry@terrymixon.com

http://www.facebook.com/TerryLMixon

https://www.amazon.com/Terry-Mixon/e/B00J15TJFM

Made in the USA
San Bernardino, CA
19 November 2018